No Behind

Louise Parker Kelley

December 2014

Street to Street
Epic Publications

This book, *No Behind,* is published by Street to Street Epic Publications, Washington, DC, under the direction of Dr. Carolivia Herron.

www.carolivia.com
StreetToStreet.org
www.EpicCenterStories.org

Library of Congress Cataloging-in-Publication Data
Kelley, Louise Parker
No Behind

Summary: An extraordinary 4th grader survives an epidemic in quarantine with the rest of her school. She uses her newfound courage and resourcefulness to declare independence and challenge the mindless tyranny of standardized testing.

ISBN 978-1-938609-23-7

Dedicated to my first teachers, my sisters:

Christine Louise Wachter Bonsby

Jeanne Marie Wachter Miller

Mary Katherine Wachter Michos

Gracias, mis hermanas, vayan con Dios

My deepest gratitude to my novelistas,

Jessica and Carolivia

and to

Rosa Parks, Ruby Bridges

and Malala Yousafzai

Contents

Section One: Outside

We had to get up and go.

When the fire alarm screeched, I grabbed my milk carton that I saved from breakfast from out of my desk, stuck it in my hoodie pocket, and zipped over to get in line. Ms. Wachter made sure everyone lined up so nobody got left behind and we left our room and went to the playground. But almost as soon as we got there they made us go down to the lower field which is really not ours to play on, but they sent us down there anyway, which has never happened before.

Then the grownups kept talking on the walkie talkies like they do and some of them were looking worried, like they usually don't. We were lined up so far away I could barely see the school any more. And then we stood around getting bored and being shushed by the teachers like usual and more and more time passed. At least it was nice and warm outside. The sky was great, so blue it could make you thirsty. The clouds were piled up next to each other, white and grey, casual, friendly. If I'd known how long it would be before I'd see clouds again, I would have looked at them longer.

It would have been a really good day for recess. Or at least finish the story Ms. Wachter was reading to us before the alarm banged, but forget that.

Maria whispered to me, "Where is everybody?" which was a real good question. Usually all these other classes line up right where we were, but there were only a few lined up next to us.

"Maybe they all went out front," I whispered back, and then we got shushed again. That's so silly, the teachers were talking to each other, why can't we? I know they say it's so we can hear the directions if there's an emergency but kids are going to talk, just like grownups do, at a fire drill. A long one, anyway, which this one certainly was.

Two more classes came down. They were walking really fast, and the teachers were at the back of the line instead of the front, which was another strange thing.

Then the principal, Mrs. Hayes-Roberson, came down to the field and I was surprised to see all these other people with her, like the grown-ups that clean the building and the cafeteria ladies. She had two kids in the wheelchairs rolling next to her and the guys and the girl that are in the autism class right behind her with their teachers. And then we heard the sirens and I thought that we really did have a fire, how cool. But the sirens were the police cars and they pulled up on the road next to the field and didn't even park in the parking lot. One of them drove right onto the grass! And they came out of the cars and they looked like men from Mars because they had these masks on. Some kids screamed. I thought it looked strange but I didn't scream at first. But when they got closer I did even though I kind of recognized they were still people. But it was still kind of creepy. You could hardly tell they were police.

Masks are not a good thing this way, not like on Halloween.

The teachers tried to stop us screaming. I guess they felt like they had to try.

The policeman handed the principal a piece of paper. I just realized now thinking back about it that he probably gave her a paper so he wouldn't have to take his mask off to talk. Plus he should have given *her* a mask. We all should have got a mask if he had a mask because there was something going on. It's not fair otherwise.

Anyway the principal read the paper to herself and I saw her shut her eyes for just a minute. She looked around at everybody and she looked right at me for a minute. It seemed like that, anyway. Then she kind of pulled her shoulders back and stood up straighter and used her loud voice and said something like, "Students, we are all going to e-vak-wait."

I didn't know what that was exactly but the teachers seemed to know and they got us quiet and straight in our class lines. The principal went around telling the teachers something real quietly and some looked upset and some didn't show it but they were all upset, I just knew.

One teacher moaned, "I don't have my purse. It has my medications."

That made another teacher look really scared. Or maybe she was already scared and knowing she couldn't have her purse made it worse. I don't know, I just know they were upset, and some of the kids could tell. And then they took attendance again. We had to say our names. Usually they just look and count or something. But that day nothing was the same.

So it turns out one thing e-vak-wait means is a long walk away from school. The whole school got in really long lines and the policemen and the teachers stopped the traffic on the parkway and we all walked up a hill and down another two blocks and past this shopping center. The whole school, all in line, and the teachers sort of running up and down next to the line.On   the   way some of the little kids went into this little wooded part to go to the bathroom! Outside! Since they couldn't hold it and no one could go back to the school bathrooms. Couldn't believe it. That's not how they do it in America.

Really I wanted to go myself, I really had to go, but it was too embarrassing.

I turned so I couldn't see where they were going and saw the long line of kids following along, the classes all mixed up together.

Mostly I was trying not to be scared. I started making up a letter to my mother in my head. This is what I do whenever I can, and if I'm lucky I remember most of what I made up when I get home and put it in my next letter to her. Auntie complains about the postage, but not too much, because she knows I'm allowed to write to her. Daddy said.

Maria held my hand part of the way when we walked. That helped. Having your best friend around always helps.

They let us talk then, a little.

"What's going on?" that sniffly Mary Katherine asked everyone. She sniffs all the time. She has allergies. Mary Katherine got shrugs, and some people started making stuff up. One kid said maybe it was a field trip. As if.

"I'm tired. I don't think I've ever walked this far in my whole entire life," I heard somebody say.

I can believe that. American kids don't do much walking. Not like back in Cameroon, where it's expected. That's what legs are for.

Of course I'm American now, but I don't mind walking, I haven't forgotten how.

Jerry, a kid I know but not in my class, started marching when the teacher couldn't see. His knees went straight and his arms went back and forth like a robot. Some other kids did the same thing, giggling and stopping when the teacher turned to look. It was a good game for a while, but they got bored with it, especially after she didn't stop them when she finally did catch them. She just shook her head and turned back around. Talk about ruining a good joke.

There were cop cars in front of us on the street and at the end of the long line, lights flashing, but at least no sirens. It was bad enough without that.

It was warm for November, but I was still glad I had my hoodie. It's kind of like having a blanket, it's made out of really soft warm stuff. My t-shirt was almost the same color blue as the hoodie. I also had my good shoes, the ones with the purple and green stripes and the rainbow shoelaces, and my jeans were all decorated with sequins. The kids with flip-flops and shorts were complaining that they were cold and their feet hurt. Me, I come dressed for recess, and I've learned my lesson about flip-flops. Fine for when it's really warm, but you can't play soccer in them right. It's painful to watch kids try.

I thought about drinking my milk, but I already needed a bathroom. When I first got here I always got a stomach ache when I drank milk, but it got better, which was good because ice cream is one of the best things ever made. Yogurt with cherries in it is also okay, but ice cream, I'm glad I don't have to miss that.

Finally we went past this old church, turned down another street and stopped in front of this big block of a building with stars and hard to read writing on it. We waited there while some grownups came out of it to talk to the principal and teachers, at least I think so, it was hard to see and people were talking more while we waited.

It turned out it was a Jewish church called a synagogue. Synagogue is a really strange word and I had to ask how to spell it, for sure. Then we went inside and sat down in a big room with these nice soft chairs like in a movie theater. Then the littlest kids went downstairs to the basement and a little later the principal made an announcement. She called out some classes, and some of the kids left and went walking down another block to this old church school called Saint Patrick's, and some kids walked to a special place called a mosque, which is another kind of holy place for praying. We found that out later. At the time, we just knew they left.

(The other kids in those other classes left because there wasn't enough room for everyone here. We found that out later. Personally I would have said that there wasn't enough room for those of us still left, but nobody asked me at the time.)

Practically every teacher tried to use their cell phones and the phones didn't work. And we all got to go to the bathroom really slow because there were only a couple of bathrooms for everyone to use and man were they smelly! At least I *finally* got to go.

Then there was more waiting around after that.

Still nobody told us why or what was up or *anything*. Plus, of course, I was hungry, and I wanted to know what was going to happen next. That's what everyone was talking about, naturally. Wished I'd brought a book. It would have been nice to think about something else while we waited and waited to find out what was going on. We were just sitting around, even Ms. Wachter, who was starting to look very tired.

It wasn't until around that time that I really looked around for Jamarr. I saw him back when we were out on the field at school but I didn't think about him after that. I'd been busy.

He is such a nuisance but when I couldn't see him right away I got real upset. We weren't supposed to leave our class, but I needed to find him. The room we were in was real big and there were lots of kids, but maybe some classes were somewhere else. Or maybe he, well, I didn't know and my mind was starting to get all closed up like it does when I worry. Then I saw him down a couple of rows and he grinned and waved at me and I wasn't even embarrassed to see him like I am sometimes.

My brother's here with me. I can't believe I'm *glad* about Jamarr being here.

When I looked at him, I noticed for the first time that he's not so skinny any more. His face is not so thin and his smile is still really big but it doesn't look bigger than his face like it used to. I felt so good when he waved at me. Right then I decided to stop calling him Big Head. I know he hates it.

Maybe he'll stop calling me teasing names too. Well, I can dream.

We're all in this new place and there aren't any classes and that's so weird. It's like the air was quivering, everyone was so confused.

I didn't know what was going on either. I *hate* that.

I tried to look around and see exactly who was around, but it was impossible. I could recognize some teachers, and my two friends in the other Fourth Grade, but the place was jammed full of kids everywhere. There was a lady and this man standing outside in the hall, they were not part of our school. The lady had on a long dress with long sleeves, a pretty dress with skinny flowers on it. The man was wearing a suit and a little beanie on his head. They were talking to teachers and the principal and pointing at things, but I couldn't hear what they were saying. They gave the principal a piece of paper which I think was a map, but it was hard to tell exactly from where I was. Still, I wanted to know, and I had this idea that the two of them belonged to this place. Trying to see through to them was hard, kids just sort of in every spot there was, and then I lost them. Somehow they turned around, went somewhere else and I never saw them after that.

Some of the kids were upset and crying and there was nothing anyone could do. There weren't enough teachers to go around to listen to kids and anyway we all knew what was the matter. "I want my mom!" I heard, and I thought, me, too. Except I need a plane ticket.

One of the teachers started crying and she went someplace maybe so no one could see her crying but everybody knew. Then principal came and talked to us a little bit and she said we did all this so we could be safe and she said she was proud of us. She didn't say safe from *what*. And somebody called out to ask why and she didn't even remind them not to call out. I already knew it was serious but that was when I knew it was *really* serious.

And she said the weirdest thing I have ever yet heard a principal say in my whole life. Ms Hayes-Roberson said she didn't know why yet herself. "This was necessary and it is an emergency but the authorities (I guess she meant the police in the masks) just told us it was important to get everyone here to Shalom Israel synagogue."

Then she said something else, but I couldn't catch what she said because my friend Sade started to whisper to me and the words got lost. Finally she said that when she finds out exactly why we had to come here she will tell us.

That's all she said.

Then she left and went upstairs.

She didn't even ask if we had questions, like teachers always do. We had about ten bazillion to ask.

I mean how can she not know. That's a mess right there.

And Jerry from the other class announced that what happens next will be that our parents will come to get us but my question is, how will they know where we are if we're not at the school? Who told him anyhow, the big know-it-all? I don't think anybody went back and put a note on the door like we do when we go to the computer lab. Actually I bet we wouldn't be allowed to go back to the school because this is an emergency thing. It's like Code Red only more. Code Burgundy maybe. Not Code Purple because that's my favorite color.

That was how quarantine began.

I learned a new word the next day: contagious. I don't think I'll ever forget it.

People sometimes ask me what was the biggest deal about quarantine.

For me it's when I wake up in the morning. I'm really glad I woke up again.

Because you never know.

There was TB2. That was bad, sure. Quarantine for that was tough. But.

There was . . . there used to be my sister, Angelique.

The worst time ever was last year when my oldest sister died of cancer. I still miss her. There were days afterwards when I woke up and it hurt so much I thought I would die. She wasn't there to talk to, to joke with, to argue with, never never. I couldn't wait for time to go by so it could be in the past and not hurt so much.

We didn't have enough insurance for her to go to the doctor and she got so skinny and my daddy blamed himself even though she told him was a grownups and supposed to take of herself.

When this happened she was living in her own apartment near us. So it wasn't his fault she got cancer with no insurance. Cancer is bad and can kill you but cancer with no insurance will kill you sure and faster. So she's dead and daddy still thinks he should have done something about it. I know it isn't true but he doesn't. He still talks about it like he made it happen.

Oh well. It's all just no good. She isn't here to talk to any more. I could talk to her about anything.

I miss her but it's not as bad as it was. I used to act kind of bad at school and even bad at home last year because I missed her so much. One teacher said I wasn't living up to my potential. I got no idea what she meant by that but I wasn't interested anyway. I got another big sister left but I miss Angelique the most.

When she died I got left behind. I didn't want to die with her but I do feel so bad without her sometimes. Sometimes I think my heart will fall right out of my chest. Other times I have bad dreams. They are bad because in the dreams she's not dead and I can talk with her just like before and then I wake up and it's so bad. Because she is still dead. I hate that part.

Somebody who didn't know asked me if she moved back to Cameroon. No. She lives in me only. I am her whole country.

How can she be gone for all time? If I were in charge of the world nobody would be allowed to die until they were more than 50 years old. However I wouldn't make it that nobody ever dies, because around where I live now there are already plenty of people and in Cameroon there are even more so it would be really bad and crowded if nobody ever died and more kids kept coming. But if I could make the rules, nobody would ever die so young that it was a big honking hurting mess.

I mean we had to find money for the funeral and that was no good either. It wasn't much of a funeral for someone as great as my sister but it was all we could do. So we need to change things about funerals. I wonder if my dad would have enough money to bury me if I died from the TB2. Since I don't make any money, I cost money, so I couldn't help much. Maybe it is cheaper to bury children because they are smaller. Maybe the government has a way to help pay for it like the free and reduced lunch. That would be good. Funerals can cost so much. But you have to have a funeral. To say good-bye. And to remember. Usually I can remember lots of stuff. Especially about Angelique.

Back in Cameroon I heard there was somebody in the next village that died from the war and they never found their body and there was no funeral. That was really bad. I can't remember the name. That's what happens when there's no funeral, you can't remember right. That's what happens when there's no body and no funeral.

Over in Rwanda they had a terrible war and there were many bodies but no funerals allowed. That's what I heard. The river was choked with bodies from the soldiers killing so many. Not funerals, just sadness and fear.

Terrible things happen here in America too. Every night it's on the news, who's been shot, who died from guns. I don't watch the news any more. Didn't. Too sad.

Now in quarantine I can't watch TV anyway.

I miss cartoons but not the news.

The way the year started was pretty good.

The first conversation I had was before the first day of school, on the bus, when I was glad to find out my BFF Maria was going to be in my homeroom class. We didn't know anything about our teacher because she was new at our school. Then we got off the bus and after that the first question is always, where?

Wait, the first question is who, who is going to be in your class and then who is your teacher going to be. That one I knew. So me, Darryn, and my friends Maria and Rachel, and other kids, have a teacher named Ms. Wachter and that's the who part. Then the question is where, where is your classroom and where is the bathroom and then when, when do we go to lunch and recess especially you have to find out are we stuck with the first lunch at 10:30 like last year and we aren't doing that time this year so that's good.

I knew where the classroom was, actually outside, in the special Fourth Grade area, where the trailers are, which I found out even before, when I was in Second Grade and I asked the lunchroom parent what those funny flat buildings were, and she said Fourth Grade trailers. I never forgot because I didn't know we had classrooms outside our building before. Ms. Wachter says they are portable classrooms not trailers but they sure look like trailers.

It's very important where is the closest bathroom that you are going to have to use and we didn't have to use the haunted one near the playground again so that was another good thing. It probably isn't really haunted but every year somebody says that there's a ghost and somebody screams and gets hysterical and then people believe more that something scary must be happening or why would they scream? Anyway we don't have to use that bathroom all the time this year. On the other hand we have the farthest to go from our rooms to get to the busses at dismissal.

Not that I mind walking. Just don't want to miss my bus. They won't let you walk home if you feel like it without special permission from your parents. Parent. I only have one here in America. After school I walk all over, exploring, sometimes with friends, sometimes by myself. The city is very interesting, and so is the park. There are about a million squirrels flickering everywhere. Even on the electrical power lines. They are fearless.

That's how it was when school started, a long time ago, before the quarantine came.

Breakfast that morning at school was boring. All there was, was cereal and the lady did not want to give me two milks but I took them anyway. Right before recess I get real thirsty and water is just not enough for me. So I hid one in my desk behind my journals because we're not supposed to have any food in the desk because of bugs. But the bugs can't get in a sealed milk carton. Maybe if they chewed on it a really long time. Or they had a bunch of bugs and took turns chewing. Or they all got a pencil and poked it.

There were lots of kids absent that day. Some sickness was going around, like always. Now we know what, but back then, we didn't. There were some teachers out sick too. Ms. Wachter was fine. I was glad. I don't like it when we have a substitute. It's bad but I kind of like when we have a smaller class when kids are absent.

It isn't that the classroom is too small, exactly. When we're all sitting down it's fine. It's when we want to do the math games or the read around the room stuff or we want to dance at indoor recess, that's when the room is too small. And it seems too small when we want to make noise, like cheering people during the spelling games or whatever. The ceiling is kind of low and I remember from science about the vibrations of sound and how the waves can echo and stuff in a small space. When we make noise in this room, we really fill it up quick.

We had it good then and didn't know it!

That day was especially good because Mrs. H was back. She's our regular music teacher. Her real name is Hamadashiru-Ngyuen, but she says we can just call her Mrs. H, which is easier. And shorter. So we had a real music class that day, which was way cool. Also we had music first thing, before reading even.

Mostly, I liked the songs. Lots of songs with animals. So far I have not learned any good squirrel songs. There are songs about bunnies and bears and mice, but I noticed there are hardly any about rats. Rats are not so cute animals.

Once I saw a rat outside at the dumpster. So I wondered if rats ever get sick of being outside and wish they could go inside. I guess they have nests and places they can go if they feel like that. Rats and mice like to go inside and outside both. I know because I've seen the rats around the dumpsters and I remember when Miss Charles complained about the mice in the teacher's lounge. They were lucky it was just mice, not rats.

The animals in the book Hatchet that Ms. Wachter was reading to us were not cute. It's about this boy stuck in the wilderness and the animals in it are serious and scary mostly. But it's not a fairy tale so that's why.

I'm not scared of mice. How can a mouse hurt anybody? Rats are creepy though, not only will they bite you but I read where they helped spread the plague a long time ago. Plague was a bad disease a long time ago that killed people from the germs that got in the fleas on the rats. I already didn't like rats!

Unfortunately, there are rats living under our trailers, uh, portable classrooms. One of the second grade reading teachers joked when we saw a rat, "Oh, that's Henry. Don't you know Henry?" Some kids didn't get that she was kidding. They just looked at her.

I thought it was pretty funny, myself. Imagine pretending you knew a particular rat. They're all ugly, how could you even tell them apart? Unless you were another rat.

So since there are rats and bugs by which I mean ROACHES, yuck, we can't keep food in our desks. Usually I'm okay with that rule but sometimes you just have to do what a Fourth Grader's got to do.

That's why I stashed some milk after breakfast, before we went off to music. Amazing, when I look at it, that my milk was the biggest deal to me that day. The secret milk was my huge concern. Like it was important. The main thing I worried about that day was reminding myself to drink the milk during snack time so it wouldn't go bad. Sour milk is the worst!

And I would drink it fast, so if she saw me Ms. Wachter wouldn't say anything to me until it was too late. (I read once that cheese is made from milk that has gone sour. That doesn't make any sense at all, cheese is great, sour milk is not.)

There are lots of things around that don't make much sense, however.

Like what all happened next, on that day. After we got back from music, after we started our work in reading class, after listening to a funny silly story.

Quarantine.

We got extra time outside that last day. Then we came back in for reading.

Our reading lesson was on sequencing. Putting the events of the story in order. Take all the juice out of it, tell what happens 1,2,3, done. Was it some fairy tale? Part of a chapter book? It was good, and I was sorry when she stopped reading aloud, because I liked it. I know that.

It was a good story about to get ruined because we were going to have to take it apart and suck most of the best part out of it, as usual, by talking about it too much, but exactly which story it was, I forget. I do remember because I had the work almost done, writing what was in the beginning middle and end, and I was getting bored when we heard the announcement.

It was a Code Blue announcement.

Now Code Blue means the teacher checks to see if everyone is in here that is supposed to be, so we wait until Ms. Wachter the teacher checks. This happens a couple of times a year. It's practice in case something bad happens, which can be a bunch of stuff, like a bad guy in the building or some kid takes off and leaves campus and they have to check every class. Usually during Code Blue we can't leave our portable classroom to go in the building until it's over.

Code Blue is no big deal. I've done it plenty of times since I've been going to this school. It was a lot more scary living in Cameroon, because the grownups used to say there was nothing we could do if the bad men came with their guns and machetes.

Because of the announcement, our teacher said don't go to your groups, and she read to us from this other chapter book, which she said was one of her favorites ever, while we waited for the Code Blue to be over.

She read us Betsy and Tacy Go Downtown. (Not our downtown, Washington, D.C., another town somewhere else.) It was about a couple of girls being friends and having adventures about a hundred years ago, which doesn't sound like much but it was pretty good. Completely different from Hatchet, which was our other read-aloud book, but that was fine. I like all kinds of stories. We get to hear both books on different days.

Ms. Wachter had just asked us, "How can you tell that this story happened in the past?" when the fire alarm went off clanging and wow, is it ever loud in the portable classroom. We all jumped, even Ms. Wachter. So now there was a fire drill happening on top of Code Blue, which was strange.

With Code Blue and Code Red, the whole point is stay put in the room. Not this time.

But you never know what grownups will do. Sometimes they don't know themselves.

This was one of those times.

— Betsy-Tacy and Tib

by Maud Hart Lovelace

Section Two: Inside

Quarantine in a synagogue place is interesting at first. Now after a few hours I'm getting bored. Also hungry.

The grownups keep whispering to each other and I wish they would just tell us. We all know something is wrong, but nobody is saying anything to us.

I suppose there are worse things than grownups trying to pretend they are not in a panic. I can't think of any right now but there must be some. They are all walking around looking freaked out and then trying not to look that way. If it wasn't so weird and scary it would be funny.

Later: Ms. Wachter is trying to explain to everybody what's happened to us. I don't really understand it all but I'm trying to. No one else is listening as close as I am. Dionne is just humming to herself and Jeannie has a million questions and Davide keeps making jokes under his breath and Rachel is scratching her head and Ahmed is trying not to cry, so he is being angry. I know how Ahmed gets. Rachel just looks upset and Maria is praying I think. In a way I'm glad they are all here with me, in another I wish they'd all go away so I could understand, just me and my teacher talk about it.

So to start, there is this germ. It used to be this regular germ called tuberkulowis and it was not a big deal for Americans most of the time. I mean now. It was a big deal back years ago but isn't so bad now except now it has changed and it's really bad. Again. This changed germ is killing people all around and they can't find any medicine to stop it.

The germ change is called mutation. Ms. Wachter spelled that word for me. So when it changed it started making people really sick. They started coughing and that makes it spread. Some people who got it coughed spit all out in public, yuck, and other people just regular coughed, and it got spread around. Some people who work at our school got it. But nobody knew it was this new germ thing until like a day or so ago. Because this new germ can kill people and I guess they didn't find out until after they died that this new thing killed them. Oh, and this new germ isn't all over everywhere yet. We are having what is called an outbreak, right around here in Washington, and there are a couple of other places, New York I think, and a place called Minneapolis, and San Francisco. But not everywhere, at least they hope not.

So we are in an outbreak of this disease. And we have to be kept away and apart in *quarantine*, we can't go anywhere, we have to stay here, which is what quarantine means.

Personally I think this isn't making a whole lot of sense. If we have to be kept apart why did we walk here? We probably left germs all over the place. Especially in those woods. I'll ask somebody about that later.

Some of the kids and two of the teachers from our school have this germ, and they are in the hospital, and the doctors and nurses are taking care of them. If anyone else that's in here with us at Roosevelt Elementary At the Synagogue gets sick really bad, this is weird, they will be taken out of here and put in quarantine in a hospital. That's doesn't make sense to me, but apparently there are different kinds of quarantine. If they get sick and they have been here with us they would have gotten their germs in here with us. I guess I should feel sorry for them but if they make everyone else sick it's hard for me to feel too sorry for them. Even though they can't help being sick.

The reason we didn't stay in the school building is really confusing. I've heard a couple different versions so far and this is what I think it really is: some grownups leaders think this germ got spread around. It's spread around the school so we had to get out of the school. That part is pretty clear. After all, we left.

Some think it was because of the mail. Somehow our school got mail from people who were sick and some teachers got mail in their mailboxes and opened it in the classrooms so they have to check all those places at the school and they want us out so they can do that. Some of the teachers that opened their mail had to go to the hospital so now there are less teachers some places. Or some teachers used the same computers as someone who was getting sick. Or doorknobs got the germs on them. The disease is all spread around already but they don't want it to spread more. And all the grownups are kind of worried because if it is contagious germs in the air you could breathe it in but you have to breathe so what can you do?

Another thing I heard is that people who went to visit another country, maybe China, got the germ when they went to visit and brought it back and it got around here first because we have so many embassies and government people traveling all over to places all the time.

Being in here is all we can do right now. It still doesn't feel safe though.

It really doesn't *feel* safe. A cough could be fatal!

We don't know for how long.

Ms. Wachter says that our parents are not allowed to come get us for a while, nobody knows how long. That is because some of the parents could be con-tam-i-na-ted or we could be. "Use the word in a sentence," they tell you. Well, I just did.

I asked Ms. Wachter how to spell it and she did and she smiled for a minute after I said I already tried sounding it out. She smiled real quick. I'm not sure why she smiled but it was better after she did. *Contaminated.* That's the word I heard.

Two new big words, *contagious* and *contaminated*. Plus *evacuate*, which I can spell now. This thing has been just one big vocabulary lesson.

But I still don't get exactly what the word contagious means, except that our parents can't come get us yet and we can't go home. So now more kids are crying and Ms. Wachter is trying to comfort everyone at once, which is pretty hard. Ms. Wachter would probably want to cry herself but she is being serious calm like teachers do during fire drills and stuff like that. After things got explained to us, there were these long tables set up with bowls and pitchers and hand sanitizer and towels and all that kind of thing. Then all the teachers went and washed their hands and face and made us do it too, fine, but if you breathe it in you can't wash your lungs out.

Right now I don't know whether I can drink my milk or not. What if it has the germs? Also I'm really hungry.

There's a water fountain here but I haven't seen a cafeteria. Now what.

I wonder why this ever happened. It's pretty scary. One of the kids said God is mad at us. I don't get it. I never did anything to anybody that would make them want me to die coughing. I don't think.

I hope my dad is okay. I wonder where he is right now? Was he in his cab when this all happened and did he breathe the poison germs in? Is he in the hospital? So I can't find out. When this quarantine thing started to happen so many people (meaning grownups really) started to try use their phones that it busted the phone system satellites. Not busted exactly, it should work again later. They say that the system is down. That's a strange way to describe a satellite. If it was down it wouldn't be a satellite in orbit anymore.

We can't watch any TV to find out what is going on either, I don't even know where the TVs are here, but even if there are some they won't let us watch them right now. I bet it is all over CNN. I bet Fox News is saying it is somebody's fault, probably the Democrats and immigrants.

One of the teachers had a laptop and tried to watch on that and they took it away from her, and when somebody else tried to find out on her iPad they took that away from her. After that they went around collecting all the phones and electronic whatevers and some kids are trying to hide theirs. I would if I had one. The thing is, the teachers are finding out some way, they are just taking the phones and things away so us kids can't find out. So instead some kids are making stuff up. It's really not good.

At least I got to go to the bathroom. I was really impressed with how long I was able to hold it. If I had had an accident I would really be in trouble, because the nurse doesn't have any clothes here for me to change into. Eeew.

A new terrible thing just happened here. What a bad day this is being . . . some parents just busted in and screamed for their kids and pushed the teachers and the teachers pushed them back and some of the kids ran to the parents and then they all left. That just makes it worse for the rest of us. The Mr. B and Mrs. H went and got poles from somewhere in the synagogue and put it through the door handles in the front so they can't get in again! Whoa! And the other teachers went to stand in front of the other doors like soldier guards. Then the cops came and stayed in front of the doors with their masks on. It was terrible.

Some of the little kids cried so hard when this happened they went to sleep. Wish I could. I'm tired but I want to stay awake in case more bad stuff happens.

Then Mrs. Hayes-Roberson says they are going to feed us soon. Maybe it will be lunch, not a snack. I hope it's lunch. Rachel says she's not hungry at all but that is the opposite of me. I don't know how they'll do it but I'm glad we get to eat. The reason it hasn't happened yet is somebody is making sure that there's no germs in the food they are going to bring. Plus there is something special about the food here that I don't understand, but you can't just bring in any food. I don't know as much as I want to, but I *will* find out.

Ms. Wachter looks really sad. I wonder what she's thinking about. I'm going to ask her can I have my milk. I've been sort of hiding it ever since we left the school.

Ms. Wachter took my milk and showed to Mrs. Hayes-Roberson. I wish I hadn't asked if I could have it. Now Mrs. Hayes-Roberson has taken it off to show somebody else and ask them about it. I bet I never see it again.

This is boring in spots but mostly scary and uncomfortable. Hope it's over soon.

They gave the new disease a name, I forgot about that. The name of it is *TB2*.

Nobody seems to know how long we will be in here. I'm trying to listen in to the grownups like usual but it's much harder to do here. They look around at us all the time, at least one of them, like they can do something by just watching us. Of course I am busy just watching them and trying to listen in, and it's not doing much good.

Maybe nobody is talking about it because they don't know. It's the kind of time where lots of grownups don't know what's going to happen either. That's pretty creepy.

They have to clean up our school to make sure there are no more TB2 germs there. Since Ms. Wachter never got her mail or opened it in the classroom she says it can't be contaminated. But the whole school could be. From people walking around with it and not knowing and coughing. We can't go back until it is all cleaned up. Other classrooms could have the poison. They have to check and it could take a long time.

There's talking and talking and nobody can hear very well but there is sure plenty of talking.

Kids are wishing they brought their toys, journals, or some books, or *something*. If I hear one more kid whine about their GameBoy I will scream, I mean it. We're not supposed to bring toys to school but naturally plenty of kids have them in their backpacks. We've got our coats and that's about it.

There's nothing to do. We got to do some fun singing games because the music teacher Ms. H taught us some, and the French teachers taught everyone a French song, but there's nothing much to do now. Some kids are trying to play games you don't need paper for, like rock paper scissors, but mostly we are sitting around leaning on each other and wishing it was over. That's me, anyway.

Maria and Rachel are playing a clapping game. They can do it really fast.

Davide and Ahmed are arm wrestling and no teacher is even bothering to stop them like they usually do. Sheesh.

They never did bring my milk back. I didn't even get to open it. Ms. Wachter said it had been out of the refrigerator too long. Ha, like I believe *that*. But we did finally get some food, cheese slices, bread, a vegetable pasta salad. Some lady that works here in this kitchen made it. Plus there was lemonade and even cake and fruit at the end. There were tables but not enough room for everyone, so some kids ate in another room and most teachers ate standing up.

They didn't ask for any money from anybody, not just the kids that always get free lunch, and the teachers were eating the same thing as us. So it was free to everyone. Well I guess all the regular lunch food is back at the school. The cheese was pretty good. The bread was nice and soft and I really liked the apple. I wanted another one but there weren't any left. In the cafeteria you can have another one if you pay for it. Or ice cream. Davide asked about ice cream but there wasn't any. I was glad he asked even if there wasn't any. It's always better to know if there's going to be any ice cream. Or if there isn't.

After we ate we moved over to the other side of the room and Ms. Wachter took a break while one of the grown-ups came to watch us. That's when I found my teacher's notebook. It was sitting where she had been sitting. I didn't really mean to but I started reading it. Opened it kind of by accident in the middle.

I found out her first name is Kathy. I never knew that before.

She wrote about what it was like having some of her kids going into accelerated math that can't read. She told them the kids can't do it but they won't do anything about it. How can they be accelerated if they have trouble reading? How are they going to do word problems? But they have to put more and more kids in it or the teachers will get in trouble. I don't understand that.

She was all upset about data tracking of kids by race too. Plus there's all this other kind of stuff that she says is like "extra homework all the time!"She wrote this on the second page:

This new Superintendent Mickey South is such a control freak. The old one's been replaced by this jerk. Constant assessment & data entry! But no choice, if I want to keep my job, that's been made clear. If you can't stand constant data entry, get out of the classroom. This weekend I spent six hours entering the formative assessments on the recording sheets. Yesterday I had to copy the running records for the Purple group. Monday I had to graph their spelling test results, the entire class. When do I get to have time to plan teaching so that it will work? First syllable of assess . . . that's what I feel like.

I'm going to put her notebook back where I found it. It wasn't right to read it but I'm just naturally nosy. Especially since we're in here and the grownups just stop talking when they see a kid come close. I wish there had been some stuff about the quarantine, but I put it back before I started to read more. I don't really understand it but it makes me feel funny to read it. Her notebook is kind of like a diary and that's supposed to be private. I couldn't resist peeking but it was wrong . . . If she read *my* secret journal I would hate that. I wonder exactly what a superintendent is. Sounds like somebody who punishes teachers.

We've been here for a week and it is so strange to be somewhere with no parents and no TV. I don't know which is worse. Okay, no parents, but really, it's awful not to have TV. The teachers keep saying it's good, because we'll have to read more, but I was reading lots anyway. I just like the sound of TV in the room, it was kind of like a friend. In my house there were always plenty of people but the TV is like a really good friend that you can have for company all the time. It never got mad at me either. Whenever I wanted I could turn on the mute when I want my friend to shut up. People would be so much easier if they came with a mute button.

There are some teachers here, Mr. B, Mrs. H and some of those nice teacher assistants like Ms. Garcia. There are over 200 of us kids, but I don't know how many exactly. I would like to know exactly. Also there is Mr. Rabin, who is a member of this synagogue and volunteered to come be with us, and Ms. Rose, who says she didn't volunteer but Mr. Rabin teases her that she did because she could have left when she heard we were coming. She said she wanted to take care of her kitchen and keep everything kosher, whatever that means. Then there is this man named Mr. Ramos, I think he said, and he was here to help cut the grass and clean and he was in the synagogue building when we got here and had to stay when they sealed it up. He is very shy but he works very hard. He is here and he has a nice smile. He doesn't seem to know much English. Alejandro can get him to talk in Spanish, but he's still very quiet and shy. There are some other grownups I don't know the names of who are in here with us but I think they are workers from our school, not the synagogue. Anyway there are plenty of people here and we can't leave, even if you're a grown-up, you can't leave. That's the way it is.

We sleep here, we have bedrolls, on mats, in a big room downstairs. It's one big giant school sleepover. Except sometimes it's hard to sleep, it's too strange. Sometimes a kids starts crying and we wake up, and some teacher comes and gets them and takes them to the quiet room up on the next floor.

There is a routine to start the day. As soon as we get up we roll up our sleeping bags and sleeping pads and stack them in the corner. Except the kids that have to go to the bathroom right away when they wake up. I am not one of them. Then the teacher (they take turns) watching us for morning routine makes sure everybody gets dressed. The girls get dressed behind this big sheet on one side and the boys on the other. It's not very private but it's not very warm either so we do it quick.

We are all working for the stars. The teachers have this star system. Everything you do right gets a star. The more stars you get the more choices you get for free time after school or after dinner. So if you get dressed fast without giggling or teasing or peeking or anything fun like that, you get a star.

If you argue with a teacher about getting a star you don't get one.

Then we line up for going to the bathroom and afterwards washing our hands in the big clear bowls with liquid soap because that is faster than waiting for the sinks. Then tooth brushing and I am so glad they take away the bowls we just spit in after that. Now I have to say the soap here smells about a hundred times better than the soap at school. Maria says the school soap smells like hospital and she is so right about that.

The farting contest cost everyone some stars because they couldn't tell who was doing it exactly. Actually I think it was worth it, it was so funny. Why don't grown-ups laugh about farts like a person naturally ought to? Farts are hilarious. The noise is funny, the smell is — well, bad, but still funny, and you just never know when it going to happen, really, even if those kids did eat lots of beans that night so they could have the contest. We all had beans. People were winning the contest and they didn't even know there was one, and kids had no way to stop farting just because the teachers said so. It would get real quiet, then bra-aap, and we'd all fall out again. The teacher standing there trying to be all serious and it was no use. Thank heaven for farts.

They tried having us use hand sanitizer but too many kids are allergic. Or they just hate it because it stings.

The synagogue doesn't have any bathtubs or showers. We kind of sponge off at night.

So anyway after getting dressed and bathrooms and washing we line up. This is something we do all day long here in quarantine, but this time it's for something good. We go into the meeting room in the basement with some other classes and play Legos and stuff while other classes go to eat breakfast. There's not enough room for everyone to eat at once, only about half at a time, plus all the grownups of course.

After they finish eating breakfast we go in after washing our hands again and they come here and play. After that it is time for class and get taken to whatever classroom in a line. In geometry we found out that a line can be an infinite set of points and I tell you what that is true in here. The lines go on forever.

Before quarantine some kids would get on the bus to get to school by nine and some would have day care before school and some would walk to school, but now we start school a little earlier and school ends a little earlier which is pretty good except for not being able to go outside, not being able to run much at all, and no screaming.

There was lots of screaming and crying the first two days. The little kids did the most but some big kids too. Also two teachers that I saw.

It has calmed down since then. Still there's plenty of sound around here. Maybe teachers are a little bit right about how loud kids get. It's good that I got plenty of friends here but I fight with them more because we're all stuck together crammed jammed in here. Plus we don't get to take showers as much so there is a strong people smell that isn't very nice.

Sponge baths are disgusting. I get so cold.

There is a much shorter line for the sponge baths though, because thery are just so uncomfortable. The other thing about the sponge bath, which is just a small tub of water you stand in and wash yourself off with a sponge, is that the towels are better. They don't get used as much as the hand towels.

Some kids want their own towel and their own bathroom and they don't want to use cold the sponge bath tubs. So they are starting to get a little whiffy.

What I mean is, we stink. For all these reasons. Me included.

They put some fans in the bathrooms because, well, it was bad. Some kids will walk in and hold their nose and complain about the smell and then go right ahead and contribute to it. Like they never had anything to do with the smell. Please.

A toilet got stopped up and that was sooo bad. One of the grownups figured out how to fix it but now we have people who check if the toilets are flushed! The patrols have to do it, and some grownups. But we have to do it. Yecch!

At least I got a change of clothes. Some part of the government sent us all these clothes, all sizes, even some for the teachers. They came in these huge boxes, boxes the little kids are using to play house and castle and stuff. I wish we had a big empty box just for Fourth Grade. But we didn't get any.

The clothes were a nice surprise but some of the French teachers are not happy and some of the Fifth Graders I heard were really upset because these clothes are kind of plain. It's kind of weird how part of our school is all in French. It's called French Immersion because the kids in it have to do everything in French, even the monthly projects. It's weird to see their projects in the hall like the ant model we all had to make and all the parts of the ant are in French. The French teachers seem nice but they're kind of mysterious. They aren't allowed to say anything in English at school. I never know what they are saying except exkusi moi. They say that in the hall when they try to get by on the stairs.

We have two French teachers for Fourth Grade, Madame Jeanne Marie Blanche and Mademoiselle Dawn DeCombe, and they are both really pretty and kind of sleek, like black kitty cats.

So what happened was that some of the Frenchies did not approve of the free clothes. The clothes were not fashionable, that's true. There were some that even were almost ugly. Still everything was clean and there was enough to pick from and all I really wear is a regular t-shirt anyway. It would be nice if there was more pretty stuff or new stuff maybe with some sequins, but there wasn't.

It's hard to live without sequins but I guess I can stand it.

Some of the kids were upset. Erin, and Maureen, they're both French Immersion students, they said wearing somebody else's old clothes was creepy. I just looked at them. You can tell they've always had new stuff, I said to Maria. The one called Erin glared at me and said no, she'd had to wear old used clothes plenty of times and she didn't like it, that's all. So after that I shut up. You never know about people.

I thought all the Frenchies were from rich families. Guess there are exceptions.

But anyway the clothes are okay with me. I figure free clothes, clean, don't smell like the ones I've got on, good enough, I got no problem.

Well I do have a problem. I wish I could go home! That's how almost everybody feels. (Except Earl. I really like Earl. He says his dad use to smack him every time he caught Earl in girl's clothes. The teachers don't hit him but they do sigh and make him give the girl's clothes back and they won't call him Shay-shay like he asked. He asked me to call him she when the other kids aren't around. Now he's trying to get everyone to call him Blinka. I think he freaks the teachers out a little.)

Maria and I both ended up crying today. I don't cry much, but today was just so bad. What happened was, Bluetooth Baruti got caught, and it was ugly. Maria says it's her fault, but I don't think so. It just so happened that we were waiting to use it next and the teachers caught us. Caught him really. And they really were upset about it and they took his Bluetooth away.

We're not supposed to have any way to call out. They asked for all our cell phones and tablets and whatever when we got here. But Baruti managed to hide his Bluetooth (so that's why he's called Bluetooth Baruti). Since we've been here he's been letting kids use it, but there's only two places in the whole building it works, upstairs in the one classroom and over near one window in the front lobby of the sanctuary part. There are usually grownups in both places but sometimes not, so word gets around and the next person gets to make a call. Meantime everyone does favors for Baruti, like letting him ahead in line, getting him an extra snack, things like that. I think that's what made the teachers suspicious, but even more than that I think somebody got mad when he wouldn't let them use it right away, and I know who did it too. It was Osumare and his brother Leo, they really wanted to call their mom and Leo even threatened to beat Baruti up if they didn't let them go ahead of everyone. Well Baruti may be kind of geeky but he's still strong and he wouldn't give in, but he was trying to get as many people as he could to make their calls so that's why we were in the classroom waiting and then the teachers came in. they went right to Baruti even though there were other people around and in between us and no one could see the Bluetooth from where he was standing. That's how I know somebody told.

Maybe it wasn't those two guys but it was somebody. Maybe just somebody jealous.

Maria was so crushed. She wanted to talk to her parents so badly. "It's not fair," she cried, "the teachers can call their families but we can't!"

One of the teachers, Mrs. Presland, looked a little ashamed when Maria said that. She locked eyes with Mrs. Davis, the teacher that caught Baruti. You could tell Mrs. Presland wanted her to back off. Not Mrs. Davis! She stood up tall and stuck her chin out and told us, "You know you're not allowed to use phones while we're here. We can't be sure you'll be able to show enough self-control to stay calm and not exaggerate about what is going on in here."

That made me mad, but I had to be careful because I didn't want to get in any more trouble, so I just said, "We just want to talk to people we love, same as you. The reason we're not calm is because you won't let us do that. People in jail get to make phone calls, this is worse than jail!"

"Phone calls are a privilege, not a right," Mrs. Davis snapped at me, and I heard her voice going up as she said it, and thought, Where's your self control, huh, but I kept quiet.

Everything is a big deal in here. There are so many of us, I heard the teachers saying. So just the regular stuff 200 plus people need to do has to be organized and changed around so we can do it here. For example brushing your teeth. There are not 200 sinks. There are not even ten sinks in all the bathrooms. So we have to take turns and what we do is line up ten at time with our toothbrushes and toothpaste.

We have to be careful about coughing and still live on top of each other! Then when we get to the front of the line we brush our teeth and rinse with water from a bottle and spit into a bucket. No more bowls. It's so gross you can't imagine. Nobody gets to use a sink, even the grownups, because they use the sinks to rinse the bucket out between every ten people, and it would take two hours for everyone to get to use a sink each. I know it would take that long because it did the first few times when we got here, that's what we did. After a while the sinks looked like — anyway, we stopped doing that. The one good thing is that nobody can skip brushing in the morning or at night. Everyone tattles if anyone tries to skip out of brushing. We have to live with the bad breath in close quarters and nobody wants that. Plus we can't go to the dentist here.

In between they rinse out the sinks with baking soda and vinegar so they won't stop up. So far that's working.

Showers are awful. We learned how to take tub baths with a sponge but oh man is it cold. Plus I never had so many people see me with no clothes on. There's another kind of shower which is just another bucket with holes in it and a hose. The teacher holds it and people wait for a turn. It's cold water because there just isn't enough hot water for everyone. There's talk of setting up a boiler that can heat water for everyone somehow but they'll have to knock out part of a wall of the temple to get it piped in and the synagogue folks don't want the building damaged that way. Some are upset they have to go to a different place for the Jewish services while we live here and some of them complained on the Internet news that we are going to ruin the building. I heard Mrs. Hayes-

Roberson sent out a video telling them we are taking good care of the temple and we are grateful to be here, which is not true. Maybe she's grateful but *I'm* not. Not really.

We didn't want to come here to start with, and we're not burglars. We're just stuck and so are they. Does it really matter what building you are in when you go to talk to God? I talk to God all over the place. I never have to make an appointment.

Well I guess it is good that they let us come in here. If I didn't have to live here it would be an interesting place to visit. Not everyone is complaining about us either. It's too bad they don't trust us more. I wonder if I would trust someone who came to my house and said they had to live there and I couldn't do anything about it? There was a village back in my country that had to do all that when some soldiers came. They had to feed the soldiers and let them sleep in their houses or get beat up.

That's NOT what we did. We didn't pick. The police made us come here.

We have to live here until we're not contagious any more because you can actually get TB2 and have it in your body and not know it and not get sick. When that happens it's called being a carrier. They are trying to make more of the screening tests for the TB2 so we can all get the test and get out of here, but there's hundreds of people and not enough tests yet. The disease is new so there aren't tests for it yet.

Keeping clean is important. Washing your hands is not so hard. Being scared about the TB2 is making everyone do it all the time. Even the boys. We use sanitizer mostly, but if you want to go to the bathroom there is always a line, all day. There's one grownup assigned just to keep the bathroom lines in order and make sure nobody makes a mess. Not all day. They take turns, just like they tell us we have to do.

Clothes are a problem. There's only so much room to keep any personal stuff, so we get three changes of clothes each and there's no place to do laundry, so they are now sending out dirty clothes every couple of days. The clothes go someplace, this big truck comes and gets the clothes which are all tied up in bags. They come back the same way and the teachers are especially mad because all the stuff is kind of wrinkled. Some teachers have to wear borrowed stuff or the donated stuff and it doesn't fit. Well it is the same for us kids but only some of the kids care lots about clothes. I'm sort of amazed that we got free clothes so fast, and we don't have to do our own laundry. There's even extra underpants and pants for the little kids who have accidents and there have been more of those since suddenly no moms or dads around.

Maria and I are trying to find a spot that no one else knows about that we can just go and be in by ourselves. So far we haven't found it but we keep looking.

Kids used to make messes in the bathrooms at school, but nobody tries it here. One reason is the adults watching, but the other is that we were told we wouldn't be able to get the plumbing fixed if we messed it up. Especially after that toilet got clogged up. If a plumber came to fix it, that plumber would have to stay with us because they would be exposed to TB2. That's because they couldn't do the plumbing work in the big Decontamination suits. That's what we were told. (That is probably part true and part they don't want us to stop up the toilets like the boys did twice last year for a joke.) No plumber or dentist or mostly anybody wants to be in quarantine with us. Some parents did want to come in with us but they wouldn't let them. We did get one volunteer doctor named Doctor Natalie and a volunteer nurse, called Jim, but so far nobody is sick enough to need them. That's what they told us. I wonder if they would tell us if somebody was that sick.

Also we have Ms. Rose from the synagogue and Mr. Rabin who belongs to the synagogue and has some other friend he talks about named Benny Bareth. They decided to stay in here with us. I like to talk to them sometimes when the school day is over. That's when we can do our own thing or go do structured activities (which means games really). If we have enough stars. If you don't have enough stars you have to do certain things and it's not as much fun. But it usually isn't as hard as schoolwork. Even the kids that can't get it together need to relax sometime.

Our apartment seemed so small and crowded to me before but now I miss it. I even miss the smell of it. It wasn't a good smell sometimes at all but now I miss it. The exterminator came and gave us stuff to spray for bugs and it smells the same now as the apartments. But it still isn't the right smell anyway. It's some other kind of bug spray. Who would have thought that a stink would be the wrong kind of stink.

I used to be embarrassed when I'd go to school and my bookbag would smell like exterminator. Now everybody's stuff smells like it. It does not smell good.

I guess stuff that kills things never would. There's that funky bleach smell everywhere around here too. They clean the tables and other stuff with it. Sometimes they've used so much in the bathroom I don't even want to breathe. Except by the time I get to use the bathroom with the lines so long I just go ahead and go. It does not work to be too picky when you are living in quarantine.

I've got my friends in here with me. That's something, anyway.

We've only been here a little while but it seems like longer. I hope this means all our regular spelling tests are cancelled. Spelling is not hard for me but the tests were boring. What I really like is vocabulary. I love finding new words and putting them in my brain for when I might need them. Like the word mysterious. I love that word. I love it enough to learn how to spell it. That is real love because it is not an easy word.

Maybe we won't have to have math quizzes on Fridays. We haven't had any real tests since we got here, I don't think. Maybe all of our tests will be cancelled because of the quarantine. We'll just read all the time, and build things and count stuff. Not too bad. Ha. I don't think so.

We're in here with teachers, after all.

It would so cool if I could help the scientists that are working on the cure for TB2. I guess they are working on a cure. They have to be. But nobody talks about it much. Some of the grownups just get so freaked out whenever they talk about the future. It's almost like they are afraid of the future. Bad stuff happened but that doesn't mean more bad stuff will happen. I think grownups are just scared of everything sometimes, they can't help it. The way things are now in here they let it show more. But some of the teachers were all scared about things before this germ attack even happened. They talked about terrorism enough that you knew they had some inside.

At least we have a doctor and a nurse. Her last name is Asher but she told us to call her Doctor Natalie, which is friendlier. And the Nurse said to call him Nurse Jim. I hope I never need to call either of them even if they do have friendly names.

Maria read what I just wrote (well I guess I let her read it) and she says I didn't spell happened right. She says it is spelled happeneded. I'm going to go look it up in the big dictionary.

She was wrong. It's supposed to be happened, not happended. I'm not going to be mean about it though. It's a big deal for her to notice spelling at all. She used to not care much about it but this year she wants to get it right.

In art class today we could draw anything we wanted as long as it had a caption. My friends drew lots of things. Ms. Wachter teaches us art now, since the art teacher went with the other kids, and she is very cheerful about not knowing how to do it, plus we don't have all the paint and clay and stuff here. So we have a good time and maybe someday we'll get some real art supplies and do something else.

This weird idea came, so I drew a picture of TB2. I just made it up.

Maria likes my drawing of the germ. Even if it isn't really what it looks like. She said it being invisible is part of how creepy it is. Exactly.

When I first got to be friends with Maria a long time ago it was because I liked her but also I felt impressed by her. That is the word for Maria Denise Ramones. She is impressive. She got to our school from Puerto Rico and she didn't speak much English. When she did speak it came out wrong. But she never gave up. The teacher had put one of the smart kids with her back then like they do but it wasn't a good idea this time. The smart kid she picked, Abby, was impatient with her and anyway Abby was kind of a show-off. Just because Abby spoke English and Spanish the teacher asked her to be Maria's partner. She didn't want to help Maria really, and she only did it because the teacher asked her. It made me mad, how she would explain stuff to Maria in Spanish a little and mostly in English. The truth was, we figured out later, that Abby really didn't know that much Spanish but she liked to say she did.

She talked to Maria like Maria was stupid or something. So two days later I'd had enough and I told Ms. Wachter I could help Maria. I was lots nicer to her than Abby. Really she understood more English than anybody realized. She could understand English, she just couldn't speak it much yet, but she caught on fast. She said she learned mostly from watching movies, especially the *Wizard of Oz*.

We became best friends. I can't imagine life without her in it.

Rachel is jealous of me being friends with Maria, but that is just too bad. Maria is the most fun of anybody I know and that's all there is to it. She says I make her laugh and I like how she laughs. She's also the one I let see when my feelings are really hurt. Not Rachel so much.

Friends getting jealous of each other is such a waste and still it happens all the time.

I heard two of the grownups talking. One of the other reasons we had to leave the school building and come here is guinea pigs and hamsters! This is because the hamsters were something called a *vector* for the TB2. I don't really understand it completely but it maybe is that the guinea pigs can get sick first and they can make people sick. And we had some classroom pets that were hamsters and a guinea pig in the science lab and everybody at our school went to Science Lab. So they had to take us out of our school and put us here and watch us to see if we got sick. The poor guinea pig got killed so the doctors could see if there was something wrong with it. Maybe that's not such a bad thing since somebody said it was sick with the TB2. Coughing until you die is a hard way to go. Even if you are just a guinea pig.

I bet this means all our class pets at school got killed.

Last night I had a dream that hamsters from Mars were the ones that brought TB2 to Earth. So Martian hamsters are responsible for all this mess. This almost makes more sense than the people who think the government invented TB2 in a laboratory somewhere and let it loose by accident. Martian hamsters, whoa. At least I know I was dreaming!

Tonight we got a special treat. Mr. B (Mr. Binwald) got somebody to bring most of his DJ music equipment in and we had a dance. I got to learn two line dances from this Asian girl named Minah. She made everybody get up and dance, she kept saying, "Let's go, let's go, why do you have to wait?" We danced and danced. My legs hurt but I didn't mind. The most amazing part was when the teachers got up to dance. Mr. B played some songs just for them and they got really relaxed and silly too.

I want to be a DJ when I grow up. All they do is play music to make people happy or make them dance. That's like having a super power.

One of the French teachers went up and gave him some of her music, which was very good dance music and all in French or some other language.

Somebody else went up and suggested something and he laughed and said in his big voice, "This song is for all the grown women in the room who are missing their men! This is Adult Swim, no kids this time!"

Then he played this song, it was so funny, called "It's Raining Men." Those women teachers got out there, most of them, and they just went wild. Some of them knew the words and were singing along. Others just danced all like, I don't know. I'd never seen this side of teachers.

They were so full of life.

There was one part, later, when the teachers were dancing that wasn't silly though. Mr. Binwald played this request, played this cool song called Born in the USA and somehow only this one guy got up to dance to it. He was a substitute teacher that got stuck here with us, Mr. Jones, and he is kind of old. He started singing along to it and dancing all intense and somehow all I wanted to do was watch him, I didn't want to dance. He was really good, even though sometimes he danced slow and he made this hand movement that was real interesting. It was like he was in his own world, which I have heard grownups say but I never really saw it until now. It was kind of spooky. When it was done Mr. B did not play any other song for a moment and then everyone applauded. So the guy, the one named Jones, did this funny bow and said, "Thank you, everyone, it was an honor to serve you in Vietnam!" When he says this, this other guy Mr. Lee on the maintenance staff jumps up, runs and gives him a high five and yells "Gulf War!" and then Mr. B hollers "Wait a minute, brother," and then Mr. B plays this song called Rock the Casbah. Mr. Lee dances around to that song like I have never seen him move before, I swear. Finally Mr. Rabin got up, and he yells WW2, whatever war that was, and Mr. Binwald doesn't play any song, he starts singing. Mr. Rabin begins to sing with him, and Mrs. H and some others, and they sing this song called The Yanks Are Coming and Mr. Binwald and Mr. Rabin somehow taught it to everyone and we ended up all singing it and marching around the room.

That's what happened. It was, like I said, amazing.

It turns out that both these guys are what is called veterans, which means they were in wars or maybe just in the military, I don't know exactly what veterans means except there is a holiday called Veterans Day and when I was younger the teacher showed us pictures of soldiers on that day. Ms. Wachter says we will have a lesson on it tomorrow. She said her dad and her brother and some of her nephews and nieces and cousins were all in the military. She says they served our country. I wonder what that means. I will find out tomorrow.

I know what veterans are now. I asked lots of questions after Ms. Wachter told us about them. . It's people who go to be soldiers and if other countries get in a fight with the United States or if we pick a fight with them, they go and shoot enough of the other people in that country so the fight stops. I told Ms. Wachter this after the veterans talked to us about what they did and she looked really sad and talked to me about it some more because it's more complicated than that. What they do is very brave, I get that, and it's sad some of them get killed for sticking up for the United States or fighting for it.

I think the fighting shouldn't happen, though. War is awful. That seems like a dumb way to put it but no matter what it's terrible. In Cameroon we know this for sure. In America they know it sometimes and other times they forget, it's like a movie to them.

After school was over today, Ms. Wachter asked me about Angelique. I had written a little poem about her, which I can't remember right now. Even Ms. Wachter asking me about it made me feel like I was going to cry for minute. She asked did I want to tell about it and I did.

Maybe it wouldn't help after all but I wanted to tell about it. To this teacher.

I told her about when they took me to the hospital to see Angelique. This was a good hospital that took her even though, no insurance. I saw her in the big white bed and she looked just squashed. Her hair looked wrong and messed up where it grew back in. Her face is not supposed to be all thin. It's supposed to be circles, full circles squeezing each other, and the cancer made it all lines instead. The cancer took and ate her smile.

She got grey. That is not a good color for nobody but especially not her. It made her look dead before she was dead. They tried to give her medicine and food with the needle spaghetti in her arm but it didn't work.

My sister just got skinnier and skinnier, got weaker and weaker. But Angelique, she sat up and tried to talk to me when I went to visit her. The cancer hurt her voice too. She didn't sound like herself any more.

Ah. She used to be able to dance for hours and hours.

She used to read stories to me and she could do different voices when she read them. Now I could barely hear her talk.

I couldn't do anything but sit there with her.

She said that was all she wanted.

Did I tell about how pretty she was? Even with her hair gone, even grey, even lying down in the bed.

She was the prettiest. She told me I was the prettiest but I know she was.

Even when the cancer ate her smile you could still tell. Even with the needle sticking in her arm with the spaghetti hanging down she was pretty. Even all grey and going away in front of me. Still the prettiest. Angelique the angel.

I never did find a way to write to my mother about it.

I can't. I still got brothers but what I want is my sister. There is no one like a sister. There just isn't.

For one thing, I am a girl. My sister was a girl. Girls are special. Some boys do not understand girls at all. Some boys think that girls just like to dress up and pretend to have tea parties and whisper to each other. I don't mind those things but that is not all there is to girls. Girls like to play tag too. I even like to play basketball and football. They say this makes me a tom girl. My name is not Tom. It is Darryn. Girls like to be smart in school and outside school too. Girls want to grow up and be in charge just like boys. Some girls want to be princesses or rock stars or maybe just normal. I actually like being a girl. I know there are girls that don't like it. At least I think there are girls that don't like being a girl and not being able to do boy things like football. I heard some girls talking about it on the Metrobus once. But then one girl said that not wanting to be a girly girl doesn't mean you don't like being a girl and the other two girls said yes that's right, but I don't know if they just agreed with her to get by. It's hard to tell with some people.

There are even boys that don't like to be boys, like that guy Earl that wanted to be called Shay-shay and then Blinka. He told me he really thought he was more a girl. No matter how mad his Dad got about it. I looked at him. He looked like boy. A skinny boy with big glasses, but a boy. I wonder what happened inside him that makes him feel that way. He didn't ask me to promise but I won't tell anybody what he said. Earl is a very interesting kid and you could really have a conversation with him about anything. I wish he was around right now but he is off talking to the school counselor. He does that a lot.

Good thing the counselor, Ms. Bondanza, is in here with us, lots of people want to talk to her. Like, every day.

What a day. I just woke up feeling trapped and I couldn't get my mind off feeling like that. I can't get out of here! It stinks. I mean it really stinks in here, because we can't take showers that much and we get hot and sweaty when we get any exercise. Like all the dancing, for instance. I want to get more exercise, really, I mean, let's move. But there isn't enough room to really do that.

I thought about how our school mascot is the panda and how the real pandas are in a cage at the zoo. I wonder if they know they are in a cage. Would it be better if we didn't know?

I finally snuck off after we had our turn at lunch and went and got a pillow and pounded on that for a while. I really smacked it good. So I did it until I got really tired and felt better. They wanted to know where I had been and I wouldn't tell them. It's not like I got to go anywhere. I just got my mad out.

Lessons can be a surprise any day in here. I was going to lunch when I heard the ESOL teacher, Ms. Nickles, talking with the ESOL kids. She gets kids from different classes to work with about language and this time they were talking about re, which is a prefix and one of the boys knew that re meant again. He looks at the teacher and says, if we do research, that means we search, we look, again? And the teacher, Ms. Nickles, her face lights up and she says all happy, "Exactly!" She gives the kid a sticker and the kid looks like the sun just came up shining right on him.

The kid says, he likes to know how words are built. Then they sit down and invent this game right then, a game they called "Prefix for Me" where each kids becomes an expert on one particular prefix and you win by helping your friends build more words with the prefix.

I was so interested I almost missed lunch and Ms. Nickles is going to tell Ms. Wachter about it so we can do it too.

Today was regular old school again. We had a math quiz and a spelling test. I should have known it was too good to last.

There was a delivery of some TVs and some computers today. I hid in the corner near the room where Mrs. Hayes-Roberson was talking to someone on speakerphone and found out about it. She was talking to some lady named Christine Johns who works for the government. This Mrs. Johns is in charge of logisticks for Roosevelt Elementary while we are stuck in here. I heard her explaining it all to Mrs. Hayes-Roberson.

Mrs. Johns said, "This is the first shipment. You'll get more, I'm coordinating the donations from the community every day. You'll be getting the big power cords you asked for by tomorrow too. We might be able to get you temporary shower rigs from military surplus, and I'm working that for more cots and futons. Can't get you beds, they'll never fit and unless that hospital comes through, we can't get the sheets. We've got blankets and towels on the way."

"Hand wipes?" asked Mrs. Hayes Roberson.

"Boxes of hand wipes coming in. Disinfectant wipes too. But I can't send it all to you now because you're out of storage space, am I right?"

"Yes, how did you guess?"

"Wasn't a guess. I served my hitch in the navy as a supply officer. I've got some idea about how tight that temporary barracks of yours has to be. It's not like it was ever intended to house all of those kids and your staff."

"What else is coming soonest?"

"The games. Some of the old kind in boxes, the rest you can get downloaded once the committee gets done screening them. I've got them on a deadline, so that's the beginning of next week. Plus you've got four Promethean boards due in soon and you can use those for any of the math and reading games and the learning game websites the county already approved."

"Thank you. We need to keep them engaged, and the teachers are getting so worn out, we do the evening in shifts but we need something to distract them, something to entertain them, and some time for the adults to relax and escape . . . I love these kids, but at least a few of them need attention all the time, late night, middle of the night, any time at all . . . "

"Hey, I understand, I'm raising five kids, I know something about that. Don't worry. Help is on the way."

Thank goodness for Christine Johns, whoever she is. I hope we can watch some TV on the computer pretty soon. I'm also going to get with Baruti and maybe Abby and then Maria will be able to send her parents email soon. Of course I'll send a message to dad.

They'll probably shut us down again but we'll go for it anyway.

We're clever Americans and they just can't keep us off the Internet and block us from the satellites forever. We will find a way to be heard! And play some new games!

Today we got to read some cool stories online and then illustrate the theme for them. For once I didn't even care that I'm not so good at drawing. Rachel helped me with that and I helped her with figuring out the theme part. The Shay-Shay showed us his/hers, and it was like an entire graphic novel about the story plus it did tell the theme, which was how important friendship can be, amazing. Then somebody had hid the colored pencils and we found them for Shay-Shay (and for us) because this project really needed to have some good color in it.

The next time we get to do our own stories, I'm going to get my friends to do the pictures. One page of words, one page with a picture.

I hope, I hope, we get to do the same thing with number stories in math. It's enough to make you enjoy decimals.

This was a really weird day. It started as usual, getting up and washing and having breakfast standing up like I like to do. Then I went to writing class. I was starting to write my new story, when Mrs. Hayes-Roberson came and got me out of there. First I thought I was in trouble but I couldn't think of anything I'd done lately. Really I couldn't. Not that lately. But I was still worried.

She saw the look on my face and told me I wasn't in trouble. She asked me if I would come with her and talk to some other people tomorrow. I said yes but I didn't even know what I was saying yes to really. It was the way she asked, I wanted to say yes, so I did.

I thought she meant people here. She didn't. She told me I would get to talk to the media about all of us being here. I nodded like I knew what she meant. I didn't.

She said we should practice. So first I had to get into some good clothes. I haven't had to get in any good clothes since we got here. What's the point? I was even surprised we had any. I guess grownups always want to have some uncomfortable clothes around for kids to wear. I have to say Mrs. Hayes-Roberson was pretty dressed up herself. She was wearing heels and a suit. Maybe she wears that kind of thing most of the time and I didn't notice. No, she wears tennis shoes usually, I remember. I got to wear my regular shoes though. Good thing, because I don't think they had fancy shoes for kids in the supplies and new fancy shoes usually make my feet hurt.

Then we went into the teacher room and Mrs. Hayes-Roberson told the teachers I would be the first one to talk to the media. She asked them to help me practice. Then I kind of got what was going on, because the teachers pretended to be reporters and asked me stuff. Sometimes they asked serious stuff and sometimes silly and sometimes confusing.

Later I asked Mrs. Hayes-Roberson why she picked me to talk to them and she gave me this big smile and told me that I don't act shy around adults usually. She knew that from all the times I've been in her office. Not this year so much, but definitely last year and the year before, I ended up in the office lots. I'm not shy with Mrs. Hayes-Roberson, that's true, but that didn't seem like it could be the whole thing because there are other kids who are good at talking. Plus I was in her office so much because I was in trouble. There are kids on the French side that could talk to any adult anytime anywhere. So I asked her why me again and she said real serious, "Darryn, I need somebody to talk to them who is a student that could be real with them about what it's like here. Honestly, I didn't want them to talk to someone who might think I wanted them to say everything was okay. It isn't and we both know it. If they interview you and the way you explain things increases the pressure on the government to get us out of here, well, that's a good thing." Then she gave me this little crooked smile and added, "Your teacher also said you did great book review presentations in class."

Book reviews have more power than I ever thought!

Truly, I didn't realize there was anything we could do to help about this quarantine. Right now I'm pretty pleased I was picked to do the talking. No pressure!

Tough day. I didn't feel good. Yesterday I got to talk with some teachers and students about what it is like in here. That was so I won't be just telling my opinion. In a way, I interviewed them, like we do for math surveys, but this was much more depressing.

I have to do it for real with the reporters and now I'm a little nervous. I want to be alone and think about what I want to say when I go to tell about it. It hit me so hard again that I can't go anywhere or do anything. What is that about anyway? I got to do so much stuff everywhere before and now I can't. I am stuck in here with these people and some of them I even like but there is nowhere to GO. No place to be alone, ever. I want to walk where the stores are and not go in them if I don't want. I don't even want to buy anything. I would like to go to a library and just look at a bunch of books that I have not yet read. Instead I have to stay in here and find stuff to do and be around all these people and have to do the same stuff all the time. Just now I heard somebody stumble out in the hall and say "ow" so I can never forget there are all the people around all the time. I snuck in here where we keep the coats and I still can't be alone to think. This sucks, it really does. I want to get OUT even for a walk and it's not safe to even try.

What do we have coats for anyhow. We never go outside.

It could be worse. I could be sick. I could be so sick I couldn't write or read. That would be worse than this. Still being stuck in here for so long is no fun and I wish it would STOP.

Then the miracle happened, we actually WENT OUT-SIDE, sort of. They've built this little . . . odd room that's attached to the side door of the temple and it's made of this clear plastic stuff. Then on one wall of it there's this speaker thing, and we can talk to people with it and they can see us and we can see them but the idea is they can't get contaminated by us. There were wires all over the place, it looked like burned spaghetti spilled everywhere.

Anyway there were all these people there on the other side and they were all reporters. They asked Mrs. Hayes-Roberson some questions but they asked me lots more. They mostly wanted to know if I was okay and what was it like being in quarantine with all the other kids and what kind of lessons we were having. It was very interesting. I explained some about hands on equations and the grammar stuff we had been doing. I also told some about how it's hard to be stuck living with each other like this. I told them I missed McDonald's, which made them laugh. I was serious about that though. I also missed home cooked food even more, no one can make spicy stew like I get at home here. In fact we hardly ever get spicy anything, it's baked chicken or fish and beans and rice mostly.

The flashbulbs going off made me blind though.

When they asked me if I missed my family I couldn't talk for a little bit. All I said then was yes.

It was cool to get to step outside the building, even if it was into a big see-through box. Seeing the sky through the stained glass is not the same at all. I miss the sky.

The principal said she's going to have some other kids do it with her next time. Still, I got to be the first, and I didn't mess it up.

I got a turn on the laptop today. They let me see what I looked like on TV.

After that they just let me zoom around on the web except they wouldn't let me see YouTube.

That was pretty cool, kind of like winning a prize for doing the right thing. Then I got this from Wikipedia, that online place to look up stuff.

Tuberculosis (abbreviated as TB for tubercle bacillus or Tuberculosis) is a common and often deadly infectious disease caused by mycobacteria, in humans mainly Mycobacterium tuberculosis. Tuberculosis usually attacks the lungs (as pulmonary TB) but can also affect the central nervous system, the lymphatic system, the circulatory system, the genitourinary system, the gastrointestinal system, bones, joints, and even the skin.

Now, this is true. I have seen what happens to the skin for some people. Since I had the laptop I did a search and found pictures of TB2 people.

I wonder what the genitourinary system is. I'll have to look it up separately. It sounds bad.

If this is regular tuberculosis is like, no wonder TB2 is so bad:

> Classic symptoms of tuberculosis are a chronic cough with blood-tinged sputum, fever, night sweats, and weight loss.

Total yuck. Sputum is spit!

Reminds me of Angelique and the cancer. She lost so much weight towards the end. What does that mean, "classic symptoms," isn't classic something good and old?

> Infection of other organs causes a wide range of symptoms. The traditional diagnosis relies on radiology (commonly chest X-rays), a tuberculin skin test, blood tests, as well as microscopic examination and microbiological culture of bodily fluids. Tuberculosis treatment is difficult and requires long courses of

multiple antibiotics. Contacts are also screened and treated if necessary. Antibiotic resistance is a growing problem with tuberculosis.

More yuck. I need somebody to explain some of this stuff to me. But it's all about the old tuberculosis. TB2 treatment doesn't rely on anything. So far, everything they tried, they tried lots, nothing works.

> Tuberculosis is spread through the air, when people who have the disease cough, sneeze, or spit. One–third of the world's current population has been infected with M. tuberculosis, and new infections occur at a rate of one per second.

One per second, how did they figure that out? Have they got people with stopwatches at all the hospitals around the world?

It also said that most people don't know they have the tuberculosis and most folks don't die from it. But some people do, about one in ten, but now this new version is much more fatal . . . .

> but, because of population growth, the absolute number of new cases is still increasing.

Eeek!

> In addition, a rising number of people in the developed world are contracting tuberculosis because their immune systems are compromised by immunosuppressive drugs, substance abuse, or AIDS.

Maybe Ms. Wachter can explain what that last part means. There was lots more and I read what I could but I got tired of reading. Whoa, is this online entry out of date. TB2 isn't even in it!

Wait a minute, it would be a different entry because they are not the same disease. I'll try again.

I put in TB2 and oh my. I couldn't even begin to read all this stuff. And it is so much worse than the other kind of tuberculosis. Anyway my computer time was up.

Ms. Wachter is still reading us that book called Betsy-Tacy and Tib by somebody named Lovelace, which I think is a wonderful name. I can picture this piece of lace with all hearts and flowers. Anyway, the book is pretty good, even though it's just about these three girlfriends who lived a long time ago in a little town. We've been reading it since we got here, off and on. Today the boys, well some of them, complained that this book isn't as good as Hatchet. That's about a boy who survives living by himself in the woods after a plane crash. Hatchet was a very exciting book and I liked listening to it, but I like this one too.

So we got into talking about both books and I guess we got kind of loud. One of the other teachers came over to us to see what was going on. She said to Ms. Wachter, "Is everything okay?" and she smiled back and explained, "Yes, this is our compare and contrast genres lesson."

Whatever that means. I don't know what she was explaining but the other teacher went away and we went back to arguing.

Alejandro didn't say anything about Betsy-Tacy in class but I happened to know he was reading Betsy and Tacy Go Downtown because I saw it in his desk. I hope it's still in there when we get out of quarantine and he can finish it. I also know he would hate it if I offered to let him have my copy, which I snagged when we got those free books sent to us. He plays soccer — back when we could — really well. He likes to argue loud with the other boys. So I don't think he would want anybody to know he likes a girl book. We got Hatchet in French but Sebastian, that tall guy with the muscles, who is in French Immersion, is keeping it to himself. The other guys in French Immersion want it and he keeps saying not yet. Maybe it takes longer to read in French?

Everyone is bored with the food. We haven't had long noodle spaghetti with sauce even once, and that is just about my favorite food of all. Maybe if I get a bunch of kids to ask for it with me? We did have those shell pastas once but it's been weeks since we got here and that's only once. They gave us little personal pizzas but I think something happened to them because they were all dry and awful.

What a meal. Last night Mrs. Hayes-Roberson and Mr. B and Mrs. Wilson all three cooked dinner for us. I had no idea Mr. B could make fried chicken and fried fish and Mrs. Hayes-Roberson made these amazing biscuits and these flaky wrapped up rolls called croissants and these cool green beans with some kind of oil and pepper sauce and then after all that Mrs. Wilson the secretary made these wonderful desserts. Then there were cookies, five different kinds of cookies, chocolate chip and butter-scotch and oatmeal raisin and sugar cookies with pow-dered sugar and these sesame toffee cookies that I never had anything like them before. I think I had the most of the sesame toffee kind.

There was fresh mango for dessert too. I got juice all over my face. Mango, the fruit that eats you back.

I really thought my tummy was going to bust. There was Mrs. Hayes-Roberson, in an apron, waving a spoon in Mr. Binwald's face and telling him he wasn't cooking fast enough and he laughed at her and it was great. There was Ms. Wachter, teasing Mrs. Wilson about hogging the oven with the desserts, so she couldn't make her stuff, and really most of the night we kind of forgot that we were stuck here in this building while the doctors watched to see if anybody dropped dead. It was a nice change.

Ms. Rose just made sure they weren't messing up the cooking part and the keeping it kosher part. You could tell she wanted to be in there cooking too but she'd agreed to let them do it so she had to step back. She went to check on something once and Mrs. Hayes-Roberson called out, "Ms. Myra Rose, you're off-duty," and she threw up her hands and went back to her stool but I don't think she was that mad, really.

Now I know her first name.

The next night Mrs. Pang made our class some traditional Chinese food like I never had before even though I have been to plenty of Chinese restaurants. It was weird but good sticky rice cakes and a doughnut that had bean paste in it. I didn't think the doughnut would be good but it was. I guess it pays to try new stuff. Sometimes the grownups forget to worry if kids are going to get the runs.

Rice fixes just about anything wrong with your insides, I think. At least rice pudding does. You forget about feeling bad because it tastes good.

It turns out sometimes all you have to do is tell people that they can't do something and they find a way. Hooray! The school PTA and some of the community groups like CASA and these other Jewish groups have all gotten together and figured out a way for us to get a real Thanksgiving meal, which will also be kosher. There's a TV channel just about food, and they helped organize it, and all this food is going to be cooked and brought to us by a Jewish caterer that only does kosher stuff. They have done big weddings and so on, the difference is they make it all ahead of time and seal it and when it's dinner time we heat it up. Well, Rose and the other folks will. I will get to eat it, and I hope there will be seconds.

Now it doesn't matter about the quarantine, the stuff gets delivered the way our other food does. I already got to watch that, it's not all that exciting. A big truck pulls up. A guy in a moon suit thing comes around and loads up boxes on a hand truck. He rolls it around to the door with the plastic walls around it, and Mr. Rabin and Mr. Binwald and Rose put it away in the big walk-in refrigerator or the pantry. This time was a little more interesting because there were men in Army uniforms helping and they were not wearing the whole moon suit thing, just gas masks. They had all that food unloaded in no time and then Rose had to figure out how to put it all away until dinner time, which was going to be early but not right away.

No one noticed me until the end, and I got told to go play. What they really meant was go away, so I did, and told Maria all about it.

Some kids were complaining afterwards that there wasn't any ham (not ever kosher) or other stuff they have at home like dulce de leche or mashed potatoes (which we couldn't have because mashed potatoes get made with milk and butter and if there's no milk the instant kind of mashed potatoes is horrible. I know dad buys it sometimes when we have no choice.) I mean there is no pleasing some people.

We almost didn't even have any Thanksgiving!

It's a good thing we got here after Halloween. I don't want to think about how much complaining there would have been about no trick or treating or candy!

I did have seconds.

One glorious thing about being here is that doing homework is usually quick, fun and easy. The teachers really don't want to have to help us with it, and there aren't any parents to do that part either. Still parents want us to have some, even if we are at school for longer in here. Still eating and going to the bathroom take a long time, much longer than before, so maybe it works out the same.

Tonight we were doing our homework, which was to make a play out of the chapter we read in class. I love getting to do this, especially if I get to be a character, but it really doesn't matter. I'll make the costumes and props out of stuff we find, I like doing that.

Sometimes we just use cardboard to make puppets but not this time.

We are doing the Wizard of Oz from the book, not the movie, but we are doing some of the songs too since they are so fun. Maria is getting to be Dorothy and she is so convincing, all wide-eyed and bewildered in Oz. Marion gets to be Toto since she has the best yap of anybody. Plus she did not mind having to help make the dog costume and fix it so it really looks more like a dog. Rehearsals are hard on the costumes. Stephanie is getting to be the Wicked Witch because she can do the creepy laugh and I have enough green markers to do her face. (It doesn't always wash off but nobody really cares in here.)

So while we busy with our show, in comes a little girl with a clipboard.

"I have to find words for homework," she announced loudly, "it's very important that I get as many words as I can that start with buh," and when Ernie laughed she looked at him sternly and added, "the letter B which makes the sound buh."

It was interesting, how we all stopped to look at her and somehow felt we had to stop our homework to help her with hers. It was something about she stood there, looking so serious even though some kids wanted to laugh.

Rachel spoke up first, "What color is the rug?"

"I already have blue," she said scornfully.

She did have a few words on her paper. I decided not to see what they were, but looked around the room, trying to see what there was that started with the buh sound.

Then John, who was wanted to get back to being the Cowardly Lion, said, "We're buh-busy," but she shook her head and snapped, "You can't just tell me. Then it doesn't count." I think she knew there was a hint in there, but she decided to ignore it.

So Erin pointed to Baruti and whispered, "Ask him his name." So she did and he told her and her eyes lit up and she asked him, "How do you spell that?"

He spelled it, and pointed to his ear, and then he realized there was no way for her to know he ever had a Bluetooth, but she nodded and said "Boy," and wrote it down on her paper.

"And what's your name?" Baruti asked her.

"My name is Elizabeth."

Carrie squealed, "Oh, you can use your own name then, you can use Beth."

She stood up as tall as she could and said very slowly, "My name is Elizabeth. Not Beth. It has never been Beth. It will never be Beth."

Having explained all that with great dignity, she wrote down Beth.

I pointed out The Wizard of Oz. She looked puzzled for a minute, then got it and wrote down book. I pointed to the author's name, she wrote down Baum.

Robert started jumping up and down, and so did some other kids, just to do it too. Pretty soon we were all doing it. "Bouncing!" she exclaimed and wrote it down.

"Boo!"

"Doesn't count, you can't just say it, she told us that!"

Now other people were into it, running around, pointing at things, trying to give hints, and sometimes arguing about what they meant.

"Wall does not start with buh."

"I know that. I'm not pointing at the wall. I'm pointing at that."

"That what? That's a wall."

"That's a board at the bottom of the wall. Now you made me say it!"

Of course Sebastian — who is not even in our play, just hanging out in the room — has to point to his butt. That makes some kids laugh so hard they can't talk. Elizabeth does not write it down. She's trying to get some other words, and every once in a while I hear her wail, "How do you spell that?"

Dena feels sorry for her and gets everyone to stop running around and hollering. She helps Elizabeth (not Beth) figure out a few more words and then tells her to try somewhere else.

Elizabeth is not pleased about that idea.

"I only need five more and I'm done."

Then Rachel, who is the Scarecrow, gets a great idea, I have to say. She looks at Elizabeth and says, "Imagine you're in the kitchen."

"We're not allowed in the kitchen."

"That's why you have to imagine it. Besides, most kitchens are the same, just bigger or smaller."

"Not on Food Network."

"Just think about a kitchen, okay?"

I am amazed. Usually Rachel doesn't have much patience. Or maybe just not with me.

"Okay, you're in the kitchen. Look on the shelves. Look in the refrigerator. What is there that starts with B?"

Elizabeth shuts her eyes. So do some of the other kids. I think about a kitchen but I don't shut my eyes. I can think of a few words right away, but I don't say them.

It's more exciting if she finds her own.

Elizabeth starts writing. "How many T's in butter?"

"Two."

"The way I wrote bowl doesn't look right."

"It's B-O-W-L."

"That doesn't look right either."

"I know. What's that w doing there?"

"Making it hard to spell."

Everyone laughs, Elizabeth too.

"Box has an x at the end."

"Yes, it does."

"I need two more words."

Maria grins and says, "What is it called when you cook something in the oven?"

Elizabeth looks confused.

"Rhymes with cake."

"Bake!"

One more. My brain is blank. Then I realize.

"It's not in the kitchen, not really, but you've got one more buh word," I tell Elizabeth, "I bet you will like this one." She taps her pencil on her clipboard. I give her a look, because little girls do not tap their pencils at Darryn, especially when this is not my homework. But then I give in, because I want her to win this buh word game.

I put my finger on my head and start to hum. I can't remember just how the song starts. "With the thoughts I'd be thinking . . . " Maria joins in, then John, and Rachel of course since it's her song. "I could be another Lincoln, if I only had a —"

Her face lights up. "Brain!" she shouts, and we all finish the song together.

"And then I'd sit, and think some more!"

Now that's the way to do homework.

One of the worst things I know about TB2 is you have no appetite on top of the coughing and fever and stuff. Well, the worst thing would be dying, excuse me. People are dying all over the place. Even though we can't watch the news, we know. The grownups are not so good about hiding what they hear.

I am so glad I haven't gotten it! Yet. You never know.

Mr. Binwald talked to Ms. Wachter yesterday and I think she was trying to make a joke. She was complaining that she couldn't get to see any sports in here. He said, "Well, there's not much to watch these days, because of TB2."

So she said, "Well, I bet the baseball players aren't spitting as much. That used to gross me out, they did it so much."

Mr. Binwald stared at her and said, "It isn't baseball season now."

"I know," she said, "I was just trying to find something to be glad about. Do you miss watching football?"

"Yes, and so does everybody else. Didn't you hear? They cancelled the rest of the games until they get this thing under control. They're worried about it spreading among the crowds in stadiums."

She cried out, "No!" and put out her hands like Stop.

Not just baseball and football, but soccer and basketball and hockey and everything! Imagine that, no big sports games. Of course I didn't always want to watch, but it's got to be really bad if nobody gets to go to it or see it or even play the games now.

It also means lots of people are out of work. No games to play, no work. Sad.

So the PTA sent us food twice. They pick out the food at the kosher grocery store online and then we get it. That's the Parent and Teacher organization, which doesn't get to do much since we are all in quarantine. The food was nice. It was some good salads and soups. I tried something called tabboolah. That was my favorite part of that meal.

Funny moment of the day today: Ms. Wachter stood up and called her yellow group for reading and kids from all over the place started coming towards her. She even had fourth graders and second graders coming at her. I guess all the teachers have some kind of yellow group!

Whenever I find a book I really like I tell myself to try to read it real slow to make it last. I always think that and I hardly ever do it. I read straight through to the end of all the Pooh books and all the Anansi stories I could find when I first started reading them and I was sorry when that was it, there weren't any more. I did write my own Anansi story but I still wanted more that I could read.

I'm so glad this synagogue has a library. Some lady who belonged to this synagogue decided this place should have a library and so it does. Mostly it is books for grownups but there are some kids books. Thank goodness for books if I have to be stuck inside!

I got a tape recorder from a radio reporter today. Any kid that the teachers thought was a good writer got one. Everybody is jealous of course. The thing is, I can't use it for fun, really, we got a lecture about not wasting the gizmos (what a great word, gizmo, sounds just like what it is) and playing around with the tape recorders. We need to use them to NARRATE what we later write down.

So let's practice a little narrating here and describe all the important details of this special SETTING that I'm in right now.

Hello, all the people out there not in quarantine. This is Darryn Yochangko Thomas, reporting to you from the new location of Roosevelt Elementary School. We live inside a synagogue. It's really something, to learn how to say that word and even more to spell it right every time. The s-y-n part doesn't have anything to do with the other kind of sin, s-i-n. This synagogue was built a long time ago. The walls inside are mostly very plain, not decorated like churches I have been in. No stations of the cross. Well, of course not. There's some stuff on the walls but it's way high up and it's just designs, not of people. So this wall goes up about, I don't know, way over my head, way over Mr. B's head, and it is a grey brown color. There are narrow windows up high, maybe twenty feet up. I wish I could estimate how high the walls go. Mr. B is six feet something. So if someone as tall as him was on his shoulders, and then another one, and a couple more . . . if the Wizards team all stood on top of each other . . . if it was a bunch of kids standing on top of each other it would take like twice as many . . . so at least 30 feet high. I think. These are the side walls.

The back wall doesn't have any windows. It has a big balcony where most of the teachers live and sleep and under that is kind of like the lobby, where you come into the building. The lobby has big glass doors with padlocks on them. There are two rooms right there off the lobby and the teachers use them, one for sleeping and one for a teacher's lounge because it has a bathroom.

There are not enough bathrooms for all of us. Everybody takes turns. We also had to invent our shower which is funny the first two times you use it and then it isn't funny any more.

On the back wall behind the balcony upstairs is a just a wall. There's no art or anything on it. The teachers carefully put up some paper on that wall and then some of them put up pictures of their families or just pictures they liked. They did it really carefully so the wall would look the same and no paint would come off when they took it all down. There is a special kind of mounting tape they used that comes off easily.

They put up other posters and papers at school with tape, lots of tape, and the stuff still comes down all the time. There are some special posters hanging from the ceiling in the classroom on some wire and they don't come down, but there isn't the same kind of ceiling in here. I remember one poster at school said, "Every child can learn, but perhaps not the same way on the same day." I remember that one because I agree with it.

There's a very cool thing out in the front on the wall where the steps stop and it's called the Tree of Life. I've never seen anything like this Tree. It's a tree made of some kind of metal that is flat but mounted on the wall. Instead of leaves it has these little rectangles with names. Next to every name is this little light and they never turn the light off. The names are of people that died and somebody wants them to be remembered so they had the rectangle made with the name on it right on the metal. It's one of the coolest things I've ever seen.

In the lobby part there is a painting. The painting shows Noah and the Ark. It's done a very cool way, with lots of unusual colors for the animals and drawn with these interesting lines and angles. We used it for our angle lesson in geometry, that's how I know. There's a lot going on in this picture. The Ark is a boat, which I didn't know, I thought an arc was like a half circle, which it is, but spelled differently. I can look at it for a long time and not get bored. So if you don't know and you're listening to this, Noah is this guy in the Bible and God told him there was going to be a flood. So Noah was smart and built a boat and put two kinds of every animal he could find in it and when it flooded he didn't drown but made it okay, and his family too. There is more to the story than that, if you really read the Bible like I did because that's one of the books they got lots of here. Grownups have all these movies we're not supposed to see, and then they have these Bibles all over that tell more nasty stuff than most of the movies. Anyway Noah gets drunk after they all make it through the flood. The painting doesn't show that. It wouldn't be as interesting if they did. Plus they wouldn't call it Noah and the Ark, they would call it the Hangover and the colors would be lots darker, I bet.

The next place is the sanctuary, I hope I said that right. There are rows of seats and a balcony area. The front wall in the front of it is the most interesting. That has the bima which is like a platform or stage where all the serious business of the synagogue happens. But Bima doesn't mean stage. It is more special than that and only happens in a synagogue. It's the whole thing up in front, with all the stuff for a synagogue service. There are a couple of podiums (another new word I learned, glad I get to use it) where people stand to say stuff and read stuff. Both the podiums have stars on them. The stars have six points instead of five and they are called the Star of David after the king in the Bible and I guess he invented it. Anyway these podiums are made of marble, they are not going anywhere. When we do stuff up on the Bima we can't move them out of the way. Still it's good to get to go up there to read a report because they are big and impressive and they have microphones that really work. The mikes we used at school didn't always work.

Behind the podiums is, are? the best part. There are two big wooden doors. It is a neat golden kind of wood. Behind the doors is the secret wonderful thing that Jewish people think is the most important sacred thing. It is not the dead Jesus. It is not a picture of God the Father or a statue of anyone. It isn't even made out of gold.

It's words on big scrolls that tell the story of the Jews and God. They call this the Torah, and they keep it locked in a little room they call the Ark. The most important thing in this place is the Word. Words, I mean. This is a great place to hang out and be a writer. And a reader. And a pretty constant talker. So I must belong here!

We only got to see the scrolls two times. The two Jewish teachers and Mr. Rabin got special permission to show them to us. Some kids thought it was weird but I thought it was awesome. I can understand not taking them out or letting us see them all the time. Putting them behind the fancy doors makes them special and keeps them safe. So far.

Maria says one of the worst things about being here is not seeing or playing with her dog, and one of the best is there are all these books she's never read. I have to say that's a pretty good summary.

Right now is the break we get between school and dinner. We can do some stuff on our own and people have some games out and stuff. We got all these free Legos from the Lego people and some kids are building towers to see who can make the biggest ones. It's funny, kids start out making different things like towns and things and it always ends up a couple of kids making the biggest tower. That's what Jamarr is doing right now.

That's enough about setting, let's do characters. Let's see.

There is a boy Bill, he is telling the Declaration of Independence again to a bunch of little kids. He's different, this guy. He sure does know the Declaration, though. He's been telling it to everybody since we got here. He told me he got to see the real thing at the Archives in D.C. He knows all about it and how it got written, he told me more than I would ever think to ask about it. I wondered if maybe he was so into it because his family is from the Philippines, but it's not because he's new to America. I found out he was born here, actually. He was born with something called Ashburgers syndrome, which means, as far as I can tell, he's just different. It has something to do with how his brain works. He's real smart though, not just about that Declaration. He can do sixth grade math already. Also he knows like a million knock-knock jokes so when I need one I always go ask him.

Some other characters in here are my friends. I think these are the most interesting characters but I am biased. Maria is my best friend and she is funny and smart and very beautiful, that is not just me saying that, I have heard other girls say she is beautiful, especially her big brown eyes and long dark brown curly hair and unlike me she has good eyebrows. My eyebrows are too big and fluffy but hers look fine, just big enough around her eyes and just long enough. Okay you would not be able to come in here and ask for the girl with the good eyebrows but if you get to look at her for long you would notice, I promise. Maria is normally fun to be around but today she is having a bad day. She misses her dog. She misses her family too a whole lot but today she is missing her dog. She told me she wrote three pages in her journal about her dog, Caribe. She let me read her journal, which she hardly ever does let me do and what she wrote about the dog is pretty good. Some of it is in Spanish but the part in English that I can read is excellente.

Reading it makes me wish I could play with Caribe and pet his soft fur. He sounds like a calm sort of dog. I would like that kind best.

So some of my other friends wanted to know what she wrote and I asked her if she would read it to us which she did and now a bunch of kids are writing about their pets, except Jackie and Kurt who are drawing about theirs.

I would write about mine except I don't have any. I talked my dad into letting me have a goldfish once but it died. I can't decide if I would rather have a dog or a cat or what. More kids seem to play with their dogs. It doesn't matter, I can't have one anyway, but in here no one can have one. They might be vectors like the hamsters which means they could get sick with TB2 or kind of get sick and make us sick. That's what happened with the class pets. Eww, I don't want to think about that.

But the real reason we can't have dogs here is I bet that you could not take a dog for a walk while you are in quarantine. After all they won't let us go for a walk.

Instead we get to write about pets in our journals. I get to record it all with this tape recorder. That's how it is in here, and goodbye to you, people out there.

One thing that really bugs me about being in here is the food. It is bland boring food. I wish so hard for a spicy food. When I was a little little kid in Cameroon we would have this wonderful spicy peanut stew. With fufu which you can't get here. My grandmother would make it, and it was so good. I always ate a little too much. Here we can't have spicy, and no peanuts allowed. Because someone is maybe allergic no one can have it.

When we talk about food, the other kids mostly talk about McDonalds and KFC and good pizza. Everyone wants something hot and greasy. I don't know if I want the greasy but I wish it was hot. By the time everyone gets it it's not hot anymore. They don't have a table to keep it hot like we did in the cafeteria.

Actually it was never all that hot by the time we got it then either.

The kitchen here is special and we can only use part of it. There's a member of the synagogue we call Ms. Rose, and she is in charge of the kitchen. It's what's called a kosher kitchen and she wanted it to stay that way. She has been trying to keep it kosher, but it is hard and now she says they may just have to re-kosher some of it when we leave. It's a big deal if they have to do that but she says our lives are more important than that. There is supposed to be a rabbi to supervise the kosher part and we don't have one around. So the teachers and Ms. Rose use the kitchen to make meals and heat up the meals and we use paper plates that go right in a trashcan. We can't even recycle anything because of TB2. It gets taken away in trucks that say Hazardous Material on them. I tried but I can't see the trucks but I got told about them by Mr. Ramos.

The only serious rule is, no pork allowed. Ahmed is okay with this, his family doesn't eat pork either though he is not Jewish. Ahmed is Muslim. Erin's a vegetarian so she is fine with no pork too. I will miss sausage but it's not too bad.

I really got interested in this whole kosher thing from the man who is the go-to guy about the synagogue, Mr. Rabin. Mr. Rabin volunteered to stay here with us when we got sent here for quarantine. He says he's so old he figures he doesn't have that much time left anyway. He laughed when he said it but I didn't. (Mr. Rabin is not the rabbi. The rabbi is like their head guy, but it's not the same as the priest. As far as I can tell, the rabbi is more like the teacher, but it's hard to understand, because he does marry people like a priest does. Their rabbi was visiting somewhere in South Carolina when the quarantine happened. So he by the time he got back he couldn't get back in!)

It took us a while to walk here and by that time Mr. Rabin, who is retired and was in here for a meeting, had figured out that somebody needed to stay. He said the other people tried to talk him out of it because he might get TB2 from us. He laughed and said he was 70 years old and if that was enough for God it was enough for him.

I think that's an interesting way to look at things.

Anyway I'm glad he's here.

I found out about kosher stuff first when we couldn't have cheeseburgers. Cheeseburgers aren't kosher. You can't have dairy stuff like milk and cheese with meat stuff. There's some stuff you aren't supposed to eat at all, like pork or shellfish. That means stuff like bacon, crabs or lobster. Which is too bad since crabs and bacon taste pretty good to me. I want to find out how come they can't eat those things. He says it says it in the Bible and I never read that part. He told me it says you can't cook a calf in its mother's milk. EEWW, I never thought about it being like that and now I won't be able to stop thinking about it.

So we can only use some parts of the kitchen and we have to be careful and some kind of things we won't eat while we're here. On the other hand, hummus is pretty good and some of these salads really rock. Kosher seems to mean more crunchy stuff to eat.

We do get that sad dry pizza sometimes but it is not good. We get it with this weird cheese because some kids can't digest dairy, so this is fake cheese made out of something else. I don't even know what. I don't want to know what. Oh and because of kosher we can't have it with pepperoni. Maybe we could have fake cheese and fake pepperoni and it wouldn't count. Of course it would taste pretty bad!

Even the food we get that is supposed to be spicy isn't. It's just sort of sad no taste paste. Last night Maria was complaining about the nachos we get, with the beef in the sauce on top, and she made me laugh. She held up the little tray in the air and said, "Can I have some hot sauce? Can I have some medium salsa then? Can I get some Tabasco sauce please? Can I have some jalepenos por favor? Can I get some old Texas Pete sauce in a bottle so old it has turned brown?" Then she thought up some more things and other kids started chiming in, saying what spicy things they wanted, and we started giggling and they were saying just silly stuff, like "Soy sauce!" and "Maple syrup!"

We were still kind of talking about it when Ms. Wachter walked by, so she came over to say hi and we had to tell her about what Maria said. She smiled and agreed with us about the no flavor but she did explain there was a reason. The first reason I could figure out for myself; lots of kids don't like spice much. The other reason, yuck, is what might happen if lots of kids get the runs from the spice. Sheesh, eat rice with it, like a normal person. Or fufu except of course there isn't any. The final reason is because the ones who have sore throats, they can't eat the spice. It will hurt. I can see all that and I still think it's a shame that nobody gets to have it intense because some people can't handle intense. Life is supposed to be hot sometimes!

Like a Gloria Estefan song. I know Gloria Estefan is old, but Maria loves her so I do too. If you can't handle her song the Conga, don't listen, don't dance it. Maybe you'll learn something wonderful. Maybe you'll just get to watch.

But nobody gets the hot because some people can't handle hot? Makes no sense.

Ms. Wachter said she would see what she could do about getting some hot sauce. I bet they don't allow it but it's good that she wants to try.

What I really really want is a meal that got made in my very own kitchen and I get to eat it right in my own house. Sometimes I wonder if we'll ever get out of here. Living with all these people is so different. I thought it was crowded in my house until I got here. You have to negotiate or get in line for just about everything. There's stuff that should be private but everybody gets to see here, like flossing. It just bugs me, seeing people floss their teeth and having to floss mine in front of folks. But we can't help it, we don't have nearly enough room or time for everyone to do their flossing there in the bathroom.

Actually we probably do have enough time but the grownups want us to hurry up so they can talk to each other about grownup stuff after we're asleep. Except I get up and sneak upstairs to listen, of course. I have gotten so good at sneaking around, like an international spy, I mean I am super quiet. I can open a door and I hardly let it make a sound. If you do it real slow there's hardly any sound. Then I put my feet down real soft. If somebody does wake up or the grownups watcher sees me I just say I have to pee. I say it like that, not the polite way, I don't say I have to go to the bathroom, I say I have to pee and they always let me go. Something about that word pee. Then I go around to the balcony and slip up the stairs. If I get caught at that point I just say I had a bad dream. I can always make up a bad dream or tell an old one. But I don't get caught often and I don't want to get caught. I want to hear what they talk about. It's super important to hear them. They don't always tell us what's going on. Also they don't always know what's going on, and so it's interesting to hear what they say. Some of them are more scared than the kids. Some of them are really cranky. Some of them are really sad, and I think there are a couple who actually like it! Not forever and ever, but it's like an adventure and that's how they see it.

The science teacher has changed what he tells us. He used to just teach us some about weather. Lately that's all he talks about. That's kind of a mess because nobody can go out in the weather, so who cares, really? He showed us this website, called NOAA, which tells all about weather all over the country. There is this weird robot voice that tells what the weather forecast is going to be. Then the science teacher explains what it means exactly. Like what it means if there are inches of rain, how they measure that, and what temperature it needs to be for sleet. I hate to tell when he's so excited about it, but I do not care. If it's going to snow I don't want to know because I can't go out and enjoy it anyway!

He does answer questions and show us how to do research about other science things. Also we get to do cool science projects about how gravity works and we made this ecosystem in a soda bottle. Some things we can only learn about from the computer because all the stuff for experiments is back at school and they won't send it to us here.

Lots of the teachers just teach one thing now. Or they teach different kids than they used to when we were back at school. They're teaching us what they remember and what they're good at, they have to because all the books and other stuff are back at school. They talk to each other all the time about what the next lessons are going to be. There's no way to avoid hearing about it in here and how some of them find it so annoying.

The thing is, I like listening to the teachers grumble. I had no idea that they grumbled so well.

One teacher was talking about how much she loves to travel and of course she can't now. Another teacher said she went to a whinery and then she kept whining about it. Then somebody else, I think it was Madamoiselle La-Fontaine, said everybody deserves a happy hour. I think they deserve more than an hour myself. For a little bit they all started to talk at once, but then they stopped and one or two talked and it ended up that they're going to have a Happy Hour here. I don't get it but they are excited about it. One teacher said I need time away from all of you, not another hour together! But they kept planning, saying who they were going to call and how they would arrange it. Teachers seem to need to have events to plan no matter what.

I wonder what makes one hour happy and another not. From what they said it seems to have something to do with tea, a tea called tea keel ah.

I heard one teacher tell another one not to complain too much about being in quarantine and having to plan all their lessons together. She said that in Texas, they tell you when to breathe, and in Florida they tell teachers to retain kids in second grade if they're concerned they won't do well on the big test. Some other teacher said that her sister told her not to move to California until they get it together because schools are falling apart.

How can they tell teachers when to breathe? I don't get it.

Most of the time the lessons are pretty good, I have to admit. We have invented a bunch of new games since we've been in here. I don't know where we get all our ideas. We played some that we thought of because there are all these Jewish Bibles here, that they call . . . the Torah or the Five Books, I think. There are more than five stories but that's what they call it. One game that everybody likes is Moses and the pharaoh, because there's some movie, which I never saw, about it so everyone who saw the movie knows the story. The boys argue over who gets to be Moses. The girls can only be Miriam, who is Moses' sister, who is interesting to start with when she puts Moses in the basket in the river but then she doesn't do much. Oh and there's Pharoah's wife that saves Moses but she doesn't say much either. I wanted to write the story myself so she could say and do more but they wouldn't let me. They just like to do the part where Moses and the Israelites get away from Pharoah after all the plagues. They love the plagues. Here we are living through one and they still love the plague part.

Rachel and I like the Ruth and Naomi story. That's pretty cool. I like the mother part better because she is one who finds the rich husband for Ruth. That's a good thing to do for someone you love, find them someone with money, like a prince in a fairy tale only without the dragons and all that. Devorah likes the story that has Devorah in it, naturally, only sometimes it's Deborah instead of Devorah and she's a judge, but not like the women on the Supreme Court. In the bible Deborah was a leader who could pick who could be a general, kind of like our president, and she picked pretty good. They won, the Israelites that is, and I really liked that story.

One of the stories we all like is the one about Esther. There are parts for everybody and the synagogue has costumes to go with all of the people in the story. Also there are noisemakers and flags and all kinds of stuff for us to use to act it out. I tried to record it with that recorder they gave me but it didn't work very well.

Somehow everyone is cranky today. Little fights all over, and you can hear how grumpy they all are, the way they talk. It doesn't make any sense but contagious cranky doesn't have to make sense anyway. There's no way to fix it exactly because the arguments don't make any sense to start with. I can feel the mad in me, for sure. Maria wanted to borrow my book and I just did not want to give it to her. Plus somebody went and re-arranged the books in our Fourth Grade space and it's not the way it ought to be. That just bugs me no end. The way I had it was the right way. They ought to know that. I certainly am going to tell them. There was even a book that wasn't put on the shelf correctly and the pages are crunched up. That is so wrong! To make it all even worse, nobody will say who did it. Ms. Wachter is annoyed too, I can tell. It's the way she keeps rubbing her eyes. I bet she doesn't even know she does that when she's mad.

I'm not going to be the one to tell her either. Not today. No way. Not on Cranky at Roosevelt in Exile Day.

Joe, Thomas, Eric and maybe John all got in trouble for wrestling. They said they weren't fighting but that was sure what it looked like. Still they weren't mad at each other, that I could tell. I think they like bouncing off each other sometimes. They seem to like it. Boys. They don't have to make sense.

We really ought to be able to pick our own school holidays. Today would be a good day to call one. Except of course WE CAN'T DO THAT BECAUSE THERE'S NOWHERE WE CAN GO.

A radio reporter interviewed me on the phone today. Her name is Liz Hunt and she has a very good voice. I guess that is important if you are going to be on the radio. She picked me to interview because she really liked what I recorded on the tape recorder. I forgot after a while that it was for a radio show. It was just easy to talk to her.

I hope I didn't say anything I wasn't supposed to say.

Things have gotten pretty interesting. The teachers decided they were going to group us starting now by what we could do together and how we matched up. That's what they said, anyway. What it means is that I'm in a writing group with kids that are all different ages. I got two Second Graders and one Third Grader, lots of Fourth Graders and one Fifth Grader in my writing group. And it works. One of the teachers said that age was a dumb way to group kids, it was arbitrary (it's my new word, I like it) which means that using our age isn't a good way to measure kids. Anyway we are in groups according to how we learn and it is kind of cool. For one thing I don't get bugged by having to stop and read the directions again because some kids in my group can't understand what they are asking us to write.

So everybody in my group is in the same category, so to speak, and I can talk to them about how to write it without having to slow down or just stop while the teacher talks. We get in a group and talk about what we wrote and we can ask each other questions and it's not just pleasing the teacher all the time. Some times that's the last thing in the world I want to do but sometimes I just had to do it so we could get the work done. Really it's amazing how teachers just insist on teaching you the way they think it ought to be. There ought to be more room for doing it different, although maybe not for certain rules. I can see not saying that nouns aren't nouns anymore or something like that. And I think adjectives should stay adjectives. You need some kind of rules for language. Even the French Immersion students know that. French word order is different, though. I want to say the words go backwards but that isn't right. They go in a different order. Vive la difference, as they say.

I think the language with the most music already in it is Spanish.

In some parts of Cameroon they speak French but I never learned it. America has more places with Spanish I think.

When it's time for writing I like working in my group. It's so much easier doing stuff with this group. They are talking about doing the same kind of grouping for reading, and maybe partly for math. The thing is for math we already are in different groups, but that doesn't always work. The big problem with that is that the group doing the accelerated stuff sometimes doesn't remember as much as they think they do. But they go around saying they are the smartest.

Really, I don't think they are because I have played with those kids and I'm in reading with some of them and they are not that smart in everything. They are just good at school math. If I work hard at learning something I can get smart about it if I really work at it. Math in school isn't always like when you use math in real life.

School math is when they ask you to solve all kinds of problems and memorize stuff and those word problems but I guess you have to learn some of it. I hate those stupid formative assessments that look like they are easy but they're not. Some of the teachers don't like those formative things either but they sure give us lots of them all the time. You can always tell a formative because there's only one or two problems on a page and it says you have to explain how you got your answer. That is really dumb sometimes. Like how did I get 3 times 7. So I have to draw an array, which can be like this:

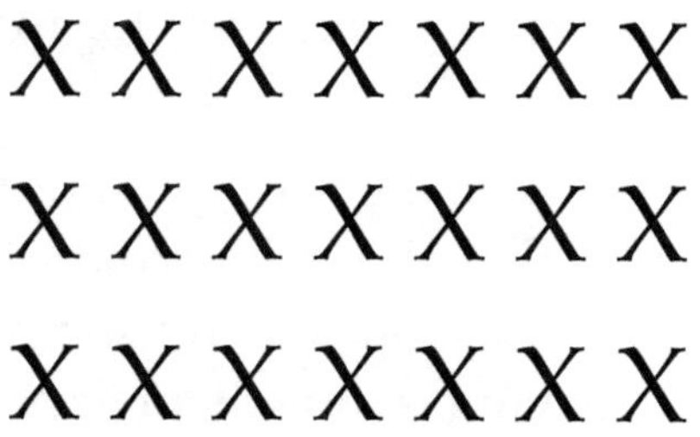

or even just circles instead of some dumb smiley face and that shows a MODEL of what 3 times seven is, except the thing is, it's always 21, no matter what, so who cares what I draw? But I have to draw something to show it. I don't really *mind* the drawing part. Sometimes I get so into it I have to hurry up and finish the rest of the multiple-choice part. Then I have to write words with it like, this is three times seven, in case they didn't know that. It's called a math BCR. That stands for Brief Constructed Response, which means, explain your answer, no really, explain it a lot.

I told Ms. Wachter I was allergic to BCRs and she laughed, but I still have to do them. She says the point is to show I understand how to solve the problem, write it out step by step. I bet the other part is to show you didn't cheat and copy it from the person next to you. Of course you could copy the BCR too, but if they are exactly the same the teacher will smell a rat.

So I will be sure to make mine very unique. I think I ought to draw little fish or something. Or maybe now I'll do rows of that David six point star that is all over the place here at this temple. At least that would be something new. My friend Abby just makes dots. Or little circles. She's says it's boring already so why make it interesting? I say why not make it interesting so it isn't boring?

We do not see it the same way for making a math array.

If I was going to make rows, I would make ones that make some sense, that show the groups in my math class now with captions. I would draw something interesting instead of just having a bunch of letters or circles.   It would be like this:

Group 1   Group 2

Group 3   Group 4

I am in Group 2. Now Group 1 is the fast group that gets whatever it is done and then starts talking about movies or something until the teacher catches them, then they go back to work. There's always more work, another worksheet, it's never just do it and take a break. Oh no.

In Group 2 we do some of the work and then we whisper or pass notes. Usually then we do the rest after the little whisper break. We don't get caught goofing off as much as Group 1 because we're not stupid enough to be so loud about the not-math stuff.

Group 3 is the group that argues. At least they argue about math, mostly. The teacher has to go and referee sometimes when they do group work. They get it done after they argue and sometimes they get it right and sometimes not.

Then finally there's Group 4. Group 4 can't get it done. They almost always need help and have the teacher explain it again. They don't seem upset about it though. Last year we had a Group like Group 4 in my class and they would get all frustrated and stuff and say they were dumb. If you say you are dumb and not good enough long enough you will convince yourself and everyone else. But this Group 4 is perfectly okay with asking the teacher to explain it all again and then sometimes they get it and sometimes they don't and so on. Group 4 is the group that doesn't know or at least mind that they don't get it. Some of them are downright rude about asking for help, from the rest of us or from the teacher. Maybe they think if they don't understand it's the teacher's fault or our fault. She should have explained it better or find another way. That's the thing about Group 4. It's not their fault. It's somebody else's, practically all the time.

I don't think they're dumb exactly. It's more like they're stuck. Too bad they get stuck lots. It's kind of sad all the way around.

They are going to need to understand math when they get big and get a job. Dad explained that to me a long time ago and I know he's right.

I thought that one good thing about quarantine is we could never have a substitute. It happened today anyway. Ms. Wachter did get sick (**NOT** TB2, just regular sick) and we had to split up between two other Fourth Grade teachers because there aren't any substitutes to come in. The principal was the substitute for one of the other teachers a couple of days ago, but I guess she couldn't do it today for some reason. Anyway it was worse than having a sub. I felt ignored and invisible. I wasn't doing anything wrong. It made me want to do something just so the teacher would notice I was there instead of just giving me work to do.

The day just dragged on. I know I didn't learn anything much new, like Ms. Wachter says we should. Wait, I learned that there's something worse than having a sub. I also learned again that nobody knows when we are getting out of here and we won't get any help from outside. Sometimes I can go for a long time not remembering any of that. Not today! Now let me get back to my wonderful math work before I get in trouble for not continuing the monotony.

I snuck up to listen to the teachers talk again tonight and it was really upsetting. One of the teachers was crying about how much she missed her husband and her kids. Another teacher told her to shut up and stop complaining and then the two of them got into an big argument. Ms. Hayes-Roberson stopped them but you could tell that they weren't over it, even though I couldn't see them or hear them I could feel it.

Since I wasn't supposed to be there I didn't dare sneak a peek to see who it was.

Then some other teacher said in this real high voice, "Too much noise."

Then Ms. Wachter had a complaint! I was so shocked. She said something like, "We never get a real break. We're on stage all the time now. I can't go home, watch adult movies with cuss words, can't say any bad words myself of course, don't have any quiet time to read without some interruption. I feel like I'm saturated with children all the time, I have no life of my own and I get sick of talking about school and the kids!"

She gets sick of us? Well, that's not what she said. Not exactly. Close.

I never thought too much about how the teachers don't like being here any more than we do. Also I kind of forget that they have families. Or other stuff to do besides school. One teacher was talking yesterday about how much she misses going to conventions for knitting. I never even knew they had conventions for knitting. Do they have contests for who can knit the most or the fastest?

Other teachers do other stuff, one of them swam all the way to Alcatraz Island, which I don't know what it is or where but it sounds like a big deal. She got to swim for miles in freezing cold water. I do not like cold water at all.

The secret lives of teachers. Who knows what they get up to when they're not at school. Inquiring minds want to know.

I don't think I wanted to know this much. I don't think I'll come up here to listen to them much any more. Imagine how mad they would be to find me when they feel like they never get a break from us.

We don't get a break from them either. There's always some adult keeping an eye on us. I managed to find a spot to be by myself sometimes but if they knew where it was I wouldn't have it any more.

It's terrible, Mrs. Hayes-Roberson got sick and they took her away to a hospital! She's going to a special place called an *isolation ward*. She's going to be all the way in Virginia in a place called Inova because all the hospitals around here already have too many TB2 patients and they all have to be isolated somehow. Everyone is scared and worried about her and some are worried about whether they will get it from her having it.

So no matter what religion they had there were people praying all ways today about what happened. Me too. I said a Hail Mary and an Our Father for her. I sure hope God heard.

Last night was really cool. I was watching the teachers. One of them is a dancer and she told the others about what kind of stuff dancers do to relax. So one thing is, they tell some jokes for fifteen minutes. Any kind of joke. So they did that, and they all started laughing like I don't know what. I have never seen teachers laugh like that. They were falling all over the place and some of them even started holding their stomachs and saying stop and like that. This was after dinner and they didn't seem to care that we were watching them.

I didn't get some of the jokes but it didn't matter. One teacher told a joke half in Spanish and everybody still laughed hard, they got it. Then one of the French teachers, Madame J they call her, told a joke in French and somehow they all got it and were laughing, even before she translated it. Then, this one teacher, she got into doing a bunch of jokes that she said she knew from watching this comic called Whoopi Goldberg. Now I know who that is because she is on Star Trek, this old TV show I like to watch on the computer. I didn't know she was so funny. This teacher was really funny, doing some Whoopi

Goldberg jokes. Another teacher said Whoopi (what a great name) was "on the view," but I don't know what that is. We don't have much of a view here.

When we get out of here I am going to get some Whoopi Goldberg movies and shows to watch on the computer at home.

The next thing that happened was the dancer teacher, who teaches second grade, told about massage. Seems like dancers are all the time needing massage, because dancing is really hard and it hurts your muscles sometimes. So this teacher explained about how dancers get in a circle to massage each other and some teachers said well let's try that and they did and some of the other teachers just watched but most of them did it and it was really peaceful to see. I didn't want to say anything, in case it broke the spell.

It wasn't that big a deal. Just a bunch of people rubbing each other's backs or feet and not much talking. I never expected a bunch of grownups to get so quiet but they did. It was a sure enough miracle if you ask me.

It was a big change from the night they were all complaining.

When it was time to go to sleep one of the French teachers, the kindergarten teacher, I forget her name, she started singing a lullaby to us. It was this French lullaby. I don't remember the teacher's name but I sure will remember her song.

Today the Internet news was very interesting. There was a school somewhere in Texas that had an outbreak of TB2. So they were supposed to go into quarantine. But it was a private school with lots of rich parents and they wouldn't let them do that, and they knew about what happened at our school and a couple of others. So they went and got their kids, went right through the teachers and the few cops that were there, and took them home. Now every one of them is in quarantine in their homes, with soldiers keeping them there. It's a couple of hundred kids and the government is mad because using the soldiers is expensive, and other parents are mad because the rich people didn't go by the rules and they did, and the rich people are mad because they have to stay in their houses and take care of their kids. Some of them said they would pay nurses to come and take care of them and they got even more mad because hardly any nurses would agree to do it and because even if they got a nurse they still had to stay in the house themselves.

Plus some wanted a refund from the school since their kids are not going for the next six weeks, and some are suing the school for exposing their kids to TB2, and the school is in quarantine anyway for the few kids that didn't get grabbed.

Oh, and all the parents who did it are going to jail probably after they get out of quarantine except some lawyers say they had the constitutional right to do what they did.

Or, as I read online, there's this belief they have that the rules don't apply to rich people, if the rule is inconvenient.

There are plenty of kids who feel like that. They think the rules should not apply to them.

But these are grownups, you would think they would have grown out of it.

One parent is already in quarantine in jail. He busted out of his house and the soldiers chased him and he fought them but they didn't shoot him. They just held on to him and he gave up. Then he tried to claim police brutality but the whole thing got shown on a video on the news so that was no good. The soldiers that got him are now in quarantine too! But not in a jail, in some military hospital somewhere.

There are people with cameras all over the town where this happened so they film everything, and they won't go away. The rich people have formed a group online and they call themselves the Bunker Hill Heroes. They blog about what it's like and they are trying to force the government to stop the quarantine and not send them to jail for being a menace to public health, whatever that is. They say all the cameras and media are an invasion of privacy and they're going to sue the reporters too. I bet before too long they decide to sue each other for something.

None of them can go to their jobs either and they're upset about that too. A couple can just work at home on the computer but not that many, and some of them might oh no even lose their jobs! Then maybe they wouldn't be rich anymore. Which is fine by me. No work, no pay, get used to it. If my daddy couldn't drive the cab he wouldn't have any money.

I do feel different about the people who didn't take their kids out of the school. They shouldn't lose their jobs. But then how can they go to their jobs because they are not in quarantine. Are they? I don't know.

And it's good that people love their kids lots and didn't want them to be in quarantine. I understand that.

But. The quarantine is a necessary thing. It's terrible enough, how many people die of TB2 these days. If you break the quarantine there could be more. It's kind of like what happens if you don't sneeze into your elbow. The germs break loose and could get on anybody around you. More people could die.

I am a little sorry for the rich people. It turns out they didn't solve it at all by defying the law. Plus, bad as what we are going through is, at least I'm not stuck in our apartment with everybody else all day every day with a soldier with a gun at the door. That would have been even worse!

Once again this afternoon I was trying again to help other kids to write stuff. Not my regular group this time. These were just different kids who hadn't finished some assignment or didn't know what to do with it next. We have lots of kids that can say what the book is about but can't write it. So for instance here is what Eric said about the book about Thurgood Marshall:

```
Thirgood can't go the law school
in merry land because he is black and
you're not allowed to be black
```

So I had to explain to him how to write it so Thurgood Marshall can still stay black and not be allowed to go to Law School in Maryland and hey let's put a period at the end of the sentence, okay?

I really like helping people write about stuff. They could write lots and lots if they only figured out how to put it down in words. We would never get bored in here if we just told each other our stories all the time.

Like when I was helping Veronica who is in French Immersion. Her family is from Guatemala so she knows Spanish and English and now French. She was writing so hard in her journal. It's her English writing journal. She has two different ones, because mostly they learn in French but they get taught in English a few times every week in Fourth Grade so they don't mess up when they have to take the standardized test in English. She was supposed to write about your favorite country. Surprise, hers is America. So this is what she wrote:

```
     My favorite contry is amerca becus
they have cotton candy, popcorn,
likrish and choklata too. They have
moives and pizza and shoos that lit up.
     The music is good to. It is hard
to get here but then it is fine. We had
to ask and ask to got to amerca and I
could only take one sutcase.
```

I fixed how she spelled things in the first draft and had her talk to me about it so we could figure out a better way to put things together. Like the pizza part should go with the popcorn. Did she want to say anything else about the shoes? Teachers are always saying add details. That's what we did.

She had lots to say about how hard it was to get to America and she needed to write it all down, not just say it. I thought that was actually more interesting than the food part. I told her to write it all down. Then I showed her how to spell chocolate. Everybody ought to know how to spell chocolate, it's important.

I didn't write it for her, I got her to write the whole entire thing over. She didn't want to do all that writing but I convinced her. Veronica even put a picture with it when she was done, of three girls and she told me it was me and her and Maria. It was odd but when she told me that, I felt like crying even though I was happy she did it.

Ms. Wachter gave her an A. Then she came over to me and said, "You get an A for editing," and I was embarrassed but glad.

This is what Veronica finished up with:

My favorite country is America because I am never hungry here. It was very hard for my family to get here. It cost lots of money and took a long time. My parents were scared we would not be allowed to stay. They came secretly first.Then we got the card from the government and now we are allowed to be Americans.

I can go to the movies and have popcorn and chocolate and licorice. We can eat pizza for a treat and they bring it right to your house. In my old country it was not ever safe to go outside at night. You could hear the guns going off.

Momma saved up her money and bought me shoes that light up. I like to dance to American music and make my shoes light up. Now I have new friends in America. That is why it is my favorite country.

Now to me that is some good writing. Sometimes I find out someone has just done a journal entry that is good and they should just re-write it on loose leaf paper and give it to Ms. Wachter. They don't even think of stuff like that.

Still if they did I wouldn't be able to help kids write, which I like to do, so it's a good thing they don't think of using their journals or other stuff.

Of course some kids just hate writing and it doesn't matter how you try to get them to do it. Sometimes I have to just tell them it's work and you have to do the work and that's it. If you do the hard work you can feel so proud afterwards, but some people don't.

So here is something that Stephanie wrote and we barely had to change anything at all:

Thanksgiving Story
By Stephanie Chavez

This thanksgiving my dad was sick. He had a bad fever. It was 103 degrees which is bad. He stayed in bed watching T.V. boring. I was tring to take care of him. He did not want to eat. Imagine that, wow! He was sick for a week. He had diary, yuck, and had to go all the time. Then a little while he was back to normal. His tempecher relly moved down. Now it was 99.2 which was better. Hory, thak god, all right. My mom and dad decided we should make a turkey. It was my mom relly since dad was too sick to do the turkey. He got up and came to the table to eat. So we had turkey of

```
course, cranberry sauce grave stuffing
and apple pie. I didn't like the cran-
berry sauce. It was sour. I had two
helps of stuffing with grave.
        It was achually pretty good at
thanksgivng this year. Last year was
better. Dad was not sick and we didn't
have cranberry sauce.
```

So all we really had to do was fix the spelling like turn Hory into Hooray and make some sentences better.

Sometimes I have to fix so many things that it's almost like starting over. That makes me frustrated because I have to do so much work. I'm not supposed to be the one writing. Still if the story they want to tell is interesting, I just keep going. I use a purple pen and sometimes it looks like I spilled purple all over the page. Sometimes what I write needs lots of work too, but I hate fixing my own writing. Now I get embarrassed when I read some of my old journal entries. They just seem so dumb. This is what I wrote for my first draft when we did our independent research project last year:

I like cheetahs. I like the way they look and I like that they run fast. Sometimes I go to the track with my dad and run. I would like to be a cheetah because they like to run. I also like to run on a track. I like the colors of the cheetah. Cheetahs have spots. They run to catch their food. I don't like how they bite their prey. If I had my own cheetah I would take it to Mcdonalds so it would not have to bite and eat other animals.

Now that is just embarrassing. It's not organized, and it's boring to read. Except for the McDonalds part, and that doesn't even make sense because there's meat at McDonalds which some human killed, not the cheetah. Also I forgot to make the D in the word a capital.

That was not what I turned in at the end, but I remember that I didn't want to fix it. I didn't want to start over though, that would be worse. So I worked on it. Then I did two more paragraphs about where they live and how they raise their babies and it turned out pretty good. Writing can be really hard. Other times it just goes and all I have to do is try to keep up with what my brain is thinking. I wish every time I went to write all I had to do was keep up. It's when I can't think of what to do that I hate it. I hate feeling stupid. When I can't write that's how I feel.

Since I hate that feeling I don't really mind helping other people. I don't want them to feel that way. Anyway, they *aren't* stupid. There isn't anybody stupid in our class. They do stupid things sometimes.

We're not supposed to call each other stupid so of course it is everybody's favorite insult. I've done it too. If somebody says something dumb it's almost impossible not to say they are. Maria is the one who got me to understand how much that word hurts. She told me that was what kids would say to her when she was in kindergarten and couldn't speak much English. I remember her when I start to say it and then I don't say it. Sometimes.

Being friends with Maria has taught me a lot about how people ought to be with each other. When she tells me to try a new food, I'm willing to try it because she's tried it and she likes it. When we go to a new place, she sees things I don't, and she knows things I don't. I can tell her things she doesn't know. That doesn't sound like much but it really is the best. The very best thing about a friend is the conversations you can have with them. Well it is one of the best things. Playing is good too. So is dancing. Maria can *really* dance. I am not bad but she is better. When she starts dancing like in music class everyone wants to look at her. I told her she is like that lady we saw in the video, Gloria Estefan. She laughed and said she is not that good but she is, really. Her legs flash and her hair flares out around her and it is like magic to see her move.

Tonight we got to hear a Spanish lullaby, Mrs. Garcia sang it. The teachers are taking turns singing to us at night. It's really nice.

Today has been sad bad story day. That's how it turned out, at least for me.

There was this girl Allyson who is Second Grade. She told me about how she had this friend, a real good friend, and she wouldn't tell me who it is even though this girl is in here with us. It turns out this girl is homeless, that is what she told Allyson but she doesn't want Allyson to tell anyone. Her mom told her not to tell people. They do have a place to live but they are not supposed to be living there and they don't want the landlady to find out. So really they are still homeless, her and her mom. This girl told Allyson she is really scared that she will get out of quarantine and her mom won't be at that apartment anymore and they will take her and put her in a foster home.

So Allyson told me about it and I had to promise not tell and it makes me sad but I promised and what could I do anyway? If I tell the teachers they might get them thrown out of where they live. This girl says the only good thing is that since she is in quarantine, her mom doesn't need to worry about her and she can maybe find a job because she can look all day and not have to be home after school lets out.

It is amazing how kids can find a little bit of good in so much bad.

That was just the first sad bad story.

My friend Mary Katherine told me about a terrible thing that happened at her old school. All her teachers left her school during the summer. In September they got almost all new teachers. She didn't understand how it happened but her mom explained it to her. Her old school, which is in another city, did not do so good on the tests. Everyone has to do good on the tests, more and more each year, until everyone gets an A on every test. If they don't the teachers get fired.

So one thing they did is that if the kids didn't do too well on the second grade reading tests they kept them in Second Grade another year. They were kept back because this big test happens in Third Grade and the kids who were having trouble might not do good on the test.

She said everyone in the Third and Fourth and Fifth grades had to go to special classes to get ready for it and for two months it was all math and reading practice all the time. So like for instance in music they would just read song lyrics instead of singing and they had songs that had lots of sight words in them. I asked her what was the point and she said she didn't know.

I was so shocked. I asked if she was making this up. She said no and got all mad.

So I had to coax her to find out more.

First, some kids lost their recess for months before the test and had to stay in and do work especially math stuff. Second, if they didn't do well on the practice tests the school would make the parents bring in proof of where they lived and that they were American citizens and if they couldn't they kicked the kids out of the school.

Also everyone got extra homework that was test practice but some of the homework had mistakes on it so the teachers got in trouble for that even though they didn't make this test practice homework, the school got it from somewhere else.

Then, there was a program after school especially for kids who they thought they wouldn't do too good on the test and the kids who didn't speak English at home had to go to it no matter what. She said she heard some parents got really upset, but the people at the school just told them that "based upon assessment," the after school program was the only way that these kids were ever going to make it.

She said the teachers were looking all worn out and sad because they knew it was going to be hard for some kids to do well on the test. Like there was one kid, she had lost her grandmother and her aunt in the same year and was out of school for weeks but she still had to take the test and somebody at the school sent a letter to her family saying it was not okay that they kept her out of school so long even though her grandmother's funeral was in New York City, so it took time to go there and come back and how about some time to cry about it, huh?

What if I had somebody in my family die back in Cameroon and I had to go for the funeral? Would they send some nasty letter to my dad saying I should have been in school? Don't they know that going to the funeral shows respect? Where is their respect? I guess all that matters is how many numbers you know and how many words, not what your family has been through and had to deal with in life.

Well, actually nobody we know died in Cameroon and we did the test in Third Grade last year and we must have done okay because none of that ever happened to us.

We could not afford to go back to Cameroon anyway, when I think about it.

When Angelique died everyone was very sad for me and sent me cards and called and left nice messages. The funeral — I don't want to think about that right now.

I can't remember the next thing Mary Katherine told me, something about the tests they had to take on the computers every other week to see if they were getting better. I mean it just sounded awful, and it kept happening the year AFTER all the teachers were fired since the new teachers had to make sure they all passed the test also. By the end of the year the teachers and the kids looked like they all wanted to be somewhere else.

Boy I'm glad I never went to that school. It sounds like a nightmare.

For some reason every single class I went to today was great. I was in such a good mood by the afternoon.

Then we got this great snack, this special kind of fish called lox. Rachel didn't like it but I did. Then we got to play statues and freeze tag and four square in one part of the big auditorium after school.

I got to sit and talk to Maria and Rachel and this boy Robert for a little while about music we like, and that was good too.

Dinner was great. After that we got to see the new Disney movie. Well it's not that new but we got to see it on the big screen TV and eat popcorn (no butter though) and I just enjoyed myself practically the whole day. By the time we were brushing teeth and getting into pjs I didn't even mind how long it takes like I usually do.

The lights stayed on later than usual tonight. It was because Mr. B was cutting hair. We don't have any barbers in here so he's learned how to do it and he and Nurse Jim do all the boy haircuts now. They have to do some boys every night just to keep up, except for Sunday. Mr. B says he deserves one day off.

Mr. Weissman, the science teacher, tried to help, but he's no good at haircuts. The boys found that out pretty quick.

Ms. Wilson does the girls' hair — she can do micro braids! When my hair grows out some more I want her to do mine, but it's not long enough yet. I like it natural too, like it is now. Mrs. Bondanza, the counselor, also helps with trimming the girls' hair, and she does some of the teachers as well. They are trying to learn how to do styling off the Internet, and I think some of them are getting pretty good at it.

The thing is, it turns out some teachers do not have the color hair they had when quarantine started. Ms. Davis, the Second Grade teacher, says next weekend they are going to take care of that since some hair salon sent them hair color "for our roots."

I want to see what they do but they say kids are not allowed because spills could happen. Hey. I have seen grownups spill plenty of things. Come on.

Lights out. Hope the whispering stops sooner than usual tonight, I want to sleep.

Yesterday some boys tried to break out of here. Two from the French side and three from the Academy side. Tried to bust out of the door that says EXIT but it isn't. I know how they feel but it was no use, they got caught and didn't even get very far. There are cops outside this place all the time, I didn't know that. One of the boys says they are going to try every day until they make it. It's weird, I wish they wouldn't and I wish they would and I was going with them. Even though they haven't got a chance.

I can't stand it. Some teachers died. Our teachers. Not my teacher, not Ms. Wachter, but a kindergarten teacher and another grade teacher. TB2 got them all. Also our great principal, Mrs. Hayes-Roberson, is still real sick with it but they say she might not die. And a Fifth Grader, who was with the classes at the church, died, but they won't tell us the name of the kid. Somebody will find out eventually. We do know about the teachers, Ms. Elage who taught kindergarten and Mrs. Miller who taught Fourth Grade. Ms Elage was young and wasn't married with kids, and Mrs. Miller was old and had three kids and two grandchildren too. I knew what Mrs. Miller looked like from seeing her at dismissal and so on, but I didn't really know her. She wasn't real old, just kind of old. She had red hair and a nice laugh. That's all I really know about her.

Ms. Elage died first and they didn't want us to know. Then Mrs. Miller died and the information about her memorial service was up on the internet so I guess they figured they had to tell us. It is so awful.

Mrs. Hayes-Roberson is still sick but not dead. Not dead, they said she wasn't.

They wouldn't lie to us about it. I don't think. Hope not.

I knew Ms. Elage from when I was in kindergarten. She wasn't my teacher but sometimes the kindergarten teachers did some things all together with all the French and Academy. Sometimes I got to talk to her when we did the class things like the picnic and the zoo trip and the musical. I liked talking to her about books. We both really liked the If You Give a Mouse books and the ones with Max the Duck by that woman named Jackie something. Ms. Elage actually knew the lady that wrote the Max the Duck books and she had a signed copy of Duck at the Door. She loved funny books. She could also speak French and Spanish. She even has the Duck and Cover book in French and she read part of it to me. It was still just as funny because I knew the story and because of the pictures. It made me feel like I knew French, but I really don't.

So now these folks are dead and we can't go to the funerals because we're all still in here maybe contagious. That made me cry, knowing we couldn't go. Also being reminded that even if we want to go real bad, we can't leave.

These are just the people we know and it doesn't even count all the other people dead that we don't know. There were a bunch of soldiers that died in some places where the TB2 is, since they were sent to guard places and take care of the sick people and got sick themselves. These special soldiers are called the National Guard. I didn't even know we had one.

What they are going to do is let us see the funeral through the internet with something called WebEx. Thanks a lot. That's so personal.

They'll show it on the big screen in the downstairs room and anybody who decides to go has to stay for the whole thing, no getting bored and leaving in the middle even if it is just on the computer. That would not be respectful.

One of the teachers wrote a poem for Ms. Elage and read it:

Ode to a Teacher

It is possible to
Be petite
And a powerhouse
To be the one to embrace a
Sacred Trust

To be willing to do whatever it takes
So that child knows
Here's a safe place

In which to work and play
To learn, to read and count
And you can make mistakes
And try again

It's possible to be the one who is willing
To take seriously
The difference between
The b, the p, the d and the q
And write all four letters on the board
Again and again

To be the one to cheer
The first time you count all the way up to twenty
When you are only five

To be the one to convince you that the difference
Between right and left
Is important
Really.

To be the one to celebrate the fact
That the seed you planted, sprouted!
Just like
Such a thing
Has never happened before

To be the one
To spend evenings and weekends
Checking drawings and worksheets and data notebooks
Planning lessons and field trips
And cutting out dozens and dozens of black dots

To laminate everything
Including your shirtsleeve

To find another way to
Teach sight words

Louise Parker Kelley

When you're
Really sick of them

To constantly buy fresh Play-Doh
To replace the rainbow smooshed Play-Doh
Now lumped in the Art Center

To sharpen pencils and tie shoes
over and over

It is possible
To put a band-aid on a
totally invisible boo-boo

To schedule parent conferences
at lunch time or
dinner time
or before school
or whenever
and then re-schedule them

To teach at least
Three versions of the alphabet song
Two versions
Of the school song
And accept
Whatever version
Of the Pledge of Allegiance

While remaining fluent in French, Spanish and English

To take very seriously
Whatever happened in the bathroom after recess
And then
To ignore things that
Need to be ignored
Really.

To do it all with style and grace

It's possible.

She
Proved it.

As poems go, I think it's pretty good. The teacher that wrote it is going to have another teacher read it for the funeral because she says she can't read it without crying. I can't listen to it without crying, so no wonder.

At least we can see the funeral and a teacher can read the poem for Ms. Elage from here. The people at the funeral will be able to hear it if the computer thing works the way it's supposed to, and we should be able to hear everything they say and do while they are praying about her.

I hate TB2. It doesn't make any difference if I do but I still do.

There is no way to get out of going to class around here. Seems like there's always somebody in the hallway and there's no extra room to check out that isn't occupied. Even when I was looking at the second floor hallway mural today, some teacher came by and gave me a look so I had to get going back to class.

It's a really good mural. It tells the story of Moses leading the Jews out of slavery but you really have to look close to see all the action going on. Maybe I can check it out tonight after dinner. There's no time for art appreciation during the day, that's for sure.

Our music teacher, Mrs. H, has gotten really inventive about instruments. First all we had were sticks. I mean really, just sticks, some were real drumsticks she brought with her, some were chopsticks she found in the kitchen and Miss Rose said she could have them. Then she got keys from different people and we used those to make jingle jangle sounds. Then we listened to this guy Bobby McFerrin and we got to make musical instrument sounds with our mouths. Some people were really good at it, like Ahmed. We used our hands to clap. Then we used the sticks on different things, like an empty bucket or a lid or the rails around the steps, to make different sounds. We made some rain sticks with tubes and dried peas and just got boxes and put stuff in them to make percussion instruments. We created some very weird instruments along the way and it was so much fun.

We learned this one song with just singing and percussion. It's called "You Can't Always Get What You Want," and we can really belt it out. Mrs. H changed some of the words so they fit school, but that chorus, it is so perfect. We sure can't get what we want in here, but when we try we get what we need. It's like our anthem.

I think we were driving some teachers crazy, but Mrs. H loved it and we didn't do it out and around for that long. We found a place to do it without being such a nuisance. We made the stuff and took it to the office we're using for music class. It actually sounded better there, because all that percussion and singing made a great big noise.

Then somehow Mrs. H got in touch with the guy in charge of the opera here in town. She did some training at the opera sometime. When this guy Andy got her email, he got to work. He got us recorders, shakers, and even a synthesizer thing! It's a big deal because we probably can't take the stuff back out of here when we leave. They might be able to sanitize it but probably not. All this stuff could just be destroyed later on. In the meantime, we make music with it. Not very good music, not yet, but it's still music. Mrs. H played this old song for us that so fits what we're going through, this song called Band on the Run, and afterwards we made up our own lyrics:

Trapped inside a quarantine
Stuck in here for months now
Never seeing new music videos
Or movies again
Oooh, Movies
School on the run
School on the run
And the Roosevelt Pandas and Mrs. H
Were singing to everyone
For the school on the run.

Okay, so it needs work. At least it's something we can sing and play besides the school song, which I have to say I am so sick of hearing on the recorder, on anybody's recorder, that I could just scream.

And I really do miss seeing movies at a movie house on a big screen while eating nachos.

Minah from the other class is going to help us do some dance moves to the song, and she can really sing too. I will just let her take the lead on that.

I found out Mrs. H's first name is two names today. She's called Mary Elizabeth. That's pretty, and she gets two instead of one, just like Mary Katherine. Maybe you always get an extra name when your first one is Mary, like buy one get one free.

Today we had a lesson about resources. It's part of Social Studies. It got really bad and sad. Ms. Wachter was trying to teach it the regular way I could tell, but it wasn't working. The whole thing cut loose on her. And us.

First she told us what resources means, and then how resources can be in different categories. She showed us some stuff like cotton balls and an aluminum can which we passed around and then pictures of other things that are too big to show. Resources are things around us like trees that are in nature. But it's also buildings and signs and tools and stuff. So trees and the ground and the sun are natural resources and that part was okay. Then there are human made resources like this chair I'm sitting in and the pencil I'm writing with. So we got that and that was okay.

But then she tried to explain about capital resources like electricity and the tools humans use to make other stuff. Then it jumped and all of a sudden we were talking about all the capital resources we haven't got much of anymore, like showers. Like the computer lab and the science lab.

Suddenly we were in an argument about whether schools and restaurants count as capital resources and somebody yelled, who cares, we ain't got either one. Then I said we did too have school we were learning in one right now and then Ms. Wachter looked liked she might cry when John said this wasn't a real school. He said it hasn't got a cafeteria or a computer lab or a gym and no playground. Then Devorah said you don't have to have those things to have a school because her old Hebrew school didn't have one and it was a school. Osumare came back at her and said she wasn't talking about no Hebrew school and then Devorah almost cried but instead she threw her pencil at Osumare and we had to stop them from having a bigger fight. When that got stopped Ms. Wachter said real quietly, well then what does make a school, you tell me, but she turned it into a writing assignment so that shut some people up. Except for them asking how to spell stuff. So it turned out to be kind of interesting. Tomorrow we'll get to share what we wrote. We'll see if Osumare can write as well as she hollers.

It's a good question. What makes something a school? If it's a place where you learn something, well, that's the whole planet, if you ask me. So first it's a building. No, first it's somebody wanting to learn something. It doesn't matter where you are. You could be on a spaceship and not be able to be in a building and go to a school. You can learn things outside. I remember what that's like! I do some of my best learning outdoors. After that you have to have a teacher. Usually you have to have a teacher. A teacher might not always be a live person right in front of you. But there has to be somebody teaching you, online maybe. If you don't need a teacher to help you, if all you have to do is read something or do something, it's not a school. It's learning but it's not a school. In a school there's got to be some way to tell if you learned it or not.

Maybe the teacher figures that part out or maybe you do, but there's got to be a way to tell. If it's a school then there's students, teachers, something to learn and a way to tell if you learned it or not. Mostly you prove it by showing you can do it. Sometimes that's a test or a project, sometimes you just do it, like singing.

Or like Lynn, who is really good at math, she just is, I don't know why but she is, and she can help other kids understand. Even though she is a kid she is a teacher. She asks kids to solve a problem after she shows them how. So that makes it school since she is teaching it and seeing if the kid understood or is just letting her do all the work and saying "uh-huh" like they know what to do.

Oh, and something else. You have to want to learn something and think you can. Otherwise it won't work. It wouldn't be school. It would just be hard.

We'll get to read our reports about what makes a school tomorrow. Then I bet anything we get to write them over. That makes it a school, for sure.

These teachers really miss their husbands and wives and girlfriends and boyfriends. And their own kids. I forget they have their own families. Mr. B started talking about how much he misses his wife and some people started crying. I could heard them sniffling, but I couldn't see who it was. Then they all started talking about how they miss going to movies, going out to a restaurant, playing music on the stereo. Then some started saying how they could order in the food they wanted, could get the music downloaded, all trying to fix it, and then one lady said, "You can't download my husband!' And there was a pause and then they laughed but it was not a normal laugh. Then somebody joked about how she misses her kids but not that much, and it turns out she has four kids, so they started teasing her about that but you could tell they were feeling sorrowful. I could tell, anyway.

This morning the teachers got up on ladders to seal the windows. I never noticed how many windows this place has. There are so few you can actually see out of at all, most are up high, they're all up high in the sanctuary. You can see the sky a tiny little bit.

I like to sit in this one spot where I can see the most sky. Nobody noticed me there.

The teachers had all this plastic wrap. Apparently there were orders from people on the outside that they had to do this. They were talking about it in low voices but I could hear them.

"How we will get any fresh air if we seal the windows?"

"If we don't do it they'll just send in those guys in moon suits to do it if we refuse."

"It's ridiculous. The virus is airborne but it can't survive just in the air for more than a few minutes. They're just in a panic."

"So TB2 is sealed in here with us!"

"It's in here with us anyway."

"I knew that."

"Well, make sure they film us putting up the frames and then send them the film."

I sat and watched them finish sealing the windows.

Afterward I realized it's all fake. There isn't any plastic or glass in the frames they put up. Do not try to bully smart people. They will fake you out somehow.

Today Maria said she wishes she could get out of here. I asked her where she wanted to go. She said El Salvador. I went and got her a book about El Salvador. She laughed and said that wasn't it, but she looked through the book anyway.

For a little while then all I did was watch her read. It was very restful.

I think it is amazing that people decided to take some trees, knock them down, mash them up, roll out the mush real thin, make dark marks on the thin stuff and it means things to somebody like me. I mean, these are just squiggles, really, but they mean things and I can see the story in my head. That's like magic.

I do use books to get out of here. I've traveled lots since we got here. I even got to travel back in the past with that guy Noah and his boat called the ark, and I went into the future when I read a Star Trek book. I even went back to visit these girls called Betsy and Tacy who lived a long time ago, and I can go back whenever I want. I am not stuck here.

Sure am glad that Shalom Israel has a library.

Except sometimes. I guess I like to complain too. Time to go find a book for me.

I was going to math class when I heard the French First Graders singing. They seem to sing all the time. These Frenchies got a song for everything, learning the alphabet, the grammar rules, subtraction, songs to sing before you eat . . . they probably have one for going to the bathroom but I don't need to hear that one.

There's been a change and now the time after dinner and before bed is very special and good. It started as a little thing for just a few of us two nights a week and now it's much bigger. For once that's not a bad thing, since if all the kids don't like it they can just go somewhere else. They generally don't though.

Ms. Wachter started it, telling some of us stories about her families or people she knew about that were interesting. Or maybe they weren't that interesting but her stories were. She told us about her mother, who was smart and funny but had problems too. Then she told stories about her dad, who was in the war and he told her stories about that, and about when he was a kid and there was no internet, imagine. Then Mr. Binwald told us stories one time about what it was like when he was growing up and it was hard because even though it wasn't supposed to be segregated, in the town he was living in, Cambridge, it still was not a good place for black people to get jobs or get treated right most of the time. Now it's better, but not then. He told us about learning to build a car by himself, and how he'd re-built motorcycles, he loves motorcycles and he really misses driving one all around.

He started telling us stories after he heard Ms. Wachter's stories about her big family and stayed to listen. The next time she asked him to tell some so he did. Now we have about five grownups taking turns telling stories about their families and telling about important things they lived through and just about anything. Sometimes the kids tell stories too. The only rule is it has to be true. (We have a different night for telling made-up stories. We tell most of those ourselves, but sometimes the adults jump in.) Ms. Wachter keeps things going if somebody gets off on something else when they're telling a story and sort of forget where they were. She does it very gently. I'm glad because I want to know what happened in the first story, they can tell the other one some other time. Plus some people cannot seem to figure out how to tell a story from the start to the finish without some help.

I got to find out some amazing things. Ms. Rose the cook has lived in Belgium, England and Israel. Ms. Wilson has family living in Greece and they have lived in the same village for like more than a hundred years, although not her because her dad moved to America and now she's in here with us. Ms. Garcia can play the flute and the guitar. Mademoiselle Mikaela LaFontaine used to be a nun!

Madame Blanche is telling true stories for the French kids once a week and for us once a week too! She used to live in France and she knows all kinds of things, like how cheese is made and wine and how to harvest olives with a net, how strange is that.

I never knew so many people had such good stories in them.

I CAN'T STAND IT. On top of everything else, we have to go to church! The parents were freaking out asking for about it, including my auntie I bet, and I figured, we're in a synagogue, so much for that. BUT NO. We get to go to church ONLINE, we go to a virtual mass or whatever church or mosque your parents want you to go to, and the toughest part is putting the computers in different rooms that have enough room for the Presbyterians or whatever the group is. I guess that means we don't have to worry about the bread and wine. Surely they can't consecrate the stuff by computer.

There goes Sunday morning. Thanks, technology. I will have to sit next to Jamarr the whole time too. I just know it. He's really going to hate looking at a computer and not being able to do anything but watch a mass. Shucks.

No Communion either. What's the point then?

But there are teachers in here that like to go to church and they are glad this is going to happen. Some of them have been reading the Bible online but they don't have the New Testament books here.

I bet they are especially glad that church is not one more thing they have to do with us, since they already have to take care of us all the time. They have what they call rotation, so not all of them have to watch us all the time but there is always somebody watching.

When she found out, my buddy Devorah was laughing at us because she doesn't have to go to services here on Saturday and besides there aren't any. She said kids go to the synagogue sometimes but they don't have to go all the time. She used to go to Hebrew School at her synagogue to learn the language, but now she doesn't have to do that even. Even the Jewish people on the school staff who know Hebrew don't want to teach it on the weekend to the Jewish kids in here. She says they say they should do something about it but since they don't know how long we'll be here they don't know if it's worth it. What will probably happen is that she'll learn some Hebrew online when they can get her a turn on the computers we have here.

She better not underestimate the parents. I bet they find a way for her and the other Jewish kids to do some kind of service here. Mr. Rabin and Ms. Rose could do it. She's the one who told me that Jewish is one of the oldest religions around. I bet they won't let a quarantine stop it.

Ms. Rose did look sad for a minute when she said "I hope we're not still in here at Passover. It's been months and it feels like longer!"

The Jewish grownups do have a special thing they do on Friday night, which is called Shabbos service. They have to have ten Jewish people to do it, which is called a minyan, which I remember because it is like minimum, and you have to have a minimum ten for a minyan. There has been some fussing about that from the grown-ups because some seriously Jewish people don't count women for a minyan but if they didn't count the women they are out of luck since mostly we have women here, so they couldn't do it at all. Which I think goes to show that you should count women no matter what!

When it's Friday night there are about six grownups who go in the chapel part here, ignore everybody else in the room, light candles and sing some songs and say some Hebrew prayers and they have some bread and drink grape juice. Devorah says she likes that and she will let me come if it is okay with the grownups.

On Saturday some of them read the Torah in the library, and some just take it easy. The rabbi is not allowed to alk to them on the computer on Saturday because it's against the rules about the Sabbath. Mr. Rabin told me.

I didn't know it but there are different kinds of Jews. They are all Jewish but there are different groups. The kind that Devorah knows the most about is called Conservative, because her family is that kind. There is another kind called Reform and she doesn't know as much about them except their services can be in English and Hebrew and they don't have to keep kosher.

The other kind of Jew is called Orthodox and Devorah says they are very serious about being Jewish the traditional way including all the rules about food and talking about God in Hebrew, even when you do the special prayers at home like for Passover. Women have to sit separate from the men at the synagogue. So really serious Jews are called Orthodox Jews.

There are different kinds of Catholics in Russia and Greece, but we are the Rome kind. My auntie is a very serious Catholic and my dad says she is devout. She goes to Mass lots and she tells us we should go more too because we do so many sins. So a serious Catholic could be a nag, but I don't think it's the same as the Orthodox Jew.

So the Jewish kids don't have to go to their services all the time like the Christians do. Except some do. I wonder what the Muslims have to do? I know Ahmed has to pray five times a day. He says he doesn't have to, he *wants* to, but even if he wants to it's still a religion rule. Maybe he wishes he were at the mosque with the other kids. I don't want to ask him.

I like talking to God the way I do when nobody knows, that's more to me than going to Mass. I talk to God lots since we ended up in here, because God listens better than anybody.

And now the rest of us have to go to church, some kind of way, on computer.

Sheesh.

Except the atheists, I guess.

This afternoon we spent some time helping Ms. Davis, who usually teaches French Immersion second grade but sometimes now in the afternoon after school (while we're in here) she's teaching everybody Social Studies. She teaches geography. She likes teaching Social Studies and she volunteered to teach us after regular classes are over. The only rule is none of her regular French second grade class can come because she's only supposed to talk to them in French. She has lots of fun games and stuff to do so you hardly know it's a lesson. Anyway today when we went in she was looking all around for something so we helped her. She couldn't find her keys.

Keys are easy to lose. I wear the one to our apartment or I would lose it too. Actually I did lose it once and after that I never took it off no matter how hot and sweaty I got playing.

"I don't understand, where could they be?" she asked, but she really wasn't asking us, she was kind of talking to herself. So we looked in all the obvious places and then the not so obvious ones.

She even sent somebody to go look in the bathroom, which took a long time since there's always a line for the bathroom. She asked little Ashley why she didn't just ask to go in and look since she wasn't going to the bathroom and Ashley just looked at her. I could understand not going to the teacher in charge of the bathroom and asking. Teachers get very grumpy about letting people in the bathroom ahead of the line, even just to wash your hands. There's always a crowd and if you're kind of quiet like Ashley there's no way you're going to ask the grumpy teacher anything. The teachers take turns checking the bathroom line but nearly always after doing it a while that person is grumpy. Anyway Ashley finally came back and couldn't find them and then Ernie had a good idea and emptied the trashcan but even after we went through everything (Ms. Davis made us put on these latex gloves to look while she did the same thing) there were no keys. We checked the hallway. We checked the shelves. Ms. Davis checked her purse three times and her pockets twice. Mr. Parker was going by and wanted to know what was going on and she told him, "I don't know where my keys are," so he started to help too.

Then she stopped searching and started laughing. We all looked at her because maybe she found them. But she hadn't. She was just — standing there — laughing in an odd way. So then Mr. Parker went over and said, real softly, "Rosemary, what is it?"

She stopped that weird laughing and looked up at him and said, "Oh, Ethan, what difference does it make where they are? I'm not going to my house or my car or to anything I've got keys for. Here I am spending all this time looking for something completely useless since I'm not going anywhere."

There was this long pause and then Samantha, who is actually in Ms. DeCombe's class, whispered, "I see them." She pointed someplace but nobody paid much attention to her. We just watched Ms. Davis crying and Mr. Parker giving her a hug.

I thought the dumbest thing. I thought, now I know their first names, like that mattered.

She got her keys back. Still not going anywhere.

Who got God? That's what the fight is about today. It started with the Bibles. Some church sent us a bunch of boxes of books and some Bibles. We were supposed to have them for whoever is a Christian. So there were these boxes in the multi-purpose room.

A bunch of us were already in the multi-purpose room waiting for lunch, which is usually later on Sundays. We were playing Simon Says.

One of the teachers was unpacking the Bibles. Mr. Rabin, the man who decided to come in here with us, was over in the corner doing something. Then this teacher holds one up and says, "Oh good, real Bibles."

Maybe she didn't mean to be so loud and maybe she didn't know Mr. Rabin was there. Anyway he turns around real fast and says, "So, I should probably collect the others that are not real. You know, the wrong ones that we already have here."

So the teacher says, "Oh no, that's not what I meant."

Mr. Rabin says really quietly, "Yes you did."

He started to walk towards the door and I called out to him, "Don't take the Jewish Bibles away! I like the stories in them." Which is true. Also I like that the books are printed backwards. You have to start reading at the back. Also there is funny writing in them that is Hebrew that I like to look at even though it makes no sense to me. I didn't say that though.

He turned around and looked at me and looked over at the teacher and then said, "Okay, since you like to read the scriptures, I'll leave them there, in the library."

Then he glared at the teacher and said, "Read Isaiah, who said, 'and a little child shall lead them.'"

The teacher dropped the Bible back in the box and looked at him and then at us and then she went away and I don't know where she went.

Naturally I went over to look at the Bibles, which are actually pretty nice, with pictures. Jesus is white as usual though. You would think being out in the sun so much walking around Galilee he would at least be brown. But no.

But that wasn't the worst part. Some kids saw the Bibles that the teacher opened and started talking about what religion they were, or no religion, which I found interesting. I went to the bathroom and while I was gone, things went bad. This boy Jake got to arguing with this other boy, I forget his name but he argued with Jake about which kind of Christian is the best kind. I don't know which kind either of them is, because by the time I got there they were already fighting and punching and rolling on the floor. The other kids weren't doing anything to stop it, just hollering. Then two other kids started fighting because why? I don't even know.

Today we were supposed to have our P.E. class right after kindergarten had theirs. We went to the downstairs hall to do it. Nowadays P.E. is a big deal because the teachers had to figure out how we could do it at all, with no gym and no way to go outside. How do you do Physical Education with no room to get physical? The teachers figured it out. We don't get to run in circles or throw balls around but we do get exercise. So do the teachers. They do their exercise at night, after dinner. Not all of them, but most of them do. Sometimes they dance to music and sometimes they do yoga stuff or what they call calisthenics, which look pretty funny, I have to say.

So we went in the big room, where there were other classes going on in the corners. It was like when we do small groups, except these were big groups. So one corner was Writer's Lab, one was Science, one corner was doing Algebra and one corner was empty. So Mr. Parker was teaching the little ones "Head, Shoulders, Knees and Toes." We were just watching and waiting to start our P.E. and then Pat started doing what they were doing, then Jeannie, Chrissy, Robert and Davide, and after that I just had to do it too. Then we were all doing it. Then the Science class fourth graders started doing it and the Writers Lab and the teachers looked mad for a minute and then somehow they all laughed and started doing it too.

It was amazing because for a hot minute we were all doing it all at once!

I couldn't really see it because I was doing it myself, but I could feel it and it felt great. It was like a corny musical. Then the Algebra kids started saying, using the same song, Find A and B and C, solve it for the unknown, so we all said that twice, then the Writer's Lab kids said, Make Complete Sentences, Add Details, and the Science kids said Prove This Hypothesis. We maybe could have come up with something better than Two Eyes, Two ears, two arms, two legs, multiplying by two, but that's what we did. Then we went back to Head, shoulders knees and toes. We did it faster and faster and finally we just stopped. Everybody started laughing and applauding and bowing to each other even. The teachers were laughing really hard. It was all so wonderfully silly! Then the Kindergarteners went off to their next class and we started doing our yoga stretches and it was totally cool.

I hope that we get to play other games again someday when the quarantine is over. I miss the playing we used to get to do at P.E., like basketball and the scooter and hula hoops. Oh well.

If it were up to me we would have less school time while we're in here. We never get a day off from learning really, because on weekends the teachers still teach some people and after the regular day too. They seem to think there's got to be something structured all the time. It's not like a boarding school where we could go to our rooms and just hang out, or even to the library or something. It's too many people in to small a space. I guess they have to organize it and it's great that there's always somebody to read to you, but please, can we just have some down time?

I found a little place to hide when I'm sick of all the people, but I have to be careful. It's this little storage space behind a secret door inside a closet and I don't want anyone else finding out about it. Not even my friends.

You never know what's going to happen in a math lesson. Ms. Wachter was teaching us the fives table for multiplication. We were coming up with all kinds of stuff to count by fives, like cupcakes and diamonds and then Michael said light sabers, so we got off on a discussion of why anybody would need to have five light sabers at a time (because Michael likes swords and guns, that's why) and then Jamie said, who cares and it was about to be a fight. There's usually a fight when somebody says who cares. They only do it to annoy, like it says in Alice in Wonderland, that book dad used to read to me.

Ms. Wachter said, who cares about what, Jamie? So he said, trying to get out of Michael being mad at him I bet, he said, who cares about counting by fives.

Jamie is smart not to pick a fight with Michael. Michael is not tall but he has lots of muscles from all his bike riding and when he fights he just goes at it with everything he's got and you do not want to be on the other end of that.

So Ms. Wachter says to Jamie, do you like parties, and of course he says yes. She asks him, do you like parties with lots of people and he says yes again, and he's looking at her like what is this about, and she says, if you like parties and you want to have parties with lots of people then you want to learn multiplication.

Then she explains, if you have a party with ten people then you need to be able to have food and drinks for ten people and you need to know how to count by tens to make sure there is enough. Actually you need to do multiplication and division usually.

So Abby says, so if I order pizza for the party I need to know there's enough slices of pizza for everyone.

And Rachel says, you ain't gonna have just one slice for everyone and Abby says of course not and I couldn't hear what everybody was saying because they started arguing about how much pizza was enough for ten kids. Something about pepperoni and pizza with everything and I swear they were making me so hungry! Then Ms. Wachter pulled it back together and said, "If you want enough for a party for five people, you need to do the math. My mother always had to do the math for the seven of us, she had to count by sevens all the time."

Then she said, "My big sister had to count in eights. And divide by eight. All the time." Somebody said, how come, and she told us, because my mother had seven children but my sister Christine had eight.

Somebody said, "Eight!" real loud and Ms. Wachter smiled real big and said, yes, eight, two boys and six girls. Then she said, and the oldest boy is named Robert and he's married and has a son named Jason. And the next boy is named Joe and he's married and he has two children. Then she stopped and said, "If I invited Robert and his wife and their son and Joe and his wife and their kids, how many people are coming to dinner?"

She's always doing that, turning a conversation into a word problem.

Then Maria said, "Will your sister come to the dinner?'
ner?'

I don't understand how this happened, but it was like time slowed down. Just from how Ms. Wachter's face changed. It was like there was just . . . more time, suddenly.

Ms. Wachter looked at Maria and said, real slowly, "No, she won't come to the dinner. My sister Christine is dead."

Davide said loudly, "Was it TB2?"

Ms. Wachter said, "No, it was the old threat, cancer," and then she looked at me. And I thought, over and over, my sister died of cancer too, my sister died of cancer too, and we thought that at each other for what seemed like a long time and don't know what anybody else said while we were looking at each other. They were making some noise and we were looking at each other.

I know she read what I wrote about Angelique.

She said to me, "She died last year and after she died my brother's heart was broken and he had a heart attack and he died too."

Nobody said anything when she said that.

There is nothing you can say when somebody tells you such a thing.

Somehow time went back the way it usually is and Devorah said, so your mom doesn't count by sevens anymore, but by fives.

After that, I don't remember what anyone said. I don't think anyone said anything for a while. We were just all quiet together with her.

Last night dinner wasn't so good and lots of kids threw it away. I remember when my Grandma told me to eat all my rice when I was in Cameroon. Now I always do that. Nearly always. I can't stand to waste any food. I mean, there were garbage bags FULL of food. I remember there were even food fights back when we had lunch in the cafeteria. There was a big one when I was in Second Grade. It was incredible, they threw the food instead of eating it. I've never seen anything like it before. I liked watching the food fight at first and then I felt awful. It was a mixed up kind of thing.

Sometimes I really feel overwhelmed by all the people here. When I woke up I looked around and there they were, everybody, sleeping all around me. I could trip over them. Then I got up to go to the bathroom going really carefully and it was early so there weren't many people awake but there was still a line! I had to get in a line for breakfast. I felt crowded like that in our apartment at times but here with the whole school living here I really feel it.

A kind of mean pointless thing happened today. Mr. Parker went around to all the classes today and hollered "Fire drill" and at first we all just looked at him. It was really strange, him just saying it. Where was the alarm sound? He smiled at the teachers and said, "No, really, fire drill." Then he yelled it in French. So then Ms. Wachter said line up quickly and we did, and all the classes lined up next to our teachers. Right there in the rooms. And we just stood there. But we can't leave the building, except I hope if it really was on fire we would. Then we walked upstairs in our line following Ms. Wachter to the main door and there was everybody else, except I heard there were a couple of classes lined up at the back door. So we just stood there until the assistant principal went all around the building to see if we were all present and we just had to wait being quiet. All we could do was look outside but not go there. That used to be my favorite part of fire drill, getting a break and going outside. Plus the drama of it all. Well these days we have all the drama we can stand, being in quarantine. Except for the long dull parts, of course. Anyway that was the mean part, just standing there not able to go outside. And we had to be quiet but that took awhile to get everybody hushed. It was like a regular fire drill that way. Then Mr. Parker went back around telling everyone all clear. I had to laugh. A fire drill where you can't leave, that's just stupid and a little mean. But still funny.

Basically all we did was practice lining up and not talking. That's not a fire drill, that's just . . . following directions.

Apparently this building does have a fire alarm and we'll practice with the real bells sometime, but the problem is the fire marshal can't come in to set it off or he (or she I guess) would have to stay in here with us. Somebody could set it off the regular way but then they couldn't shut it off. Also I bet the fire engines would come. That's what happened when one of my cousins pulled the alarm in our building. He got in loads of trouble for that after everybody tattled on him. And no one here knows how to program it and it's not a school so it doesn't work the same way so we can practice. The teachers will figure it out. They're good at that.

I found out about a teacher that isn't sad she's in here. Her husband's brain is dying. She feels guilty because she is getting a break from taking care of him, but she told this other teacher that it's also a relief and she can't pretend it isn't. He has some disease that starts with an A but I can't remember what she said it was called. So he doesn't have TB2 but he's still dying. Someone else is taking care of him and she's in here. It's too bad his brain is dying. When your brain dies, so does the rest of you. Poor guy. Poor her.

She was talking to her friend, Ms. Meredith, who is the Special Education teacher here. Ms. Meredith was patting her arm and just listening to her. Ms. Meredith has a very kind face. The kids she teaches say she is a very good teacher and funny too. It almost makes me want to be in Special Ed.

We found out more about where some of the rest of the school is, since they're not here at Shalom Israel with us. There wasn't room for everybody here. So Roosevelt in exile is all over the place. Some classes are at St. Patrick's Church and some are at the Golden Spring Islamic Association Mosque. They got computers donated from the Methodist church and we might be able to send them email soon. The kids at the mosque are lucky, they have the art teacher, more rooms and especially more bathrooms because it's a really big place. I heard they have these stained glass windows over at St. Patrick's and these cool curved windows and tile pictures at the mosque.

It must have been tricky sealing off the curved windows. Nobody has more books than we do, though. I went and checked and there are books in every room here, the little classrooms upstairs and even in the chapel and sanctuary parts.

Grownups are so weird. Sometimes they just don't make a bit of sense. Some of them think TB2 is something the government invented and then let loose by accident. Not all the grownups think that, but lots of them on the Internet do. Not so many of the people living here believe it, but I did hear two teachers talking about maybe, just maybe, this was a government germ warfare thing. I heard the counselor, Mrs. Bondanza, say back that people want to believe this partly because if humans invented it, even by mistake, we have some control. Whereas if TB2 just happened, just a real bad thing that just happened somehow, we had no control. The two teachers got real huffy when she said that.

So I guess they think it's better if it's a government experiment that got out of Fort Detrick and got in the air all over town than if it just changed by chance. It did start someplace, maybe even around here, so what? What difference does it make what caused the disaster? TB2 is here. It's what they call a mutation, how the original TB germ changed into this. Of course there are other theories out there on the Internet. There's the one that says that some other country that's mad at us invented it and sent it over to us. There's the one that says it came out of Africa. Another time they turn a continent into a country! There's the theory that says it came from China. There's even one that says it came from Malaysia and it came in the spices that people brought with them when they went on vacation. That theory is interesting because it has that detail in it, but I bet it is wrong all the same. There's even one that says that some guy in Australia actually says he made it and he's sorry but somebody stole his research and let it loose on America.

Now America will never be the same.

Well, wherever it came from, however it happened, because of it there are now 220 people living at Shalom Israel synagogue and as Devorah pointed out only about 40 of them are partly or completely Jewish!

Today Johnny started coughing so bad when we were in the hall going to class and he couldn't stop. It was terrible, instead of helping everyone started to back away. Yes me too. I couldn't help it, it made me scared.

Then little Earl, I mean Shay-Shay, he went right over to him and gave Johnny a tissue and stood right next to him while Johnny tried to stop. After all the times he's been teased about being a wuss and all, and there he, or she, was, Shay-Shay willing to stand by somebody who might have a contagious disease.

A teacher came, Mademoiselle Laotian, and she helped. I saw the look on her face first, though, and she was just as scared as anyone but she made herself go over and she sent Chrystal for some water and Sebastian for Nurse Jim.

Johnny finally stopped coughing, drank the water, and they took him down to the nurse's little office and all, but I just felt awful. The teachers gave us sanitizer but I wish they had something for how stained I feel on the inside.

When I remember how I backed away. I didn't do a thing to help. Shame on me.

Johnny doesn't have TB2. He has something else called pneumonia and now the grownups are in a fuss because his parents want him in a hospital to get better and none of the hospitals can take him. Or so they say. I wonder if that's really true or if it's because he's in quarantine with us. Who would have thought that big concrete hospital buildings could back away?

Maria and I and Sebastian talked about it. Maria and I decided to say some prayers, but Sebastian said that wasn't his thing. Instead he went and got some of the Legos from the indoor recess collection (really it belongs to the synagogue, but we get to use their stuff) so he can have something to do.

Poor Johnny.

We had a science lesson about germs and contagious things. It's about time. By this time we could give the lesson ourselves.

It was on the news that they don't have a treatment that works for everyone but some medicines they are trying do help some people. Some big company is also saying they have a test, which is a really big deal. Also some people are getting TB2 and surviving it and nobody knows why, because when they got sick they didn't tell anyone because they didn't want to go into quarantine. So why tell now?

Adults don't have to make sense, I keep forgetting.

A wonderful thing has happened. I don't know how he did it but somehow Mr. Parker got his church to donate some P.E. equipment to us while we're in here and he got the synagogue folks to agree to let us have it to use in here. All the stuff has to be put away every day, but so what? We got mats and those big balls you can roll around on your stomach on and best of all we got a TRAMPOLINE! It's not very big but who cares, we can take turns! It's about the same size as the one in Rachel's aunt's yard. I got to try it today in class and it was so great. It's like flying when you jump on it. It's the best thing. If we have to be stuck inside at least we can do somersaults and cartwheels and bounce up high and do tricks on the tramp. We even named it. I named it, actually. I named it Chrissy because Mr. Parker got it from his church which is called the Church of Christ but I didn't tell him that was why. I thought maybe he wouldn't like it since it's God's name. I just said we ought to name the trampoline and so I did. Actually I do like the name and so did the other kids and now we ask if we can have a chance to play with Chrissy. Chris will lift you up, that's for sure!

We were doing our map work this afternoon and I was showing Maria all the countries around Cameroon when it happened. First the lights went out and I was frozen because that could be really bad. That's the first thing I thought.

Then I saw Ms. Wachter and all the kids coming towards me with this CAKE with CANDLES burning on it and they were singing "Happy Birthday" to me!

I was so happy I couldn't talk.

While they were singing the cake was put down right in front of me on the table and I just looked and looked at it. My name on it, and Happy Birthday, in icing. With candles. It was just unbelievable. I didn't even ever say about my birthday, or ask for anything, and here was this cake and people smiling all over their faces at me and it was so fine. Even if my stomach felt like it was flipping on Chrissy the trampoline.

I hadn't forgotten it was my birthday of course. But in my family we don't always have a big deal about it. I know that there have been birthday celebrations at school ever since I've been going to Roosevelt, but I've never had one. I asked Dad twice about it and the truth is cake and stuff costs money we don't really have. I even told one teacher I would make my own cake and bring it but she said that wasn't allowed, you have to buy it. So I never had a birthday at school. Only with the family, and only sometimes, and mostly it's not for kids, it's for the adults in the family to get together and talk and see each other. Once before I got to hear the birthday song with my name in it. Rachel sang it to me that time but hardly anyone sang it with her. Since we've been here there have been some birthdays but last month at least there weren't many parties. Maybe there were and I never knew because it's just your class.

It doesn't matter, I was having one and it was fabulous. What a surprise.

Ms. Wachter laughed and laughed when she saw my face. She had to tell me to make a wish and blow out the candles because I was just standing there staring. The candles were burned down real low by that time.

Some people were hollering by then and I looked up and there was Maria. After I looked at her my stomach stopped flipping but then I started to cry. So she came over and squeezed my arm real light and I took a breath and tried to say thank you.

The tears stopped but the words wouldn't come.

"She can't even talk!" Ernie yelled, and everyone laughed, because it was true and I am not known for being shy.

There is such a thing as too full up with happiness to talk. I found that out today. It was the best birthday I've ever had.

Also I found out that cutting cake doesn't require talking. Which was good, because those kids weren't going to wait much longer for the treat, no matter how impressed I was.

Later on, Ms. Wachter whispered that she was sorry there couldn't be presents. Without thinking I said, "You are crazy. This is the best birthday present I ever got, lady." This is not the way to talk to a teacher, but I was lucky and it just made her laugh and she hugged me.

Maria told me all about how they planned it, how they asked her my favorite flavor cake and everything, and how Ms. Rose made the cake just last night. Then Maria gave me a drawing she made for me, of the two of us, and I gulped and had trouble with words again for a few minutes.

We talked about lots of things after that. Then we just sat there while we remembered things in our heads but at the same time.

The birthday party is not over yet. Maria said Rachel was upset that there would not be goody bags. That's understandable, because Rachel's family always has big birthday parties with goody bags and games and all. But this time it wasn't really that she wanted it for her but for me, because Rachel said I should get a good birthday.

Anyway it seems that there will be some candy coming later this week and we will get to share it.

Grownups continue to be odd. There's been "discussions," as they call it, because some teachers want to give out candy on special occasions and others say we should not have any. Like ever. They say some teachers give kids candy for finishing their work on time and that's not good. Mrs. Hayes-Roberson settled that one by telling teachers that if they did not want their classes to have candy at birthday parties or on any other time that was fine, but she didn't want to see any more M & Ms in a bowl in the teacher's lounge when we got back to school. So after that they agreed on a compromise and candy is okay only if a parent provides it and if the nut allergy kids can have fruit or something else and the M & Ms stay in the lounge!

Then Mr. Binwald asked what about kids who have parents that can't afford to send any candy?

They figured that out — ask the parents who can to send enough for a class to share — and then they saw me standing there and told me to go find my friends, this was a meeting. Well, I knew that. I just like to know things.

Winter is here like no kidding. Not that I can feel the fresh cold wind of it in here. But I can see the snow go by next to the windows in the sanctuary and I'm so sad I can't go out and let it fall all around me. I love snow. It makes the world so quiet and soft. Except the big snow-storms, they are noisy and impressive. But this is one of the soft ones, and the snowflakes are big and how I wish I could feel them on my face.

Plus I would like to make snowballs and see if I can nail Jamarr with a few. I used to hate playing with him sometimes, now I hardly ever get to do it since we are in here in different classes. So I miss it.

Sometimes it would be nice if I could be more logical, but right now I can be as mixed up as I want.

God did a very good thing inventing snow. Once you learn how to live with it. You don't have to wait for art class, you can just go outside and make stuff. If you fall down in the snow it can be fabulous. You can eat it, even if some people don't like it, I do. It wraps all around trees and bushes and they look so magical and stark.

You can also get off school if it snows lots, but no such luck in here!

I went to the library and looked for a book with snow in it. I found one called Snow Treasure and it is so cool. The kids in the book help get the gold out of this country where the Nazis are trying to take over.

Mr. Rabin told me about the Nazis because part of the library here has a special section called Holocaust and I didn't know what that word meant.

He told me about the man named Hitler. How when he was in the Army there was this big war and how America went to help save the world from Hitler. How Hitler blamed everything that was wrong on the Jews in Europe and tried to kill them all, but it didn't work. How there were places called concentration camps and death camps.

It reminded me of what happened in Rwanda, I told him.

He looked so sad and told me that the lesson was supposed to be never again, but that brother had killed brother for so many years. Then he showed me one book from the library about it. It's for kids and it tells what happened to one kid who made it.

Still I have had nightmares for three nights.

Abby said he should not have told me about it and maybe it is not all true. I say I'm glad he told me and I bet it is the truth but it is so bad I wish it wasn't.

I showed Abby all the books on the shelves about it in the library. She looked scared but said, "Have you even read any of them?"

"I read one. There aren't that many for kids. But that was enough. There's a book of pictures up on the top shelf and Mr. Rabin would not let me see it. But I can go get the ladder and you can look at it if you want. He didn't say you couldn't see it," I told her. She didn't say anything. She just shook her head.

There's even a museum downtown about it.

I bet Abby thinks they made that up too.

I wish I could go back to not knowing, but it is too late. It's the same way I feel about the people in Rwanda. But if it is a true thing that happened, I need to know. Even when it is terrible. It's better to know what's real.

We found out that we won't be going to classes during the winter break, but almost everyone is sad and droopy because we won't get to see our families for the holidays. We can say hello with the Skype and so on, but it is not the same. Computers are fun but real humans in the room with you is lots better.

At least we get to do some cool Art projects. We got to have lots more choices and we can make presents for each other if we want. I'm making my own Advent calendar, since I can't get one from church. Cutting out the little doors to hide the pictures behind is harder than I thought it would be. Still, it's fun.

We played Twister last night with some kids we didn't know at all until we were all in here together. It was fun and silly. Later I found out that one of them speaks hardly any English, but with Twister you don't need to.

If I don't play a game or read a fun book after dinner I have trouble falling asleep. I get to thinking about things too much.

Twice I wrote my dad a letter and one to Auntie, but they won't let us mail them out. I wish I could send it by email but dad doesn't have it and I never get enough time at the computer to type it all anyhow.

I used to spend lots of time with computer games. I still like them, but in here it's more fun to play with the other kids. Mostly. When they don't argue . . . I argue sometimes myself, but that's because I know the way it ought to be.

Wow. Just wow. We are being serenaded by a choir outside. We went up to the front glass doors where we hardly ever get to go and these people stood on the big steps outside and sang hymns to us. There is no room to move in here and it's hard to see, but there's no keeping that wonderful sound out.

They just did Adeste Fideles, my favorite.

Everyone is being so quiet.

It's not just that they are singing. It's not just that I love some of these hymns. It's that even though the doors are still between us, we are not locked away out of sight and forgotten. It just feels so good. Tonight some kids will light a menorah too.

Tomorrow night some Jewish musicians are coming and they are going to sing Shalom Aleichem, Devorah says it is very nice. Plus some Chanukkah songs. The group is called the Klezmer Mavens. Is that a name you can't forget or what.

Ahmed says some people from his mosque are coming later this week to perform too, even though Ramadan and Eid is over. He doesn't know what they will do but it will be some kind of wonderful. People are coming to visit us even if it means they stand outside. Like that church choir is doing! Right now I just want to listen.

Yesterday we found out that they have made a sort of hospital in a building nearby that used to be a community center that went out of business. They needed it for all the people that can't fit in the regular hospitals. I asked if any of our teachers got sent there but nobody knew.

No tree to decorate. But we get to have kosher turkey and baked potatoes both kinds and four kinds of salad and green beans and challah stuffing and I don't know how many desserts for our holiday in here AND the PTA is sending us presents too. Some will get more presents at home when we get out of here but we are getting ones we can leave here when we finally get out if we ever do but at least there's a big meal, a feast for all of us and presents for Christmas and I love the PTA and all those other community and church and whatever groups, I really do!

What a great time in reading class. We got to do something called Charades, where you act out the name of the story and people try to guess what it is.

It was hilarious, we got better at guessing but we got to laughing so hard we lost track sometimes. We did it for a long time, I think. Watching Jack try to do Huckleberry Finn was the best. He kept trying to do huckle, but he finally gave up and did berry and fin and Abby guessed it. Then she was mortified because she didn't want to do one herself, which is what you win. Instead she picked Dionne, and then it got peculiar, because she did a book and Alana guessed it, Alana did a book and Dionne guessed it, and this went on until Ms. Wachter stopped it and whispered to them and they giggled and picked someone else to have a turn.

Found out later that they both know American Sign Language because Dionne's dad is deaf so she learned it from him and Alana learned it because she is Dionne's friend and she likes ASL. The teacher finally caught on about what they were doing but it was a mystery to us. I couldn't stand not knowing so I made them tell me. Frankly I think they were pretty proud of themselves, tricking us all like that.

We did a game for math that was sort of like it, with people trying to guess what number you were thinking of after you gave them clues. But it got messed up because we didn't have enough think time to come up with good clues and some kids, not that I'm going to name any names but they know who they are, tried to change their number after it was obvious that somebody guessed right. So we started over and wrote down our clues and did them in teams instead of with the whole class.

Later I realized that we had fun and ended up making up our own word problems.

I'm not a fan of math word problems.

Teachers can be really sneaky that way.

Somehow we have all ended up writing a play and we are going to perform it for the little kids in two weeks. It is all about the Underground Railroad and Harriet Tubman and Frederick Douglass. It is really hard to write a play but five of us are writing one scene each and Ahmed is going to be the narrator. Mrs. H. is teaching us songs to go with it. The best one is "Wade in the Water" and while we sing it we pretend we are wading in the water so the dogs don't find us. I don't get to be Harriet Tubman, Rachel does, but that's okay, I want to watch the scene I wrote when we do it.

Everybody keeps asking about the costumes. They are even passing notes to me in class. I am not in charge of costumes, and they better learn their lines first. Ernie tried on his Abe Lincoln beard today. He looked so funny but he got mad when we wouldn't stop laughing.

Honestly I don't want everybody laughing so much they miss the lines I wrote. That was a lot of work and this show has some funny bits but it is not supposed to be funny all the way through. Slavery was not funny.

The play was great! The cast kept bowing until somebody finally pulled the curtain because the applause was kind of going away but they were enjoying the bowing too much to stop. Now I'm so tired I think I could fall asleep standing up.

Vocabulary test tomorrow, and I haven't hardly studied but I'll probably do okay.

Some kid asked me to sign her program. That made me smile. I told her other people wrote it too, but she only wanted me to sign the program.

We are studying about the famous Reverend Doctor Martin Luther King this month. Wow did he do some cool stuff. We got to hear part of his actual speech that he gave here in Washington D.C. in 1963 when they were trying to get justice for everybody. He is a Reverend Doctor because he was a minister for a church and he went to college for a long time to be a Doctor but not medicine, which is kind of confusing but it shows how smart he is. Was. Somebody shot him. But not before he changed the way things were being done.

Still, I wish he hadn't been killed. He and his wife had four children and she had to raise them all by herself after that. That must have been so hard.

I have the most mixed up feelings. Tonight they told us that we're getting out of here the day after tomorrow and we all shouted. Then later I was not excited about it. I couldn't understand how I was feeling. I still can't, but the one thing I did figure out is that I've gotten used to being here. I really have, and now that's what's normal. I'm still leaving and I still want to leave but this has been a fascinating place to live. It's as if I've been to another country. A very very small country. Without its own flag, or language, or national costume. It doesn't have special food or interesting geography. Still, it has some good music and some mighty cute and smart citizens, I just saw one in the mirror.

We get to go home. At last. Before February is even over. Because there is a test and a treatment and they think the worst is over. I sure hope so.

I do know one thing it feels like and that is, a miracle.

We can't take much with us. Even though now they have a test to see if you have TB2, and if we haven't gotten sick by now we probably don't have it, they don't want us to take lots of things we have here with us. So those stuffed toys and other stuff will be thrown away. Even Chrissy the trampoline. The computers will be cleaned carefully and eventually the school will get them. The books are okay, we can take them because they did tests on them and found out the germ can't live on paper.

There will be a bus to take some kids back to school for parents to come get them, but most kids will be picked up here.

Dad is coming to get me and Jamarr. I don't have any mixed up feelings about that, I am all glad. Goodbye, quarantine. What a bizarre couple of months you have been. I can't get no satisfaction but if life goes back to being regular again I will get what I need!

It is the view of the Ministry that a theoretical knowledge will be sufficient to get you through your examinations, which after all, is what school is all about.

— Harry Potter and the Order of the Phoenix

by J.K. Rowling

Section Three: Inside Out

I'm stuck inside again, and I want to be out.

The beginning of being back at Roosevelt was good. We got to be inside and outside. Fun stuff to do and talk about. I got to see my buddies. Jamarr was somewhere else for hours instead of tagging around after me all the time.

Our second day of school, Ms. Wachter passed out these pretty notebooks, that she says we get to have as our secret journals. She is not allowed to read it! She told us, "You can write anything you want to in it." Plus we can decorate the cover. Immediately I put lots of stickers on mine. Also we can draw anything we want in it.

But not today.

Thing is, most of the time I don't mind learning something. Sometimes I don't even catch on that I have until there's some sort of test. That kind of test is not so bad, even if it is kind of boring, but this kind of test is horrible. I hate this long boring test we have to take now so much.

This test, no, it's awful, and there are times when I'm done. Really done. And then I want to talk to somebody or draw and sheesh, just get out of the classroom for a minute. For real, take a walk or something. But you have to stay where the teacher says. Unless you go to the bathroom, so everybody tries to go all the time and the teachers catch on about that and only let us go sometimes. Or unless you go into quarantine, then you stay where the government says. Until they are totally sure you are not contagious any more. Like we did. For months.

It used to be that I could write some things in my journal and then draw some stuff and I put funny captions with the drawings. I did drawings of my family and my best friends forever, I put both Rachel and Maria in my picture since we are all friends together now especially since we lived together in quarantine.

I drew my dad with all kinds of expressions on his face, and auntie looking sleepy.

I drew my mom always smiling because I love her smile.

Also I put my dear sister Angelique in my pictures. It's where she should be. I can't draw her as pretty as she was. I remember so that's good enough. It's good to be part of a big family. Usually.

We don't all live together in my family though. That would be impossible. Me and my dad and auntie and Grandma Sarah and my little brother Jamarr live in our apartment. My half-sister Hope and my other big sister Halima and my big brother Malcolm and my cousin Ben and my other Aunt Anaiah and Uncle Eli live in other apartments. That's all the family that lives close here. Nobody has a house yet. Some of the folks in Rachel's family have a house. We don't.

She has a big family too. Rachel calls herself my cousin but that's not it really. We are just kind of cousins from far back in our families in Cameroon but not really close cousins. Not like cousins are in America. Rachel has really big poofy hair that she is always trying to get me to braid for her but I can't get it to stay braided. She had big brown eyes and I have to say that her eyes are nice. Except when she is really mad. Then it's like lightning bolts are coming out at you and you better find cover. Rachel is a little chubby and she does not like you to mention that. She does not like to read as much as I do but hardly anyone does. She is very good at playing dress up and making up stories about us being grownups. Also sometimes she plays she is a talk show host and it is amazing how good she is at that. I get to be different famous people and she interviews me. That is lots of fun. We both get to be famous when we play that game.

Since we live so near each other, her mom is friends with my dad. Some of Rachel's family have got a house as well as the apartment here but she lives in the apartment with her mom and dad and goes to visit her aunt's family, they have the house.

The house is not very big but the yard is great. They even have a brick barbecue. That is where they have such great parties. They have a really good outside to their house.

Really her family is not closely related to mine, just in kind of a way from some of the marriages before we got to this country. Actually I was born there but sometimes it doesn't feel like a big deal because most everyone else was born back in Cameroon including my dad and my grandma. So anyhow Rachel is always coming over to play with me. Which is all right. Except Rachel tries to get me to say she is my best friend but she isn't. My best friend is Maria, she moved here from El Salvador with her family, which is bigger than mine, and they all live in a house together. And they can speak Spanish which I can't. And she has her mom with her and I don't.

But now we are the three amigas so it's all okay.

School is different than home. I don't have a desk in my house that says "Darryn Yochangko Thomas" on this nice decorated nametag and I don't have a water cooler with cups sticking on the wall next to it with my name on my cup again and I don't have to sign my name on a piece of paper and take a pass to go to the bathroom when I'm home. Of course at home someone is nearly always in the bathroom anyhow.

School is better than home in some ways. There's more interesting things to do some days. Science experiments are fun. I love doing math games and I'm good at place value so that's good. And I like to read if they let me pick a book I like instead of something lame. The Beverly Cleary books are not bad. Except I haven't found a book yet with a kid in it that has a life like mine. There's some stuff that's similar but it isn't really like how I live. The kids who ride on the bus to school in these books never have a bus ride like mine. Like the one when somebody dropped his pants yes underpants too on the bus and holler bad words about wanting to do you-know-what. All they did was suspend him.

They never seem to have such big fights when Ramona is on the bus and there's nobody named Jamal or Julio in her books. She never gets to see two guys screaming and calling names and punching the heck out of each other so bad that the bus driver stops the bus and tells them they are going to have to get off and he can't really do that but at least they stopped the fighting. And they got suspended too and they got in a fight this week again anyway! And if somebody called me the n-word I might get in a fight too, look out!

Now this kind of thing does not seem to happen to Ramona.

I did see two kids fighting over a pink eraser once just like in the book though.

But when this kind of thing happens to Darryn she stays cool. I just write about it later in my notebook and duck when necessary, like the food fight the other day.

Food fights are not good for journals. You can't ever get the grease stains out and it smears the words. That's why I've given up trying to write when I'm having soup.

Everything that happens can go in my journal. I write it all down and figure it out later. Or at least write it all down. That's how I learned the school song in Spanish. I copied the words Ms. H gave us and Maria helped me pronounce them right, but it was writing them down a couple of times that helped me to remember them.

Really, I am pretty lucky to have Maria as a friend. I wish I could learn another language but they don't teach you one until you get to middle school. Unless your family has money and can pay for you to have a tutor. Or your family won the lottery to go to French Immersion. Daddy won the visa lottery already. That was good enough.

Maybe I ought to pay Maria to teach me. Oh, yeah, that would take money. Never mind. Maybe I will just watch Spanish television.

I wished it worked the same way for me remembering multiplication but just writing it down doesn't see to work for numbers like it does for words. Oh well. I get to draw stuff for the numbers and that seems to work okay.

2 X 5= 10

When you draw multiplication it's called an array. But when you do geometry this is a ray too: ➤ and there's a singer well he's dead now and he's a Ray, too. And there's Betsy Ray in the book we read.

And me I'm a little ray of sunshine. If sunshine were purple.

That first day of Fourth Grade was so cool. I wanted to learn to write the date with just numbers and a slash just the way Ms. Wachter did on the board: 8/26. I never wrote it that way before. Seems like a long time ago now.

Underneath the date on the board she put, "This is the date that women got the vote." Vote about what?

Lots of parents came with their kids to class. What's the point of that? My dad never comes. He knows I can find the classroom by myself. He has to get to work anyhow. I bet the parents who came are just nosy to see how the teacher decorated and what she looks like. Well she put up some good pictures and she's got long brown hair, she's white and skinny. Okay people? You can leave now.

160

It's not a bad classroom. I'd seen worse. At least there were enough desks and chairs. Plenty of books and stuff you can really use in the math center. There was a bunch of posters about all kinds of stuff, I don't have time to read them all and besides some have no pictures so who cares. There were two computers, that was good. And a bunch of stuff over in the science center and a map of some country on the wall, it's not the United States. I wondered what it was. Too bad I couldn't wander over and look but teachers don't like that. When they say sit they want you to stay that way.

Later on I found out it was a place called Afghanistan where Miss Wachter's brother was, being a Marine there. She showed us his picture. Nice uniform.

Miss Wachter turned out to be all right. There are some nasty teachers that can't wait to leave at the end of the day. There are teachers that get so nasty about how your cubby or desk is or they get nutty about permission slips. I had a mean music teacher once. She just wanted us to shut up all the time. She said it was so she could hear the music we were supposed to be making but I think she just got old and cranky like my great grandma. With this teacher the only time you knew how you were doing in her class was when you were in trouble. I know some people got 3s all the time from her because they were quiet. That is a dumb reason to give somebody a 3 if you ask me. And why a 3 anyway, why not a 7? Seven is a cool number. Or a ten. I would like to get a ten. 3 as a grade just seems so small. Is it even worth it.

We used to get grades like an S or an I or a N, which were pretty easy to understand. S is satisfactory or suc-cessful, I means you almost got it and N means not yet.

My sister Halima told me that we would get As and Bs and a C or a D if we didn't do so good, but it seems like sometimes we get numbers instead of letters. But now the new rule is only As and Bs. C is not okay and D is bad. And then we get those 3s, of course sometimes you get a two instead. Like 3 wasn't small enough to start with.

On our first day of school back in August, we went out to a trailer except we're not supposed to call them trailers. Ms. Wachter told everybody welcome to their new classroom. She said she doesn't mind being in the trailers but I noticed she doesn't want anyone to call them trailers. She calls it the portable classroom. I wondered where they are going to move it to if it's portable. One time I remember I heard another teacher call our trailer a Learning Cottage and Ms. Wachter busted out laughing. I can understand that. This place is lots of things to me and to her but it is not a cottage. If it was made out of gingerbread we'd have a worse rat problem than we do now.

Some of the kids and all the teachers complain about the trailer portables. I don't mind it. It's big enough for all our desks and it's bigger than my room where I sleep at my house and it has more books. Plus the air conditioning works better even sometimes it's too cold. So I don't know what the problem is anyway. Teachers and grownups complain all the time about lots of things. Kids, for instance.

That's all right. I got complaints about them. I wrote one of my best stories about what it would be like with no grownups at all. If they could just stop bossing. It's like that's why they wake up in the morning.

I was watching the French classes walk down the hall one day while I was coming back from taking the attendance folder. I just had to stop and stare at them, I'm not kidding. They were all walking in a line with their hands on their hips. They looked so haughty. The teacher was doing the same thing. I guess it's just so they can keep their hands to themselves going down the hall but that's not how it looks. They look like they are models strutting on the runway or something. Then when you hear the French it sounds twice as stuck up. But when I hear French in a song, it sounds great to me.

Back in Cameroon lots of people speak French, but I don't and my dad doesn't. He can understand it to listen to better than I can. He's very proud of the fact that he can speak English so well and he tells me I should learn other languages. I guess I could learn French but I would rather learn Spanish. Maria speaks Spanish to her mom and I love how it sounds. To me Spanish sounds friendlier than French, I don't know why, except maybe I hear more Spanish where we live. My dad is right, I should learn another language. It could be handy later because I want to travel lots. No matter what I want to travel back to Cameroon to see my mom again, so maybe I should learn French for that. We didn't speak it when we were there but it would have been easier if we had. There are CDs you can get to learn a language on the computer but they cost lots of money. At school they don't teach you any language but English, except the French Immersion of course but I'm not in that class. Those kids all looked rich to me. I found out in quarantine that's not true.

The thing is, even before quarantine, I talked to some of those French Immersion kids at recess when we were all out on the playground, since I speak some French and they speak English mostly at recess anyway. They aren't all really stuck up. They just . . . I don't know, they just got this reputation. It's hard to hang out with them when they are in a different class and speak another language and sometimes they do better on the tests than we do. That's what I heard.

Ms. Wachter comes up with strong things for us to write about. One time she said to write about the best thing that ever happened to you. Another time she said if you had a super power what would it be. We write about it here in our secret journals first. Then we make a second draft where we fix it up more and make sure the sentences all start with a capital letter and stuff like that. Then we write it again and it goes up in our publishing center in the classroom.

Now in this boring Standard Normative Measure, SNM test there is a little writing, but nobody would put it up in the publishing center. Even if you worked really hard on the short Brief Constructed Response thing, it would not be anything anybody would want to read. Dick and Joan go to the store to buy some bread. Joan reaches in her pocket for the money . . . maybe the writing is supposed to be about the problem in the story. The problem is obviously supposed to be she lost the money, but the real problem is that this story will put you to sleep. You will not remember one bit of this story later, because it is so boring. But that is the kind of writing for the SNM test.

Once Ms. Wachter wanted us to write about if we could go anywhere where would it be and why, write at least five sentences. (She always says write at least five sentences and I always write one more than that just because. Actually sometimes I write lots more than that. If she didn't say write five sentences some people would write like one.) Maria doesn't like to write as much as I do but she doesn't mind writing five sentences. Maria wrote about how she wants to go to Puerto Rico, because her mom's best friend is from there and told her all about it. Then Maria read it out loud to the class. So Jeannie said, "That sounds cool but what if you don't have a passport?"

It turns out Puerto Rico is part of the United States so you don't need a passport to go there, and that shows what Jeannie knows.

Well I didn't know that either but I didn't ask anything about a passport.

If I could go anywhere I would go to Cameroon and visit my mom and bring her back to America with me. I think it is very sad that she can't come to this country because Daddy won't marry her.

If she came I would take care of her. I'm strong about that. I could do it. I can take care of my family.

I got a letter from mom the day before yesterday. This is a good letter, she tells me good things about the village and how her rugs are selling so well. She writes letters just for me now that I am older and I write her back.

When I was only in kindergarten here she used to send her letters to Dad and he would read them to me but he didn't like to do it. She would always put in something about how she missed me and wanted to come to

America. She can't come. He doesn't want to marry her. If he did she could live here.

That's the way it is with them.

He had a wife before he met her. That wife died. He really loved that wife, he still has her picture in his room and she looks very beautiful. Her name was Virginia, nickname Ginny. Angelique was Ginny's daughter. He had other children from her too.

I wish sometimes that my dad loved my mom Imani enough to marry her. But he doesn't want her. They lived together in Cameroon. I don't remember much of that time but I do remember hearing them arguing. When his cousin wrote to him and told him that he should come to America, my dad decided to try and he won the lottery they have for people who want to move to America. So he was very lucky.

Dad wanted to take all his children.

But not my mom.

So she writes me letters and now I write her letters. I wish . . . but there is no point to wishing.

If there was I could wish this stupid test away. It would burn up, poof. Back to this dumb test story:

"Oh," cried Joan, "how can we tell Mom?"

Be glad you've got a mom you live with you can tell something anyhow and get over yourself, Joan.

Hey, Joan, how about you figure out how to write to your mom about your sister dying and everything that happened with her in the hospital and so on. Now there's a problem in that story, Joan, for real.

Mom was so sad about Angelique, even though Angelique was not her daughter even.

One time someone asked me how I could keep up with all the different people in my big family and how they are related to me. I don't understand how you can't. I'm lucky there are so many. I just remember. Family is family forever, even if you get mad, even if they live far away. Love can travel just fine.

That would be bad, not knowing about what is going on with your family.

A thing I really don't understand is this whole thing about boyfriends. It has gotten to be a big deal lately since we got out of quarantine. I have to say this is one thing Rachel and I completely agree about. Why would anybody want a boyfriend here in Fourth Grade? Boyfriends are even more work than friends, as far as I can tell. It's like some people can't wait until they are old enough. Maybe they are old enough, but that's them, it's not me. These girls even want to go to the movies that are for teenagers. Now there is that vampire movie that started with a book about a girl who falls in love with a vampire boy. Why would you want to go around with a boy you know is going to bite you?

Not all boys bite of course. The ones that do have to go the office.

One thing I know for sure is that the boys hate to be beat in Math. I like knowing and saying the answer fast, they are just going to have to get used to it.

It's so horrible being back at school now. Just so much SNM.

One thing I hate about practicing for this dreary test is you can't talk. At all. Even to yourself, to help figure it out. It's 100% all the time ssshh.

Lots of times teachers don't like talking unless it is them doing it. But with this standard test, even they can't talk during the test, except to tell you to begin and they say how to fill in the circle for your answer. That's probably not the right grammar way to say it, but who cares. I'm not going to worry about it. If this was our writing class with those 6 + 1 traits we need to do I would have to re-write everything a zillion times before I could be done with it. Ms. Wachter says that is what real writers will do all the time. Boy oh boy do I feel sorry for them!

I remember Ms. Wachter seemed okay for a teacher. Some teachers are jerks but she's not, most of the time. On the first day of class she was really nice to us like teachers always are the first day. So I couldn't really tell yet. Now I know for sure, she's okay. Except today she seems like a robot or something for this test thing.

Living with her in quarantine showed me that.

On that first day she introduced herself to over and over everybody while she was standing in the doorway so you couldn't even go in without saying excuse me to her. Then she stayed in the doorway all the time people kept coming in. So of course I had to introduce myself mainly since she asked me to, and she didn't say anything dumb like "Darryn is a boy's name, isn't it?" or ask me if my family was from Africa when I said my whole name.

I hate it when teachers do that. First off Africa is not a country it's a continent. My family is from Cameroon which is a country in Africa. Secondly what difference does it make, I moved here because of my dad and I'm an American now. Fourth it's fake like they really care that I was born somewhere else, they don't. So at least she didn't do that kind of dumb crap. I'm not supposed to say crap. Crap crap crap. Wow, look, the world didn't come to an end . . . so much for that rule.

The first day Ms. Wachter had stuff for us to do already on the desks and she asked us to do it. First thing I thought is what are we supposed to do but I looked at it and it was just a paper for us to say our name and address if we know it, which I do and any allergies, which I have one to bee stings and then a bunch of questions about what do we like to do in school and that was easy because it's computers and recess and PE and music and science experiments for me.

There's just these questions, spread out, with lines for the answers. No place on this question paper to draw anything, not even the back. That's a drawback. Ha-ha.

Drawing is okay but I would rather be reading. No matter what most of the time I would rather be reading.

She wanted to know what we liked to read, well I didn't say it but for me it's everything. I even like to read the ingredients on the cereal box. It's one of my most favorite things, reading. Books too, of course. Thing is, if you tell a teacher that, they think you're going to want to read all the stories you've got to read in school and that is so not the way it is. I like chapter books if they're exciting and I like some picture books if they are funny and I like anything about Harriet Tubman but some of the stuff they want you to read sucks. Like Johnny Tremain was a drag and I thought the Little Lame Prince was really lame and other stuff I can't remember the titles of because I never want to read it again. Or do a summary of it. Or compare and contrast it with the two circles. Or find the main idea of it. Or predict what would happen next in it. Man. That's what I mean about how a reading lesson can ruin a good book. Sometimes it just sucks the juice right out of it. I like to read a book again and if you do too many things to take apart the story to see what it all means you can't forget enough of it to get to have the fun of reading it again. That's what I have found. Also sometimes the book is not very good. In school it seems like you are never allowed to hate an assigned book. But I do. I got a list, let me tell you.

There are books I like a lot. I can read "Give a Mouse a Cookie" over and over. There's a picture book this woman wrote about her family, called "Always and Olive," and she came and read it to us and that's one I like. Also I just started reading Harry Potter and the Philosopher's Stone and it's great. Dad got it for me from a friend of his and it's the British version, there's a different title and picture on the cover but it still the same first book. There's Captain Underpants books too but it's not so good the third time around because you know what will happen. Sometimes I like knowing what will happen and sometimes I don't want that. I like mystery stories if I can figure it out. There is also a story about this real person, called Rosa Parks, who helped change the bad segregation laws, I love that book. I must have read it ten times. I hoped that David Adler wrote some other books like that. Now Rachel likes adventure books and books about friends and Maria likes funny books and books about friends. There are lots of books about friends so that's okay. We can swap books like that.

Dad doesn't read much to me now that I'm big. So I'm trying to read Alice in Wonderland all by myself now but it's hard. It's not hard to read, it's hard to understand. I can't figure out how to do a book report on it. I'm supposed to tell the characters and the setting and the problem and the solution and there are a bunch of all of those in it. Maybe I'll just read it for fun and not a report. I could just write a report about friends. I could tell about what it is like to be friends with Maria. The thing about her is that she is different from me but we are alike too. My hair is lots curlier than hers. Her skin is light brown and mine is dark brown. She's a little taller, but my feet are bigger than hers. We both like to read but we usually like different kinds of books. I love to talk in front of the class and she really doesn't but she does it anyway. She really loves to color and I just do it because we're supposed to do it. She likes Ethiopian food and I can't stand it, but we both love burritos.

I know exactly when I wanted her to be my best friend. We were sitting around talking and eating lunch at a field trip, the first one of the year. It was this cool garden we got to visit. I never saw so many different colors on plants in my life. So we're sitting around eating lunch. I don't remember what we were talking about, but I do remember that all of a sudden she started apologizing to me. She has this great soft voice and I had to pay attention to hear her. What she was sorry about was that she was talking at the same time as me. She said she was sorry for talking over me. I hardly even noticed. At my house sometimes we all talk at once and the one who has enough breath to talk the longest wins. It's just how we talk sometimes. But here was Maria saying that she was rude to do that. It gave me a whole new idea about what rude is. Plus she wanted to hear what I said instead of saying what she was saying. It was real respect and I thought she was a classy kind of person. The kind I wanted for a friend.

Also sometimes she will do something or read a book I like just because I ask her to. Rachel will too. That's why we all read some of the Nancy Drew books. She likes the parts where Nancy has fun with her friends best and Rachel liked the adventure part best and I liked the puzzle of it, then the friends part. It's also really funny that there's a girl named George!

We have to read 25 books by the end of the year Ms. Wachter said. That's no problem for me. It's doing all those book reports. That's so much work and it takes so much time. Bet anything I will have to re-read Charlotte's Web all the way to do the book report right even though I already read it over the summer. Plus I already saw the movie with my friend Dena. But we will have to read it again in class. You watch.

If it was up to me I would just read fairy tales and fantasy books and graphic novels and a bunch of those books I keep being told are not appropriate. I LIKE not appropriate. I am not appropriate.

That can be a good choice.

Weird, to think that in most of the classrooms, everyone is taking this test. In the whole state, even. Roosevelt

172

Fifth Grade is taking it and the Third Grade is taking it. Plus all of us Fourth Graders.

We have four Fourth Grades here at our public school and there are 100 kids in the our grade here. I found that out when we did our second-day math survey, when I went around asking the teachers how many kids in each class. That was kind of fun, that's when I found out the French Immersion classes have more kids than we do here on the Academy side. Nobody told me why, though. In French or English.

Hate this test. I couldn't help it, I started reading the first story in the SNM booklet. Wow is it boring. I'm sure somebody tried really hard but honestly, it's so bad. I've read cereal boxes that were better than this. But then, they want you to buy the cereal.

Time to think about something else. We got a new kid back in late September. She had just moved here. She looked so scared. That was Devorah. She has dark curly hair and glasses. She brought her own lunch that day. It looked like a pretty good lunch. That first day I talked to her a little bit but she was really quiet and I didn't want to bug her. We agreed that we hated moving. I knew since I have had to do it a couple of times, it is no fun. She said she likes to read. My kind of girl! Now after quarantine we are good friends.

I think I might be her only close friend. I'm looking at her right now and is she concentrating on this test. Now she's putting her head down like she does when she gets a headache. Poor Devorah.

Now I'm being told to keep my eyes on my own booklet. I will need to be reminded sometimes because my mind does not want to stay on it. Even though I am still answering the questions. I'd rather think about the past. Or lunch, now at a new time because we have to finish the test up in the morning. Or maybe I could draw a nice doodle on this scratch paper they gave us. I guess it's supposed to be if we want to make notes or something. Why do they call it scratch paper? Does it make you itch?

Along time ago, in science class, back when we actually were learning new things every day instead of reviewing everything we would need for this so annoying SNM test, Chrystal passed me a note. I don't usually pass or accept or write notes to pass because the teacher nearly always catches you and it can wait until we get to the playground. But Chrystal looked so upset that this time I took the note and read it.

Wish she would pass me an interesting note right now, but that is totally against the test rules. They would think we were cheating. As if. I know some other people who might cheat but not Chrystal. She is like her name, clear and transparent. She would never try to get away with something like that.

Anyhow I remember the note. She said she was not Jeannie's friend any more. So I wrote back on the note and asked why. Here on the scratch paper I have re-done the whole note just like I remember it:

I am not Jeanies friend any more. **Why?**   She says she is not my friend. For no reason. She is mean. Do you know why? I don't know why. Oh well if you figure it out tell me. **Why not ask her.**   She said it was because of the lunch box on the butt. Just because I hit her with a lunch box. On the butt! **That's not a bad reason. I would be mad if you did that to me.**
Your mean too.

So then Chrystal got mad at me and later Jeannie too. Jeannie said it was none of my beeswax. Well I didn't ask Chrystal about any of it. She gave me the note and I just wrote back my opinion.

I don't care. What if you hit someone on the butt and hurt them and never said you were sorry and they got cancer later. You would be really sorry. These people just do not understand important stuff like that. If you ask me what I think when you get in a dumb fight like that I am going to tell you what I think. Everybody knows I am going to say what I think. I have an aunt back in Cameroon named Fern and she is like that too. We have to tell the true thing. I am not just going to be on your side when you did it because we are friends. Besides sometimes it's all my friends arguing like this time so there is no safe side to be on.

That's why I don't like notes about stuff like this.

Chrystal and Jeannie did forgive me later but it took a long time, like a week.

Last year I remember one time we all got in a fight on the playground about who was the best friend of who and we all ended up in the principal's office. It was me and Chrystal and Jeannie and Dena and Rachel and even Maria, who doesn't usually get in trouble. There was hardly room for all of us in the office. Mrs. Hayes-Roberson the principal was really mad even though she acted all calm. I could tell she was mad. That was one time when I didn't want to tell what happened and she made me tell. I knew I had done a mean stupid thing but I didn't want to talk about it in front of everyone. Really I should not have said that Maria was my best friend forever so we could not be BFF with anyone else and Rachel got all upset. I should not have said Rachel was too mean to be anyone's friend.

Rachel's uncle died from TB2 last week, which is part of why she is upset these days. The funeral was very crowded, everybody liked Uncle Feso. He was a big man could swing kids up in the air and bring them right back down so safe and fun. But the TB2 made him small and weak so fast.

TB2 is still happening, and the treatment is not a cure, and many places don't have crowds like they did because people are so scared. Sports and movies and stores are not crowded like they used to be. Still people are trying to go back to the way things used to be, while leaving time for funerals. It is not the first funeral we've had to go to since we got back. Rachel cried and cried at the funeral. I gave her all my tissues, I only needed one myself. I didn't know him like she did.

Sometimes Rachel is mean, though. She has a really bad temper. Sometimes I do too but I don't poke people the way she does. I use words. I'm really good with words, even to fight, and I like how good I am with words. Rachel can't even fight from the same dictionary as me. She doesn't think fast with words the way I do. So she pokes folks with her finger. Maria isn't fast with lots of words but she is very good with the ones she does use. It's like if it was a real fight, I throw lots of punches and

176

she only throws a few, but the punches Maria throws are stronger. Sometimes it's like pow, pow, and I have to shut up because she's better. What she says isn't mean or nasty so much as it's true. She knows it, too, I can tell the way her eyes snap. Of course sometimes I win. Sometimes it's not important who wins, as long as we stop fighting. Maria is my BFF for real and true.

Rachel did stick up for me one time when some kid that lives in her neighborhood started making fun of my skin being dark. She didn't hit him though, just blessed him out so loud he took off running.

"I won't let anyone talk to you that way," she said, and was that true.

Sometimes the best thing a friend can do is chase away an enemy for you.

Dena is different. Dena is almost always calm and funny. She's a very restful friend to have. I don't know how she got caught in the drama the rest of us were having. It's not like her.

So when we had this big fight Mrs. Hayes-Roberson did a really cool thing and told everyone else to wait outside the office and she talked to me by myself. Now I still didn't want to talk about it much and admit what a jerk I had been but when she did that I could at least start to tell about it. While I was telling on myself I kind of tattled on everyone else too but Mrs. Hayes-Roberson did another cool thing. She got everyone to come in and talk to her one at a time to say what happened from their point of view and when she did no one could tell who tattled on who. We all lost recess of course but that was one time I thought it was fair.

I spent a lot of time in the office last year. It seems like there were just days when nothing worked out. Sometimes I was just sad and mad all at the same time. I never knew when I was going to feel like that and I got into picking fights sometimes, I guess. Also there are some really stupid mean things kids say and most of the time teachers don't even hear it. Then the person can say no I didn't do it or somebody else said it and unless somebody else heard it there's nothing they can do. One time on the bus this kid Bayra was whispering all kinds of mean things about the bus driver to me. The driver had a little accident, she went up over a curb. Bayra screamed are you trying to kill us? And afterwards she kept saying stuff to me like the driver was stupid because she went up on the curb and I told the bus driver and Bayra said she never said it and the bus driver believed her, not me. So Bayra was right the driver was stupid.

We're not supposed to say someone is stupid. But sometimes it's true.

With girls it is so easy to get into a big argument about nothing and nobody ever forgets and forgives, at least not for a long time. At school anyway, that's the way it is. All one girl has to say to the other is I won't be your friend and then it's all just upset and nastiness after that.

Two girls in Ms. DeCombe's class got into a big argument, Marion and Carrie, and it was something to see. I don't even remember what they were mad about, just what their faces looked like, it was like they were all eyes and mouth.

What really doesn't make any sense is when some girl tells me she doesn't care if we are friends or not. If you don't care why are you talking about it. Here you are and you are holding on to your mad at me about it like it's some precious jewel.

I never got into a mad like that with Angelique. We got into fights but then we forgave each other, even that really bad time when I hid all of her hair stuff when she was going to go out with John Joseph, her great new boy-friend.

As long as I live I will never forget him crying at the funeral. I never saw so many men crying in my life. That was my awesome sister, so wonderful she made grown men cry. Even before she died.

I wish when bad sad stuff happened everybody would just roll up their mad into a big ball and kick it over the fence at recess so we could play together again. That would be better than all these grudges and stuff.

Somebody with gloves better bury the ball. If we touch it the whole thing could start over again.

If it were up to me we would have twice as much room on the playground to start with, if we could spread out we might not fight as much. I've seen middle school playgrounds and they look bigger than ours. Except I think they don't have swings and jungle gyms. All the schools should have as much room outside as inside, no matter what kind of school it is. Kids need the room. I need the room, anyway. That's because I like to move it move it, like the song says. That's a really good song. And if I like it I bet the other kids would too. It seems to me that grownups have most of the world. It seems to me that they could share more.

Of course if grownups could share more then they wouldn't have so many fights and then what would we get to watch on CNN?

Also, if it were up to me we would have three free snacks to pick from every day. Not those sorry snacks like raisins, either. But it wouldn't have to be potato chips, I don't have to have grease. All the time. Not like some people. Some people whatever the snack is they don't like it and then they say they're hungry. They say they're hungry over and over, like that is going to do something. Maybe they were able to play some teachers by whining like that and they got something else. Ms. Wachter doesn't fall for that. She tells them that's the snack and that's what it is. If we had my system we could pick from three and one of them is bound to be good. If there's three and you still don't like any then you really are being a diva and never mind.

At least we get extra good snacks with the test. They also told us to eat a good breakfast and get some good sleep. Except it's hard to sleep for those kids worried about the TEST, because it's all we've been hearing about for MONTHS. Sheesh.

We got people with allergies in our class so that means we never get certain kinds of snacks ever. No peanut M & Ms, no Butterfingers, no Snickers, no Reeses. One year we had a kid, she's not at our school any more, Shelly was allergic to all kinds of stuff. She couldn't even have regular M & Ms because M & Ms get made at a factory that has peanuts in other candy. It was like she would break out if she even looked at a peanut.

I felt kind of sorry for her. She had to sit a little away from us at lunch, in case of peanuts or other things in our lunch, and Halloween was just awful for her. All she could have was those fruit snacks things like jelly beans. And raisins. Poor thing.

Once in another class I knew a kid who couldn't have anything made from wheat. He had celery disease. But he could still eat celery. He couldn't eat wheat. That means no noodles, no doughnuts, NO PIZZA. Life without pizza. Now that is just pitiful.

He said his mom made him his lunch all the time because wheat is in just about everything they serve in the cafeteria. It was like this poison he had to watch out for. He ate some one time and it made him go to the bathroom for three days every hour. That's what he said. He told me all about it. I don't know if I believe him because he had to sleep sometime and if you went to the bathroom that long you would probably pass out by the end of the second day. I didn't ask him more about it though because I was afraid he would tell me more about it.

He also couldn't eat pork but that wasn't allergy. It was just important for God. Like for the Jews and kosher Ahmed being Muslim. I wonder which one this boy was, or if it was some other religion.

I can eat just about anything. Except Brussel sprouts and cooked carrots. There is no good reason for anyone to have to eat either of those things. I don't care what they say about carrots being good for your eyes. They tell me they got vitamins. I say, there's vitamins in other things. I will eat my carrots raw. Don't talk to me about vitamins in cooked carrots. If there were any vitamins the boiling got rid of them, along with all the taste. It's like chewing on somebody's ear. Only worse.

Eat carrots raw and do the right thing.

School is weird, they tell us about all the good food in Science class and then they don't give us hardly any in the cafeteria. Or in the classroom, either, teachers will give you pretzels or popcorn but that is only from one food group. You are supposed to eat more vegetable and fruit than anything else. What do we eat in the cafeteria. Burgers. Hot dogs. Pizza. They tried a soy burger once but nobody would eat it once they found out. So they quit. They should never have told people, they would have just put ketchup all over it like they do and never known the difference.

Is ketchup a vegetable? It's made out of tomatoes. Tomatoes and sugar. I read the packet ingredients so I know. I bet the sugar means it doesn't count as a vegetable any more. Sugar is a carbo-drate, I learned that in Science. Pretzels are a carbo-drate too. I wonder what popcorn is. Besides good when it's fresh.

I like carrots raw. I don't like to dip them in dressing. I don't get that. Ranch dressing just tastes like mayonnaise to me. If you're going to have dressing on something it should taste like dressing. Some kind of flavor. Ranch dressing means the salad is undressed. Eeew.

We got better food in quarantine because it tasted like it just got made which was true. Miss Rose made it and the other people helped her.

I get the food I like at home. I even like spice with some food. Some of these kids would never make it in Africa. Or Mexico. You show them a chile at lunchtime like Nasir did the other day and they scream. It's just a chile. It can't bite you. Not unless you bite it first!

Only the strong survive eating chiles. Other folks, step to the side, chile eaters coming through.

Then leave space open after that because we need the bathroom faster and more than the rest of you.

It's worth it.

I finished the first part of the test. The timer just went off. How did that happen?

Jamarr just does not know what to do with himself sometimes. He doesn't even have to take the test but he is cutting up lately like the pressure is on him or something. Last week he wouldn't stop standing up on the bus. I never did find out why. Everybody expected me to do something about it because he's my brother. I have to deal with him enough when I'm home! He wants something else on the TV instead of what I'm watching. He wants me to reach the snacks for him. He wants me to help him with his homework and it is so easy and he still doesn't want to do it by himself. First grade is easy. He has no idea.

Actually, when I was in it, parts were hard. But still, he should do it himself.

So today going home he wants to stand up on the bus again. I didn't even want anybody to know he's related to me but of course it's too late, they all know. Even so, who cares if he stands up and jumps around and makes faces or whatever else he was doing this afternoon. The only one who was really bothered was the bus driver and maybe the safety patrol.

Of course he didn't sit down when I asked him. I don't know why anyone thought he would listen to me. The driver said he would stop the bus. I didn't think he really would but I was so embarrassed, I just wanted Ja-marr to cooperate for once.

So in the end I bribed him. Now he gets that jumbo pack of gum that I've only had three pieces of but I had to do it. Otherwise I would have strangled him.

I had a bad day but got a good story out of it. It's up there in our publishing center now with that big A on it, when I told Ms. Wachter I wanted an A not a 3. So she put both. I can't really see it from here but I know it's there. It's under other things I've written since, but it's there, my words. I read it to the class and I remember it so well. It is ten times better than anything I could write in this ridiculous booklet.

It's really long too, lots of concrete details like they want you to do, and when I went to write it the words just kept coming like light down my arm.

The other kids told me they really liked it.

When The Day Does Not Go Well
by Darryn Yochangko Thomas

The day before yesterday was not good. It started okay. But it did not go well.

Usually we come to school and then we have math right away. In math we switch to different classrooms except I don't switch I still have Ms. Wachter. She teaches the Fourth Grade math.

I'm glad I'm in math with Ms. Wachter. I fit there.

To start in math class we do some warm up problems. I don't know why they call it that. I don't feel any warmer after. We turn that in. Then we listen to her explain stuff like graphs right now. Then she wants us to do it. She goes around putting numbers on your desk and whichever number she puts that's your group for the day. So today I was in Group 2. We go around in a Rotation after we do the warm up thing and the lesson with everybody. Ms. Wachter teaches us the math lesson and sets the timer and we do the activity, as she calls it, for a while and when the timer goes off we do the next thing. At the end if there's time we do flash cards or Math Around the Room or some other math game. It sounds kind of complicated but it isn't. If you're with Ms. Wachter in her group you do the graph. If you do Centers you do review work with your group. If you do independent work you do it on your own. That's when things go the right way, but this was not one of those days.

After we got done with the lesson we get to go to Centers for the rotation, Centers are usually some cool game but sometimes it's a dumb worksheet. Some kids like the worksheets. Those kids are pitiful. I want a game every time.

So we did Centers for 15 minutes like usual, rolling two dice and adding them or multiplying them. After that we switched to the next thing, except it took me a while to put the stuff away from the Centers. I don't know what it is about dice, they just kind of roll everywhere and hide. I was about the only one putting stuff back too.

So I was a little late getting to the Independent Work and when I looked at the sheet I didn't understand it. It was a way to make a line graph but I didn't know what to label the X and Y axis. The rule is you ask people in your group before the teacher, "Ask three before me." That's the rule, and I did ask people, but nobody wanted to help me. The truth is most of them didn't get it either but they were pretending to do it and really talking to each other about stuff and passing notes. The people in my group who understood wanted to get it done so they could do something more fun and they just ignored me. This is not tattling because I am not saying names.

Ms. Wachter was working with the other group and the 3s went to Centers. Since I couldn't get anybody in my group to help me I went to ask Bayra because she knows this stuff cold. Bayra is sometimes in my group but today she was in the 3s. When I went over to ask her Kateri saw me doing that and she was in the 1s who were working with Ms. Wachter and she tattled on me. So then Ms. Wachter told me to go back to my group and then I explained that I didn't understand the work so I was going to ask Bayra.

Ms. Wachter said, "Bayra needs to work with her group, the 3s. Did you ask three people in your group?"

I told her yes but nobody would help me.

So then she says to my group, "Oh, can't somebody help Darryn?"

So of course Ernie says yes he'll help me which is not good, not only do I have to go back to my group that hasn't got a clue, I have to work with a boy. He did explain it some but I was still mad. So I didn't do my best work and I just knew I would get a note later on it from Ms. Wachter that told me to be neater but really I just wanted to be finished.

I didn't even finish it, after all that, but I put it in the finished work bin anyway. If you don't finish it she sends it home for homework and I did not want it for homework.

Then when we rotated it was our turn to work with Ms. Wachter and I was glad about that because I figured I could ask about line graphs even though we were going to work on circle graphs since I could see that she had some.

But then I remembered I hadn't signed up for lunch! I just forgot, when I came in. If you don't make a check mark and pick what you want you have to take whatever is left when you go to the cafeteria. I hate that, not having a choice. Ms. Wachter let me go to sign up but I could tell she was disappointed that I forgot. I didn't mean to forget. But it was still embarrassing and when I got to the cafeteria the lady had to go find the sign-up sheet for my class and she was grouchy about it. I was felling pretty grouchy myself so that did not help. By the time I got back to class from the cafeteria math was pretty much over. I got to work with Ms. Wachter for like five minutes and then it was time to switch. I felt like I didn't get much done in math class. That was a true feeling, I didn't, and then we got the homework packet and the end of class and it was lots of pages. I hardly ever have time for homework and now there was tons.

I don't have anywhere calm to do my homework. Also I don't want to do it usually, but sometimes I do if it's projects (which are fun) but either way there's no room at home. We have to have room for people, that's why.

Next we went to specials, usually my favorite special of all, music. But not today! Which is too bad since I love music with Mrs. H. But our teacher is a substitute, this old guy who is mean and wants us to be quiet I mean totally quiet like we were dead or something, while he tells us which notes are which. Then he shows us how to put our fingers on the recorder to make the notes and we practice that but we still can't play the notes until he is sure that everyone is doing it right. Then we play the notes. Except if you took your recorder home to practice and forgot to bring it back you just play on a broken recorder which just makes a whoosh sound but not the notes. That is to punish you for forgetting your instrument which Mr. Binsbee says you should never forget it. Personally I think this guy hates kids. I don't know why he's a teacher. They say he is going to sub until Mrs. H comes back from her foot surgery . . . I hope it's not too much longer, and only until she gets back.

They say he used to be a good teacher but then his wife died and he got sad and then mean. That's what the big kids told us. Some days he is not mean but mostly he is and I hate doing that really dumb "Row Row Your Boat" song. When am I ever going to row a boat anyhow? How about a Shop Shop song?

I have had good substitute teachers, like in kindergarten when I had Miss Mary for two months. There are good substitutes. But this guy is not one of them.

He told me twice to be quiet today. I only wanted to know if Maria got the new Style Up CD. When I talked again, I was only whispering, he said I lost time off recess. He said in a really mean way, he kind of hissed it at me. It made me feel bad. It was only five minutes off but it's still not fair. I was actually talking about music, just not recorder music. He wrote a note to Ms. Wachter to tell her.

Anyway that was music and it stunk. If it was a song it would look like this:

ssh sssh ssh snore

Next we went to lunch and even though I signed up they didn't have enough hot dogs so I got chicken nuggets which I did not want. By the time I ate my dessert and the corn, and drank the two milks, I was in a really bad mood. It was like the food stuck in my stomach. Then when we went outside I had to stand on the side with the rest of the kids in trouble and watch everyone else have fun. When I went to play I tripped on somebody playing tag and hurt my knee. When I went to wash it off there were no paper towels. When I went to tell Mr. B there were no towels the other guy who works in the building who I don't know his name yelled at me that I was not supposed to be back near Mr. B's office. When I explained he just made shooing motions with his hands like I was a dog or something.

When I went back outside I got in an argument with Rachel and we both ended up in time out again on the side. Watching everybody else run around. And then it was time to go in.

I couldn't find my folder for Reading. Missed the adjective hunt. It just kept being like that.

Sade laughed at me when I didn't know the answer to the question Ms. Wachter asked about the map. I don't even remember what she asked me. I just remember getting all upset that I didn't know.

Pencil broke. Later, entire pencil box spilled.

Couldn't find Washington D.C. on the big map, that was the question she asked, now I remember. Now that was bad. I live right next to the capital of the United States and I couldn't find it on the big map.

Science was okay. The teacher is good. Mr. Pete Weissman is the teacher, he lets us call him Mr. Pete. I managed not to spill, break or lose anything. I already knew the parts of a flower so I can't say I learned anything but at least I avoided looking stupid.

I didn't look stupid in Science. In one class. The only one.

I was glad when the dismissal bell went off and they called my bus early. The bus was extra noisy and I imagined tying Mr. Binsbee to a seat and making him sit though how loud we can get when the day is over and the teacher can't say "Sssh" any more.

When I got home I went and got a book and ignored everyone. I didn't even ask for a snack. After about I don't know how long, I felt better, and then I could go and eat dinner with everyone. We didn't talk much and that was fine with me. It was a day when things did not go well and I was just glad it was over.

Until I found out we were out of toothpaste.

Auntie made me use baking soda to brush with. I should never have told her.

And that's the end of the story when the day does not go well.

I gave my story about the bad day to Miss Wachter. Then I felt like it was time to die while she read it. Parts of it were not very nice, after all. But she turned around and had me read it to the class. Even though it was so long. I showed them my picture of Mr. Binsbee. Some kids laughed. I finished reading it. Then they applauded!

Last night we had no homework. About the only good thing about Test Week.

Homework is a weird thing. When I can do it I just grab it and do it and no problem. But when I grab it and look at it and I don't know how to do it and I don't know what it means, I hate it. The thing is I don't know until I look at it and I don't look at it until later. I need to come home, turn on the T.V. or read a book I don't have to read and just forget about school. There are always people everywhere in my house and I have to shut them out. When I can't do it I get really tense and I just want to argue with whoever is in front of me. School is hard work. I hate to walk in the door and first thing I have to wash the dishes or go find stuff for a project. Also sometimes it feels like I should do the homework right away to make sure it gets done. I hate that the most.

I find all kinds of things to do if I don't want to do the homework. It is just amazing how many other things I can find to do.

I liked October. The air was better somehow. Also it's the month my dad was born so of course it's the best month. The principal, Mrs. Hayes-Roberson, visited our class in October, before all the stuff happened. All she did was sit in the back of the room and write stuff down. I still don't know what she was writing. She said to ignore her so I tried but it was not easy. I could tell that Ms. Wachter knew she was there. Ms. Wachter's voice sounded funny and she started reading the book faster. I think she was nervous. It's not much fun when she reads faster.

She asked us questions about the story and some people called out like they always do and I had my hand up like usual and she didn't call on me, which happens sometimes. Some of the people she called on didn't even know the answer! They just wanted to be noticed, I think. If you don't know about the story's setting then don't raise your hand. Dionne even started talking about how her dad got a new job at Galludet University, which was not about the story at all. Meanwhile Mrs. Hayes-Roberson kept writing stuff down.

Later on the principal stood up and pointed to our schedule on the board. Ms. Wachter looked at it and said, "I'm a little behind."

And I busted out laughing because I looked and she does have a little behind. It's not a bad behind but it's little, like she is, and then when they both asked me why I was laughing I couldn't say it. I mean how can I tell the principal that my teacher has a little behind. It's not very respectful. But it's also very funny. Behinds are funny in general. When a behind talks it is a fart and that's funny too.

This was a time I couldn't tell about what was funny. So I was stuck. Anyway I finally stopped laughing and then I was so embarrassed. Ms. Wachter looked at me and I know she was thinking of telling me what I did wrong, but then, she smiled. She looked at the principal and she said, "Darryn can see the humor at times when others can't," and Mrs. Hayes-Roberson smiled and suddenly it was okay and I wasn't in trouble any more. So I wrote on a piece of paper what I had been thinking and then I put at the end, "No disrespect," since it would be easy to think that making fun of someone's behind is disrespectful. Except I wasn't. Seriously, I can't help it if my mind makes up funny things at times.

They both read my note. They both laughed. They shook their heads. It was like they practiced it. Ms. Wachter wasn't real nervous any more either and then she started talking to Mrs. Hayes-Roberson about what we were going to learn next while we all went off to centers and everything was okay now. When we read in small groups that day we totally forgot the principal was there, we just wanted to talk about the book.

You never know when something you can't help will get you in trouble. That reminds me of what happened to Jeannie in second grade. Jeannie only wanted to draw.

194

She got in trouble for it sometimes. It was long time before a teacher realized she did this was because she was good at drawing, and she wasn't good at reading or writing. They started letting her draw things for spelling and math and she got much better. It was such a change because they stopped looking at what she was doing and saying she was goofing off all the time.

Some teachers can understand how you think about things better than others. Sometimes teachers can even tell when you think they're being boring but they generally don't like it. Or they can tell that there's something funny even if they don't know what it is and they don't get mad. That's the kind of teacher Ms. Wachter is. Now the principal can see right away that I can see funny things when other people wouldn't. Ms. Wachter can see it too. It didn't take them very long.

That's why I'm glad she's my teacher.

Mrs. Hayes-Roberson could tell that Miss Wachter is a good teacher even if she spends more time on a lesson than it says on the schedule. I think that's what happened.

I never thought before that teachers have to get good grades too. That's kind of weird. Good, but really weird.

One thing I don't like about weather here is how it gets so much colder. It got cold in Cameroon too, but not like it does here.

I've got my hair in braids now, and that makes my head so cold if I don't wear a hat. And I don't like to wear a hat because then my head gets too hot. I don't want to turn into a spoiled American though, always complaining about the temperature. In summer they say places are freezing cold with the air conditioning and in winter they say they are too hot with the indoor heating. It's like there are not any temperatures in this country where people can just be in the temperature and do things.

In Cameroon it is usually just 75 degrees or so but sometimes it is humid.

Also in Cameroon you have to pay to go to school and wear a uniform but here it is free and you can wear anything you want.

When we left in the spring from Cameroon there was an all day party and it was hot. People fanned themselves but there was no air conditioner to make it freezing. Everyone was eating and talking all the time and my dad was smiling at everyone all the time. I was not smiling so much. Moving all the way to America scared me and Mom was not going with us. My grandmother was so mad about that. She kept hissing at my mother that she should have waited until after she got my dad to the church. My mom said, he never asked me, but she was crying when she said it. I don't know for sure what he was supposed to ask her but I think it is the marriage thing again.

The party was still fun, there was food everywhere and we could have meat that had been cooked on the charcoal. They do that in this country all the time, they call it a cookout. For my family in Cameroon it was special because we were leaving and it was our bon voyage party. Bon voyage means have a good journey and good luck and let's celebrate all at once.

I just realized bon voyage is French. Some words in French mean more than they do in English. French is different that way.

Today at the end of the day I was going right past the teacher lounge to get to the bus. As soon as they call my bus I usually go, because I really don't want to miss the bus. I got left behind a couple of times last year and the year before and that was bad. Dad had to leave work and come get me and once he sent my auntie and every time he was really mad. I tried to explain about having to go back for my homework and the other time when I had to go to the bathroom and the last time when I was on the computer and didn't hear it, but he didn't care. He was just mad.

But then I did stop for a few minutes to zip up my backpack. I was thinking, I better get going so I'm not late since I was supposed to be somewhere else. Then I heard a teacher say "No child left behind" and I thought they were talking about me! But that wasn't it. She was complaining about this law called No Child Left Behind. Imagine naming a law that, like you have to make it a law for grownups to remember to take kids with them. But it's not really about grownups going places with kids, it's about the school tests. This law, the teacher said, means no one can get a grade less than a B, or be less than "proficient" on the big test they are going to make us take this year.

There's a law that says we all pass. Okay.

Some of the teachers seem pretty mad about it.

It doesn't say left behind what. I guess it just means behind in general. General Behind, who won the war!

We had to learn the positional words back when I started in school. Above, below, in front, behind. If there is no one behind who is in front?

Unless you have a mirror you can't even see your own behind. And a problem with white people is they really have no behinds. You can't see their behinds. Especially the men have no behinds at all to speak of. There is just flat. Now with black people you can see the behind. I'm not saying whether it's better or worse but you can see they have a behind. And they have all kinds of behind. They have the high tight behind. They have the big broad behind. They have the behind that my uncle calls two cats fighting in a sack.

So then when they first talked about the law called no child left behind I figured the white teachers are talking about no behind because sometimes they do not really have one. Then I saw that there were other teachers in there who were brown so maybe not.

Besides I have not seen all the behinds that there are. That's probably a good thing.

Our first day back at school after quarantine was so strange. To me it seemed like it should all look different but it was the same (only maybe cleaner). After all that happened, I expected it to look different, maybe like in some of those disaster movies. But it was pretty much the same, same tall windows, same big metal doors that are hard to open. For a little while I felt like I should be on tiptoe or something. Then we went down the hall and into the portable classroom and that was even weirder because our room wasn't the same while the hallway was.

My classroom looked so odd, so blank somehow. They came and took down all the posters and all the stories we had up in the publishing center and the calendar wasn't there and the rugs were gone! It didn't look much like our homeroom at all.

Ms. Wachter was upset. Now that we all know each other she doesn't try to hide the way she feels so much. Or maybe I just know how she shows it now. She was upset that it looked so bare. Plus she was mad that they took our writing away, boy did that make her mad. It turns out they were worried about the germ but the germ doesn't stick to paper. Plus she didn't open any mail in the classroom and we didn't have a class pet anyhow. But they didn't know that for sure so they took everything out and vacuumed the whole classrooms with these giant vacuums. I wish I could have seen that. Gigantic vacuums sucking it all up, maybe it would have sucked us kids into it if they had it going full blast.

But they did not take the desks and chairs away and they didn't open her desk drawers. So in her desk drawers were all our first drafts so when she found that out, she felt better. And then Davide reminded her that we wrote some of the stories on the computers so we could just print them out again and that really cheered her up. She also said she wasn't going to tell them they forgot to do her desk and we all agreed not to tell anyone either.

The school library is the same and the computer lab and the cafeteria of course. And some of our classroom still looks the same. The walls are the same. They did clear out the file cabinets. Of course all our notebooks were gone and our other stuff like folders and pencils. The math books were gone but I didn't mind because they were boring anyway. They are going to get us new ones but hopefully not anytime soon. So we get to do math with the counters and the dice and the flashcards and the games we make up so yay for that.

There are worse things than having all the math text-books disappear. And the computers are brand new, the keyboards that is, so that's nice. There's a new thing, a big box on the wall with a fire extinguisher and a gas mask and gloves in it. Ms. Wachter laughed when she saw it and murmured "Just one? One gas mask? How can they think that I —" and then she looked at us and shut up. But I know what she was thinking. I think.

All the indoor recess stuff was gone. That was bad. We decided to send home a note asking people to send in board games. They have to be brand new though.

We got to put the desks where we wanted them, not the old way. It looks kind of the same, but the desks are facing different ways and we only have two (new) note-books and three folders to keep track of, so that's better. We don't need to have our names on our desks perma-nently, because we might change around again. So we wrote our names on just plain pieces of tape with wipe-off markers. In cursive, since everybody got pretty good at cursive with all those weeks of practice. That chalk we used at the synagogue was easier to write with somehow. My writing doesn't look as good, but it's gotten better. All I have do is keep practicing.

It was a busy first day.

I'm still so glad that my family is okay. I can stand living so close to them better now. Living at the synagogue was pretty crowded too, so it makes it seem not so bad to go back to the apartment.

I don't have to roll up a mat and a sleeping bag every day, for one thing.

I think we got a better deal than some of the other kids. The synagogue had more rooms and more fun and more books. They got some books later but to start with all they had at St. Patrick's Church were those hymn books and the Bibles which only had the New Testament and I already heard those stories a million times. The Old Testament was better, especially the battles and the poems that they called something else. The poems were called Psalms except you don't say the P and you don't say the L much either. Why not just call it Sams. English is such an aggravating language. Good thing I like it anyway.

I wonder if this year will really count as Fourth Grade or if we will have a do-over. Davide said we had too much fun, it couldn't count as real school. We laughed when he said it. Maria said what about the no homework, we might have to have double homework now. Rachel said she wasn't going to do the regular homework let alone double. I just sat there and wondered. Nobody really knows anyway. We're just back at our school after the quarantine.

We learned all the stuff we needed to know. Plus more. I feel like my head is really full. We have to get used to the old schedule again, including the specials and recess OUTSIDE.

I bet we have to prove that we learned stuff somehow. That's usually what happens. That's what usually happens to me, anyway.

The main thing I think about? I wonder if hot lunch will be really hot today. It wasn't hot yesterday. It seems like the cafeteria isn't used to the new ovens. I guess they had to replace all that stuff, ovens and shelves maybe.

So much stuff got replaced because nobody knew if the poison was there or not and I overheard Mr. Binwald said that it would have cost more to test everything than it would to replace it. That's why they took all our stuff from the portables. Still, they vacuumed too. Somebody else said, some Fifth Grader I think, that they pretty much think that the virus has spread all over the place already in the past few months and if it didn't kill you yet, it won't. That doesn't sound likely to me. People get sick all the time from germs being around.

I bet the grownups didn't know what to do exactly so they did too much. It's amazing how stupid adults can be when they're scared. And yet there is Mr. Binwald explaining that if it cost too much they wouldn't do it.

We had a very cool lesson today about taxes because one of the kids said her dad said that taxes were going way up ever since TB2 happened. So we asked about what taxes were. Ms. Wachter explained that because of the fear of contagious germs they had to have so much classroom stuff taken away and replaced or not replaced yet but it still cost money. And tax money is what will pay for all of it. Everyone who has a job and even people who don't have a job pay taxes. So tax money went down when people weren't working for a while because of TB2 and places that housed the kids (us) had to be paid for

202

providing shelter and of course also people died. Dead people do not pay taxes. Ms. Wachter was explaining this part and Davide said just it like that, "Dead people do not pay taxes." Then Ms. Wachter laughed and laughed and then she started crying.

Rachel went and got her a tissue. We didn't get upset when she got upset. I mean we didn't feel like she was upsetting us. We knew why she was crying and a couple of kids cried a little too, but it was a quiet okay cry. There are plenty of dead people who don't pay taxes anyhow.

My sister Angelique has lots of company then. She would have lots of friends anywhere she went, everybody loved her. That's the truth.

One thing I am convinced of is that there is a heaven because there had to be a good place for her to go.

I don't want to write about Angelique right now! I want to write about school!

So we are back and some things are different and some are the same. Personally I am not too worried about when all this stuff gets replaced. I have my writing journal, plenty of pencils, other people got some things replaced, there are books to read and things to count. We'll be fine.

I wish we could have more music like we did when we were all stuck in the synagogue. I heard that some of the second graders got to dance to different Middle East music, whatever that is, since they were in that mosque that was in that tall building's first floor. I never got to even hear the rest of the music they got to hear. That's not fair. Don't worry about replacing the old stuff. Just make sure we get to have all the new stuff everybody else did while we were in the quarantine. Now that would be too totally cool.

They did something to my writing journal and now it smells funny. They put it in a machine that made germ-killing fog and now I can keep it. I would have had to fight them if they hadn't found a way for me to keep it.

Tomorrow we get to go on a Science Walk. Ms. Wachter said that one thing that will be different from now on is that we will have class outside more and more. Whenever the weather is good enough. We all cheered when she said it. She even made it one of the new jobs, the Weather Watcher will tell us what kind of weather it is in the morning when we do the schedule and we will put in when we do it, and if the weather gets bad later the Weather Watcher is the one who is supposed to re-member the next day that we will get more time outside. I want that job myself.

It is just so strange to be back here in this building where it looks pretty much the same and I have changed so much. It's like being in one of those time travel mov-ies. We do some of the same things but even that is so dif-ferent. Today we had an assembly and saw the new sub-stitute principal. Mrs. Drew is very tall and she has bright red hair. Her ears stick out. She wears glasses sometimes and sometimes they are on a necklace she wears instead. She looked very serious like teachers do when they are telling you something they think is very important. She said she was a Fourth Grade teacher for years somewhere else and now she is a principal. Well I knew that. The whole assembly was about meet the new principal! I can't say I felt like I met her. I saw her and I heard her. She said part of her speech in Spanish and that was kind of cool. She has a voice that is okay but loud. She told us Mrs. Hayes-Roberson would be back when she got better and we all just looked at each other. People do not always get better from TB2. We know this for sure but she told us that Mrs. Hayes-Roberson would get better anyway.

She told us we were great kids and she wants us to keep getting smarter every day, whatever that means. She said she wants to inspire us to be the best we can be. She talked and talked. She has a kind of round voice that can make you sleepy after a while.

I don't know if I even believe what the principal says sometimes. It's kind of a weird sound in her voice, it reminds me of people on TV that want you to buy something. It might even be a good thing to get but the way they say it, you don't want to buy it. That's the way Mrs. Drew is sometimes. I bet she doesn't even know it.

Anyway, then she said she had a writing assignment for the whole school. We are supposed to write about, one good thing that we got out of the quarantine. The little kids write a sentence. Next first grade and second writes two sentences. Third Grade has to do a BCR, a Brief Constructed Response which means at least three sentences. We have to write at least one paragraph of five sentences, Fifth Grade has to do two paragraphs. On looseleaf paper. Must have a title for all this, and a topic sentence, supporting details, everything spelled write, ha.

The little kids have to draw stuff to go with it and the teachers are supposed to put the best ones up on the bulletin boards. Everyone has to do it, she said it is mandatory. The teachers are supposed to collect all of the paragraphs and send them to the office by Friday. Mrs. Drew is going to give prizes for the best ones.

The teachers looked surprised. We sure were. We left the assembly and went back to class and we talked about it. Ms. Wachter said it was a good topic, actually, she just wasn't sure we could get it done so quickly. And just like that, we came up with a solution: we will write ours together. The people who like to write will help the ones who don't, but no one will get left out. Ms. Wachter smiled when Davide said we could all write the same one and just send it in as our class story. Osumare said Mrs. Drew would notice we only had one. Besides, people were already thinking of different things. So we didn't use that solution but we had more than one.

I never heard of a principal telling everyone in the whole school they had to write something, not even in Cameroon where the schools are very serious.

It's interesting to me that we have kids who can't write very well. I thought anybody who liked to read all the time like me would be good with words, but it's not like that. You can read thousands of words in books and like them but that doesn't mean you can put them together in a new way when you write your own stories. It's surprising to me but it's so.

We started in doing it in class.

It really wasn't going to be possible to not do it. Mandatory means you have to. It would be possible to do it really badly, and I did think about that. But that's not my way when I write. I do the best I can. Sometimes it doesn't turn out too good but that's not what I mean to do when I start!

206

I helped some people after I started my own. Then I got to read the rough draft to the class. No one wrote anything like mine. Ms. Wachter says that is a good thing, to have a "unique point of view." I wonder. So I put the first draft in my journal.

The good thing about the quarantine
By Darryn

One good thing I can think of about the quarantine is how glad I was when I got a cold. I have never been glad for a cold before. If I got sick with a cold I got tired or sad or even mad but I was never glad before. In the quarantine I was glad because the cough I had was just a cold kind of cough. In the quarantine I learned about coughs. There's a little cough when sometimes you want to talk and your throat is dry. There is a cough that happens when your friend has asthma or bronchitis and they cough when the air is dry or full of pollen. There is the cough you do when you are a little embarrassed.

There is a cough you cough when you are some sick but not real sick and you don't stay home from school but it's yucky and it's hard to sleep. There is the cough that I had, when you have a bad cold and you have to stay in bed or in the cot in this case. That is the my kind of cough.

Then there is the TB2 cough and it does not sound like any other kind of cough and I know what it sounds like now. The very good thing is that I know what it sounds like and I do not know what it feels like.

People in my class did not say anything much after I read it. Maybe they were remembering what it was like, maybe they were trying not to remember and my words were getting in the way. I don't know. They just looked at me very serious. That was better than any prize.

I don't care if Mrs. Drew even likes it. I told the truth of it for me.

Daddy told me today that he was proud of me. He read my story about the good thing about the quarantine. He looked at me from over the top of his glasses for a minute. Then he gave me a hug. We do not hug much. Then he told me he was proud of me and he whispered it. He never whispers either. So I know it was important. Then he told me he was so scared that I would get the TB2.

That made me cry a little bit. I told him about how much I thought about him and how back then I was scared about him getting it too. He gave me a little pat. He took my story and put it up on the wall in the living room. I told him I wanted to write it nice on the computer but he said no.

And then he went to work. And I looked at my story. I read it to Jamarr. He says he wants to write something so good like that.

I just stood back and looked at my words.

I love my dad and I was proud of me too.

Today I lost my temper. Like I never have since I don't know when.

It was raining so we had indoor recess. We haven't had to have indoor recess in a while.

Ms. Wachter has these big pieces of cardboard which we can use to make play houses or forts or just boxes or whatever. People grabbed them to use and I wasn't pay-ing too much attention because I wanted to play Candyland with other people. We got into the game. Then I heard like a yell and I looked over and the cardboard pieces were collapsing on top of whoever it was, and I went over to help take the pieces off and. And.

There was Davide, and he was tied up with the jump rope. Tied really tight. And he looked so scared. So I tore all the cardboard off and I got the rope off him and it was like I was ten feet tall when I said, who did this, and nobody said anything, they just looked at me with their mouths hanging open. Even Ms. Garcia was just sitting there staring at me. She was there to watch us but she didn't see this stuff, did she? Finally Ahmed said he and John did it, but Davide told them to tie him up, and I said it didn't matter, it was stupid and WRONG to tie somebody up like that. They said they were playing prisoner and he was in jail and all of a sudden I got so sad and asked them why they would want to play jail, of all things.

I guess they have never really seen what a jail is like but I have, on the news about the war in Eritrea and there were men tied up and looking scared while they were waiting to be put in the jail. Also I remembered one time when my cousins tied me up and left me in the closet and teased they would never let me out. I remember exactly what the clothes smelled like and how my throat hurt from screaming. I remember that. And what about slavery that we learned about, tying people up and saying they were slavery prisoners for their whole lives until Harriet Tubman came to let them out and after that Abraham Lincoln too. Chains and ropes on black skin, it's not right. Except Davide is white.

Well, it doesn't matter it's always wrong to make people prisoners.

I told them don't ever play that game again and so Ms. Garcia finally said it too.

John said you're not the boss of me and I looked at him and said, and you're not the owner of Davide and Davide said, yeah, who do you think you are, pharaoh? And John looked confused and we reminded him about the story of the Jews in Egypt that we heard in quarantine. So he asked us a question or something about it and then it was back to regular, with John and Ahmed just kids who decided to play a nasty game that I told them to stop and we'll see if they do it again but I bet they never try it on Davide again or anywhere where I can see them doing it. Or Ms. Garcia either.

I doubt that anyone ever tied her up. It gives you an opinion about it that can be on the strong side.

Davide told us today that we are not to call him that any more, his name is Dave. He offered to fight anyone who didn't want to call him the new name. Even Ahmed did not want to fight him, the way he looked. So now we will call him Dave. Okay.

Today's challenge in writing class: write 100 words on any subject. Okay, here is what I'm thinking about and want to write about so start counting words from here:

The Day I Cheated
by Darryn Yochangko Thomas
I don't usually cheat. I haven't thought about it for a long time but today I was thinking about it again. This time I did. It happened in second grade. We had

a test. Another test. It was the third test of the year and I was tired of the tests and I didn't know most of the answers this time. I usually do. School is not too hard for me. This time it was. So I looked over to see what somebody else was doing and I could tell they didn't know the answer either. I mean their answer didn't make any sense. So I was kind of in a panic and I decided to get sick. It is not so easy to do that when there is a test. Teachers know it's maybe because of the test. So I lied. That was how I cheated. It's not the only part of how I cheated but that was the first part. I counted, I have over 100 words already, but I'll keep going and tell the story.

I'm not cheating about the word count.

So I told the teacher I had to go to the bathroom, which was almost true, and she looked at me like teachers do when they don't know if you're telling the truth. But she nodded her head for me to go. My second grade teacher was very smart about those things. When I looked at her and said the lie, then I was sick to my stomach and I thought, let's go to the nurse. The nurse is better than this test. But I realized that saying I was sick might not work. So I got up to get the bathroom pass and when I stood up I really was sick. I felt dizzy and awful and I ran over to the trash can and I actually threw up. But what I was really sick about was the test. Because I didn't study enough for it and I didn't understand the question and I couldn't even copy off anybody.

They ended up sending me to the nurse anyway and they called my dad and he came to get me and he was kind of mad because he could have made money driving the cab with customers instead of just taking me home. He was a little worried but he knew I wasn't that sick. Dads are like teachers, they can tell. I never did tell him I somehow made myself sick. It's not a very nice story but it is a true one. You can lie yourself sick. If you cheat enough you can make yourself really truly sick. It can even cost money. So

don't do it. It isn't worth it. Especially if your stomach
is more honest than you are!

The challenge was to write a hundred words and I
did more than that. Do I get extra credit for doing more
and doing math counting on it besides? I wish when I
wrote it sounded exactly like how I think it or say it.
Sometimes when I write it is never exactly the same. Not
the exact way I want it to be. Writing is the only thing I
know that gets close to what I go through when it is me
having my life. If it was any closer it would be my life,
but it isn't wrong, when I write it. It isn't like cheating. It's
kind of like using crayons instead of pastels, how deep
the colors are, just different enough that it's interesting.
You can even write it again to make some colors more
intense. I don't do that very much.

I think it must have been like that for Langston
Hughes, that writer Ms. Wachter likes so much. He made
some words more intense. Maybe that's how poetry
always is for poets. I don't know for sure because I never
tried to write any but poetry is a good thing. It's a whole
lot of good bright colors at once. Some of them are strobe
lights.

Mrs. Wachter gave me back my challenge essay with a
high score on it. She told me I did a good job but I should
take it home, not keep it in my writing portfolio. She said
it is like an Act of Confession and that is really just private. Which is true, and there are times when I show my
writing portfolio work to others and thus time I wouldn't
want anyone asking, "What's that, can I see it?"

Today sucked. The worst thing yet. We still have to take the big test, the SNM thing. The teachers and the parents are really upset. They were saying that with the quarantine we shouldn't have to do it. Ms. Wachter is muttering that we shouldn't have to take it anyway, regardless of the quarantine. Nobody taught us the test the way they are supposed to and I think they are worried. Personally I feel like I learned plenty this year. I don't know how I'd fit it into a Brief Constructed Response, though. Guess I have to narrow the topic. Give me a BCR about airborne germs and you better believe I'll get a 3. No problem. Hey, ask me something about the Shalom synagogue architecture. What the Torah is and why they keep it locked up most of the time. How much moms and dads really matter. How to tell stories and make them better and longer. How to identify leaves. What to do when there's no snack except Tootsie Rolls. What is the Holocaust. Why too many cars are a bad idea. How to take a spelling test with chalk. How to make a little kid stop crying and eat something even though they miss mom so bad. What does kosher mean. How to make a shower. What are good dance songs. Will any of that be on the test?

We were all pretty upset about the test. I remember last year, it wasn't such a big deal. We went to one assembly where everybody did signs and cheers and wrote posters telling all about how everyone should do their best on this test. Then after that the month before the test some of the big kids got kind of cranky, well not kind of, they got real cranky! They picked fights with each other and even with kids in other classes. Some of them made a mess of the bathrooms and others made a mess of the cafeteria. Some of that was happening before, but after that it got much worse. It was better around that time to just avoid the big kids.

There was this time back in quarantine when we were cleaning up and this teacher came by and looked at what we did and said, "This isn't all clean. It's all wrong." So we went around cleaning up more and the same teacher came by and told us it still looked like it wasn't good enough and we tried to get it right one more time. But I don't think we ever got it done the way that teacher wanted it done, perfect somehow. We gave up and the teacher looked frustrated but you know what? I don't think anything would have been good enough.

I just have this creepy feeling that this test is going to be like that. Got to be perfect and we'll never get it perfect.

Mrs. Drew made this long announcement this morning about us doing a good job on the big test. She said that part about wanting to inspire us again. I thought shorter announcements would inspire me the most. It's so strange that we're back to having a box on the wall talk to us every morning.

We had a very strange lesson after that. It was something called the Balldead system and this Balldead is how we're supposed to run our class meetings. First thing we have to do is write this agenda thing. That is a schedule thing that says what we're going to have the meeting about. We can't have the meeting until we make an agenda and agree on it, which takes forever, seems to me. Next, when we do the meeting we have to make a chart that organizes everything we say. That part is not too bad, it's just it takes even more time, making the chart and writing all the stuff down fast enough.

Next part is making goals and solving problems. That's the simple way to tell it but it sure isn't simple the way we have to do it. If we didn't have to do it all together at the meeting it wouldn't have been so complicated. We solved how to write that good thing about the quarantine thing together. We already know how to do that stuff. I could have done the whole thing for my part in about a half an hour, I bet.

All this has to do with school being a business and using business tools. I didn't know it was a business. I thought you went there to find out what you didn't know and to practice the stuff you did. But I was wrong and it is actually work. Certainly felt like it today. I was exhausted by the end. We didn't have nearly the fun we usually do.

Some of this stuff might be a good thing but it was intense. Also it was a change and I've had about enough of that lately.

To make our goals, which today was about doing book reports, we have to write down first all our data (and data just means information. I looked it up. I don't know why we can't just call it information, anyway). So we write down how many book reports we have finished in our journals. We didn't have that many books anyway, when we got there, not for all of us kids. It was a shame we couldn't count the Old Testament stories, but Ms. Wachter said we just talked about them, we didn't do written reports. She muttered something about separation of church and state, but she didn't explain what it meant. I'll look it up.

So we worked it out that everyone just put on a piece of paper all the titles plus the authors of the books we had all read when we were in exile. Everybody put Betsy and Tacy and Tib, for instance, and Hatchet. Those are the ones she read to us. We did Harriet Tubman and Charlotte's Web in my group and I don't remember what other titles people said, but we got to put in the fairy tales that we did too. Some people put the other books they read on their own Kindles, stuff like Emmy and the Incredible Shrinking Rat or Harry Potter or Ramona or Diary of a Wimpy Kid. Wish I had my own Kindle.

Ms. Wachter said it didn't count if you hadn't done a written report, since some kids read stuff and talked about it but never wrote down the summary or anything. So she wasn't sure we could count Noah and the Ark, or the other Bible stories we acted out. Why not? Those were great stories!

It was a very lively discussion about what counted and what didn't. We have to have RESULTS. That's because Balldead says we have to have DATA DRIVEN RESULTS and set FUTURE GOALS based on DATA. Whether you actually liked a book and thought other kids might like it was not so important.

Ms. Wachter said that this kind of way of doing things is called a CORPORATE or BUSINESS MODEL. She also does not like it. She didn't say it but I can tell. I don't like it much either but we have to do it this way. It's that mandatory thing again. I don't even have to look that up.

Lots of kids that read graphic novels said they were going to do reports for the ones they read. I bet most teachers will not let you do a book report about a graphic novel.

It's not the same anymore, even at the grocery store. Dad and I went to get food and when we were in line the cashier said she had not seen me around in a while. Dad said, "She's been in quarantine." The cashier looked at me and she was scared. She didn't want to take Dad's money and pushed a button and a manager came! The manager woman just shook her head when the lady whispered to her, picked up Dad's cash and gave him his change. I put all the food in the bags we brought myself and then I wanted to lean over and cough at the cashier. But I didn't. But I wanted to!

I will talk to my friends tomorrow and see if anything like this is happening to them.

What a super strange Tuesday this was. Instead of our usual routine, Ms. Wachter had to give everyone this test on her tiny little computer. We are not allowed to use that little one, which is about the size of an iPod but it isn't one. It is called a Palm and she told me that is because you hold it in the palm of your hand. I'm glad she told me that because I was thinking it had something to do with the tree, the palm, like in Chicka Chicka Boom Boom. She gave me a card to read the sight words, which was no big deal because I know them. They are called sight words because you can't sound them out, you have to know them when you see them, on sight. I think sight is a sight word, actually, because you can't sound it out, the g and h don't say anything. Then we had to repeat the sentences she said. After that we had to read a story out loud to her and then part to ourselves. The story wasn't bad but it wasn't that good either. In the middle of it Rolando came over to ask her something and she was real upset, she told him he couldn't talk to her when she was testing me. Well. I didn't mind. She sure did though.

It didn't take me long to do it. There were a couple of words that I don't think I said them right because her face changed. I got the questions mostly right about what happened in the story, I think. But she said I did a good job.

I noticed she said the exact same thing to everybody. She said things like I am going to read a sentence to you and you say it back to me. She also told everyone they did a good job. I think she was reading it on the Palm computer. It was weird hearing her read the same thing to everyone. It was almost like I didn't believe her and I never felt like that before about her.

Well I happened to be reading on the other side of the bookcase and I could hear her saying the same things. Plus I went first. Ms. Wachter did not sound like herself. She was so tense about the tests. I could tell from the way her voice was different. I almost wanted to tell Maria the answers when it was her turn but I knew that would make Ms. Wachter mad. So I just sat there and listened to the same thing over and over. It was kind of boring. I don't know how Ms. Wachter can stand it. I can barely stand it and I'm just eavesdropping.

We weren't being very quiet, the class wasn't. I was quiet because I wanted to hear what she was saying. So I could tell she was having a hard time hearing what Maria was saying. Maria never talks very loud. She could hear Davide, I mean Dave, just fine, but he wasn't doing very good with the story. He did fine with the sight words. I think he got tired of reading out loud because he messed up the end of the story and he didn't know some of the answers to the questions she asked at the end. She told him he did a good job just the same. She looked as tired as he did.

But the test where she had the little computer in her hand was not bad. It was just tiring but it wasn't unfair, just long. That's my opinion.

Next we had to do some test with papers with questions that were multiple choice: what is the right answer pick one. So that you do with a pencil, you fill in the circle. She showed us how to fill in the circle! Like we would not know how to do that part, sheesh! That's one part.

The next part of the test is writing the answer to a question. These are called BCRs, which means Brief Constructed Response but that's a dumb name. First off it takes lots of time to think of one so it is not that brief. Second, construct is what you do with blocks or clay in my opinion, or maybe building a house or a office building. Third it should say writing somewhere in there and it doesn't. So the whole name of it is useless.

Now we have to do those stupid BCRs all the time. We have test practice almost every day and the kids who don't like to write are now back to being treated like they're stupid. None of these kids are stupid. I know this for a fact. I may not like all of them but there are no stupid kids at my school. They don't say the word stupid, of course. They say the kids need extra help. Everyone knows what it means, though. It means stupid, just saying sideways.

Everybody's brains are different. I don't need every-one to read as much as me. That does not make them stupid. That makes me a bookworm, like Ms. Wachter says. That does not make me better than them. It makes me a happy bookworm.

The stories on the practice tests are pretty dull. One of the cool things about the quarantine was, we kept getting new books. It was something people outside could send us and feel like they were doing something. I ended up reading more because there wasn't much else to do a lot of times. The books helped me feel like I wasn't stuck inside that building, like I could go anywhere, see anything, even stuff that doesn't exist yet like the future. Then I made up my own stories and put them in my fiction journal and told them to the other kids. Then they would tell the stories they made and we really got into it. That's how we learned to write the good way, when people want to know what happens next. You can write any kind of story, with animals being like people or stuff that's real like two people arguing, or in outer space, and if you do it right people want to keep reading and find out what happens next. It got so I had to read my stories out loud so I could figure out what to do with them or if they were done or what, and now we can't do that at all. There isn't time. We have to practice the test stuff and write the way you have to for the BCR.

Thomas says BCR stands for Boring Crappy Regurgitation.

I had to look Regurgitation up. It means throw up!

When Thomas is right, he's right.

Of course then they had to get rid of the books since we couldn't store them all, but at least they found a way to keep us in plenty of books. I wonder what they did with the books after they got rid of them. Did they just throw them away or burn them since they could have TB2 on them even though the scientists said it couldn't live on paper?

They sent e-books too but I like to hold a book in my hand. I don't mind reading off the screen but somehow I don't imagine the whole story the same way. The book is just what I'm used to, I guess.

This testing stuff is so bad. It's just not right. I think it's like we're all the same size yogurt containers, coming off that assembly line in that movie I saw about milk. We are not the same! Making it a big federal law that we are will never work. Actually I never thought about if before but what's with putting people in a class according to age? It makes about as much sense as grouping people according to height for reading. It doesn't match the way we are. It doesn't help us to read stories the same. We're supposed to learn the same skills but mostly we can't, not the same way on the same day. So the teachers try to teach each one of us our own way, but then the rest of us have to wait a turn and do a worksheet.

Then teacher gets all frustrated and you can see it on her face, when she knows you don't get it and the way she's explaining it doesn't work but there's the whole group she's got to teach and it gets so frustrating!

SNM. Standard Normative Measurement. Stupid Nasty Monster.

Maria has been having bad dreams about the test. Rachel is so mad she says she doesn't want to talk about it and then she does, all through lunch. Ahmed's father got him a tutor so he can study after school and on the weekend and still he worries about whether he'll be able to do it. Dena says she is not one little bit worried but I noticed her fingernails are all bitten down and she had stopped doing that but not now.

We spend so much on what might be on the test. And we have to do everything in the packet when it's time for centers. It's getting so I never get to do stuff with some of the other kids in class and in my reading group we have to do most of it on our own. Miss Wachter meets with some groups every day, but not us. Still we have to do the center work and turn it in and it's sometimes interesting, but I hardly get to see my teacher.

I feel like I have to make an appointment to see her. Also it helps if I can't understand something, then she'll help me, but I have to wait until she's done with the other group first.

The SNM test is all there is any more. It's like all these unknown people are pushing and pushing me to do work for this test. They are on my behind so much it feels like I have no behind left.

Today we got a paper to take home that said there was a Field Trip to a museum and I got real excited, only then we found out it's a virtual field trip. I don't know what that is exactly but one thing about it is, we won't actually go anywhere.

You know what a Virtual Field Trip is? It's a movie about a museum. That's what it is. Like Maria said, no trip, no field, what the heck. When is a field trip not a field trip? When it's a virtual field trip.

Teachers come up with some really lame names for groups. Colors. Flowers. Animals. How about some wild new names, some intense names, something that is not the same old same old. Or at least have a description with the name that tells what that group is about. That tells the total truth about what the group is about. Not dumb like football team names.

They call our city team the Redskins. I looked and not one of those guys had a red skin. Plus that's an insult anyway, calling them Redskins. They ought to call them black skins and white skins and pale brown skins and faintly yellow skins. That's what they got on the team. It's a bad name , having a bad name is never going to work.

I got some good ideas for names. It's always been something I love to do, naming. Words matter. Let's do some new naming here. Group names that would really be tight and accurate for us, and we get to choose to be in, is what we need.

The Artists, we draw what we know

> *Group that wants to sing it or show it with their bodies*
>
> *or dance about it:*
>
> *The show offs.*

I guess we can't call them the show offs. Need something else. I know, the experts! That's what they think are, anyway. And their symbol is a star.

 **Experts**

The funny thing is that the show offs would love having the star as a symbol and they would never catch on that really they are kind of bragging on themselves. The first thing they would do is show off the star! fMaybe their symbol should be a mirror. No, I like that Michael Jackson song too much, *Man in the Mirror*, they can have the star instead. Not that they'd ever know that I'm doing this, but even pretend, they don't get the mirror, forget it.

There are kids that need to find a rhythm to things. They like to talk loud. I'd call this the Percussion group. They should have a drum set as a symbol:

Percussion Group

224

Then there is the opposite kind of person. We'll call these the Bookers. You have to be quiet and read if you're in the Bookers, except when it's time to talk about the stories.Their symbol is a book, of course. They want to be left alone and please do not disturb them when they are reading, they hate that.

 **Bookers**

Then . . . there are the Insiders, since that's where they like to be most of the time. It's okay.

Group that would rather think it and write it and not have to share out loud. The quiet ones: the Insiders.

Their symbol would be . . . a set of headphones, maybe. Maybe a door with an arrow pointing inside. Actually, they could pick their own symbol.

I'm sure they would insist!

It would be so much better if we could make our own groups. It's what we do at recess.

Maybe there should be a group that only does stuff on the computer. Wait, everyone would want to be in that group and we read on the computer whenever we get a chance anyway. That's not different enough. Nobody would have to stay in the group they started in. They could go from one group to another if they wanted.

Here is a map of it.

Teacher sits in the circle, listening mostly.

Readers sit in a circle around her
reading. She gives the first
reader one question to answer
after they read aloud.

Take turns reading out loud after
you get to read for five minutes
on your own.

The one who reads aloud gets to
think of what question the next
reader answers. It's got to be a
good question or they got to
think of another one.

Especially if it's too easy! We are
going to be really fierce about
too easy.

Before we had to spend all our time studying for the test, back in quarantine, that was the size small groups we did for reading. But now we're down to three or so in a group and all we do are those short stories and poems that are supposed to be like the test is. My group hardly gets to meet with Ms. Wachter, only like two times a week. She mostly has meetings with the kids that don't read as much as we do. I used to be book buddies with some of those kids, but not any more.

It's like all we learn is how to read and how to do math. The only science stuff we do is those multiple-choice questions again, only about science stuff. We do these random map things and some (multiple choice again) questions about famous people, but otherwise no more Social Studies.

I have been sitting here thinking about what I can compare this to, only doing reading and math. We do have to know both, but it's as if there isn't anything else to learn. So what if there were only two things you were supposed to learn in school. Let's say it was P.E. stuff instead, say running . . . and . . . volleyball. So everyone would be taught how to run starting in kindergarten. For running it would just be maybe 20 feet for little kids, and further as you got bigger. Then volleyball: there would be small volleyball nets and small soft balls for the little kids, and the bigger you got the taller the net. You could have small scores for little ones and you have to get higher scores until you get all the way to high school with the biggest scores of all.

So the goal would be for each grade to go really fast to a certain distance by a certain time in the year. Which is what reading is like, really, you're tested to see how fast you read and the books get longer and less pictures the older you get. So here we go, by first grade you have to run faster, and if you are in the accelerated part of first grade you have to run as fast as a second grader. After all they say if we can do above grade level work we are accelerated so it works out! If you couldn't keep up, you would get put in the remedial running group because of course everyone's legs should work the same way if they are all about the same age, so run faster!

Kids in wheelchairs or in Special Ed would have to take a virtual running tests on a computer. They would have to practice for that kind of test just as much as we practice for our running tests, and be just as bored and frustrated as we are.

Kids with short legs would just have to learn to run faster.

Now some kids that don't know English, they would be kids who came from someplace where running wasn't the big thing, uh, dancing was. So Spanish would be dancing and English would be running. So these kids are good dancers but when they get here they have to turn into good runners because that's what we do here, running. They would get special running coaches and after one year they would not get much more coaching, they would run and be timed just like us. They would gradually have to give up dancing because dancing is not American. And if you had asthma or one short leg or just were clumsy, you would still have to take the running test but a teacher could help you take it, like some teachers read kids the test and write the answer that the kids tells them to write. For the running test the kids would tell a teacher exactly how to move their legs up and

228

down until the kids told them to stop and that's how they would take the test. To practice some of these kids would lie on their backs and pedal in the air (just like we really do in P.E. sometimes) but they would have their inhalers next to them in case, and it wouldn't matter if they weren't running on the ground because some teacher would just measure how fast they were going in the air. Running and not getting anywhere is what it is like for some kids taking the test anyway.

Playing volleyball would get harder and harder as you got bigger. By third grade we would have to be able to serve the ball, spike it, be able to pass it to a teammate and play any position since the positions rotate. Everyone would have to practice serves over and over, just like we do basic facts now. If two teams played each other and it was a low score, they would have to play it over and over until the score was good enough, just like we have to take Test B if we don't score good enough on the first unit test.

Homework would be just running in place and practicing tapping and throwing a nerf ball or something. Your parents would have to film you with a camera to prove you did it. If you didn't do that you would get twice as much practice assigned.

Anyone who wasn't a good runner or couldn't learn how to serve right would have to go to more practice after school. Teachers would check to see if parents were running with their kids every night. Everyone would feel sorry for kids who had parents who didn't have time to run or didn't run much or even didn't run any more. Rich kids would have the best running shoes and so would everyone in their family and if they weren't very good they would go to private coaches and have special running machines they have to to use at home. Some people would be lucky enough to have parents who would volunteer in the class to teach kids how to run better.

Parents would tell kids that if they didn't learn how to run faster by second grade they might never go to college. Colleges would test students by having all kinds of races, and to get in you would have to run short distance, long distance, jump hurdles and be able to do relay races too. People would talk about how America didn't have enough fast runners compared to Kenya and Ethiopia and other countries.

The only way you would be able to get a job is by having good speed. If you weren't really fast you would never get hired. If you got injured or sick and got slow, you would be fired. Slow and steady would not win the race, no matter what Aesop says.

If you were good in volleyball everyone would tell you how talented you were, and your dad might say you were in good because you are like him. Everyone would know that Asians were just naturally better at volleyball, and black people just weren't as coordinated, and Hispanic people just didn't understand the game the way Asians and whites did. If anyone said why should everybody be able to play the game the same then they would get laughed at and some people would whisper that probably they weren't very good at volleyball or running and that's why they said such a silly thing.

Kids would get all upset about their running scores and would have nightmares about missing the ball. Teachers would worry about whether they would be fired because the kids in their class couldn't run as fast as the kids in the other suburbs and people would pity city kids because it would be a well known fact that city kids could not run, jump or pass a ball properly — it isn't their fault, really, it's the terrible conditions they live in, no place to run to, the air is more polluted, too many cars around, more crime happens around the running tracks, their parents weren't very good runners either, probably, and you would hear parents saying things like did I tell you that Benedict did a five minute mile last week?

I surely have heard parents bragging about their kids at school events.

I'm trying to make fun of it but it's scary, how close this is to what people expect of us and this test. I heard one of the teachers say that it's all about how many by when. That sounded so cold.

Our bodies grow at different rates, just like brains. What if everybody had to be four feet tall by fourth grade? How can they not see how whacky their rules are?

I may not like the rules, like now is bedtime, but I know why dad has rules like that. Rules with no why get me crazy.

I've got such a headache just thinking about it.

Today I was by myself at recess, which doesn't usually happen. I was just looking at a tree and thinking about God, which I also don't usually do. I mean, I think about God sometimes but not usually at school. The thing is, I like talking to God inside my own head but I don't do it much at school. School is too noisy for talking to God. This was the one time when I did feel close to God at school. I stared at the tree and told God all about how I feel about how it is at school now. I tell my friends about it but I hadn't talked to God about it, I don't know why. But this time I did.

I told God all about what is going on. All the sad weird stuff we have to deal with since we came back. All the wrong stuff that has happened and how I feel like an evil spirit has taken over our school and is making us do all these tests for no good reason that I can see. I can't understand it.

God did not answer back but I felt better after I was done. Then I looked up and over across from me was that girl Erin in French Immersion. She smiled at me and I stood up and went over and she said "What's up?" and we went off and got to talking about other things and I felt lighter. I didn't tell her what I was doing. Talking to her was good though. I didn't need to tell her what I said to my friend God, I was clear with God and even though God didn't say anything back that I could hear I felt like I was heard and that was good enough.

Last night I was looking in my dad's room for a pen and I found this letter next to his bed. I forgot about the pen. I couldn't help but read the letter.

I know it wasn't my letter but somehow I just had to read it. Now I am really sorry that I did. He hasn't finished writing it or mailed it off to my mom yet in Cameroon. I just put it back where I found it. No matter what I can't say anything about it to my dad. But I can't forget it:

Dear Imani:

How are you? I am well enough. I am sorry your mother has not gotten the money I sent. I sent it the regular way but somehow it has not gotten to you or her. I will go down to Western Union tomorrow to find out what happened to it.

Darryn is well. Of course I keep checking to see if she is sick with the disease. You do not need to remind me to do this. Know that I care about our daughter as I always have.

I also care about you. I believe that I care about you more than you do about me. You want us to marry so you can leave Cameroon and so you can live on my money. I know this is the truth. You say you don't care about whether I have money but that is not what you said to my sister. You were angry enough with me that day to tell the truth. What was the first thing you wrote to me about this time? The money that you did not get. Next you wrote about Darryn. Then you asked how I was. What is important goes first.

I know you love Darryn and want to be with her. But I will not marry you just for this reason. You cannot use me this way. If it were possible to . . .

This is where it stops. I wish it had stopped much sooner. Or I never picked it up.

I miss my mom. I wish daddy wasn't so mad at her. And I really really wish I hadn't read that letter he wrote.

Maria listened to me talking about it almost all day today, every chance I got to talk to her. She didn't offer me any advice, she just listened. That's why she's my best friend. She listens to me like I matter. She also does not give much advice, which is another really wonderful thing about her. She understands how I feel, that it is hurting my heart to know this thing but also I feel bad that I read something not for me.

When I can talk to Maria I can live with sadness.

Sometimes things do not work out. That's just the way it is. It doesn't matter if it's Homework Help or Housework. Or someone in your family. Some folks cannot be helped and they will make you take care of them so they don't ever have to help you or help themselves. It is disgusting but that's the way it is sometimes. I know it.

Once we took in somebody in the family who was having a hard time. I call him Sorry because that's what he was. His real name was something else but in my mind I called him Sorry. He was always apologizing. He left a mess in the kitchen, he was sorry. He broke a chair and didn't fix it, he was sorry. He took the last stick of margarine in the refrigerator which did not belong to him whatsoever, he was sorry. I mean it really needed to be his name so that's what I called him. Dad was sorry too, sorry he took him in, because this guy would not leave. He would not stop living with us and go away. We didn't want to live with him forever, there were already enough people living with us. But he was all sad and he thought he couldn't go out in the world and do stuff like we could. There was always a reason and it was a sad reason just like him. He was trying but my dad said he wasn't really trying enough, then Sorry found a new place to stay and he wanted to stay right with us. So he said he wasn't going to the new place but stay in our place. It used to be just ours, but he wanted to make it his place without giving us very much money or cleaning up like he said he would when he moved in. He was not the cleaning kind but he thought he was, which is kind of extra sad. If he got a job and a place to live he would have to move out and he didn't want to, is what it came down to, and dad got sick of it. So he kicked Sorry out of our home and it was sad but it was necessary.

That was a sad ugly day when Sorry moved out. He brought all these boxes and he didn't even have enough stuff to fill all the boxes. Sorry was so mad and still being grateful, it was the worst thing I ever saw. I never want to see anyone act how Sorry did that day, mad as he could be but still being all kind of sweety syrupy to us because he couldn't dare say what he really wanted to say. In case he needed us again sometime.

I feel sick right now, remembering it.

That is what it is like dealing with some of these kids in my class. Not as bad, but they remind me of Sorry. They don't want to do their homework, they want me to do it and copy from me. They really are sorry they didn't do it but they want me to say it's okay and lie about stuff. Just like dad with Sorry, I am getting sick of it. They need to do the work and stop pretending they did. I am kicking them out of my Homework Help group. Forget it. I am not sorry for them and that's all there is to it.

Today there was more bad news. Ms. Wachter was so angry. I have never seen her look so mad. I was hoping she wasn't mad at us. She has gotten mad at us for stuff, but not like this. Like when some kids were bullying people on the playground. She was pretty mad that time. I mean sometimes we do bad stuff. All I knew was she looked really really mad. So she looked at us and then she said we had to have a grade level meeting. I didn't know what the heck that meant, since I don't think we ever did it before. What did we do? What's a grade level meeting?

It means that all the Fourth Grades have a class meeting at the same time. French Immersion too. We went to the cafeteria at 2:30, when no one is having lunch anymore, and they told us the bad news.

All fun stuff is now officially completely cancelled!

No more class musicals, no time for rehearsals for them. No more PTA assemblies with dance or music, no more guest authors, or anything like that. No field trips until late May, after the tests, and maybe not even then. No Fourth Grade Literacy Festival, no Fourth Grade original opera musical (like the Fourth Grade has written and produced themselves for the last three years at our school) and even worse than that, no more Science Walks. I can't stand it, no more Science Walks, no more hands-on science experiments in class either. What will we do? Just Reading and Math lessons, with Social Studies and Science in the lessons just as part of whatever we're reading. That means those little paragraphs about all kinds of things, I bet, that have the multiple choice answers right below them that we've already been doing.

Minah raised her hand and asked why we were being punished. One of the French teachers started to answer me, saying something in French, real upset, but then she stopped herself and looked at Ms. Wachter, who took a deep breath and said it wasn't a punishment. Ms. Wachter said it was just because we had lost so much time while we were in quarantine that we should have been using getting ready for the test. So we need to spend extra time doing it now. That's what she said.

If it sounds like a punishment and feels like a punishment and works just like a punishment, I don't care, it's a punishment. The whole SNM test is a punishment. It's the only thing that matters any more.

We couldn't go on field trips in quarantine and now we can't again. We might as well have stayed in quarantine! That darn test didn't ruin everything when we were there.

At least Ms. Wachter is not mad at us.

She is mad that this is happening.

The teachers are so mean now. Even when they are not mean and cold they are no fun. Or they just walk down the hall looking at the floor and looking beat. We go to class and it's like they don't want to see us. I don't like being in school and I don't remember ever feeling like that for days at a time before.

Mrs. H looks tired and she never ever looks tired. Usually she gets us into the music and perks everybody up. But not now. I know she would rather teach us real songs like before instead of dumb skip counting rhythms and multiplication chanting like 2, 4, 6, 8, who do we appreciate, 5, 10, 15, 20, count by 5s, you got plenty.

Plenty of boring. Where do they get this stuff?

But she can't, not until after we take the SNM. This isn't the way it's supposed to be. I mean, she's a music teacher, she's supposed to be teaching us music. She says counting is important for music, but doing it like this isn't really any good. I don't want to tell her how bad music class really is, she looks so down these days. I did try to talk her into letting us use the drums or even the sticks as we skip counted but she just shook her head. And looked sad. She wouldn't tell me why, but Rachel said she heard from the Fifth Graders that Mrs. Drew walked into music class a while ago and told Mrs. H that they should be doing math, not the kazoo and the shakers like they were doing. Mrs. H told her they were making up a song to go with the math facts, but Mrs. Drew said that they were supposed to be learning, not entertaining each other. Why can't we do both, like we used to do before this test infected our school?

Yesterday our P.E. teacher Mr. Parker went home with a bad headache. He never gets sick! Ahmed said it was because of us, we weren't doing too good with his reading lesson. I hope it wasn't us — I was trying to play Word Bingo the right way but it was hard to understand the rules. Some people didn't know how to read the words to start with, so we had to tell them when to cover the word with the red dot. So they weren't learning how to read the words anyway. When somebody won the first Bingo, Thomas got real mad and said he didn't want to play anymore because the first prize was the best one. Terry in the French class said it wasn't fair, that they should get to do theirs in French, but Specials are always in English. Somebody else said they already knew all the Fourth Grade sight words so this wasn't any fun, and Jackie that's in the other class said what everyone was thinking, which was why can't we run and play volleyball and shoot hoops like we used to do in P.E.? That was when Mr. Parker said he had a bad headache and we got dismissed early because he had to go home. He looked so bad when we left. Really. Basketball practice never gave him a headache.

Today was the assembly I never want to remember. But somehow we can't talk about anything else. There was a thunderstorm and it was like nobody cared, it kind of matched how we felt. Ms. Wachter didn't say anything at the assembly and could hardly talk afterwards. We were all talking in the hall after and she didn't even hush us. It was so bad. Mrs. Drew announced it all. First the stuff we already knew. The class musicals are all cancelled. All field trips, class parties, cancelled, also the Fifth Grade poetry slam, and even Field Day, though that might get to happen in June. No more Science walks. Even French Immersion lost their chance to do that fairy tale play in French, I forget what it was called. They already said no more Career Day, when the parents come and tell about their jobs. Career Day was so cool when parents came in and talked about their jobs, especially that guy that brought in real brains in jars and told us about studying how brains work at NIH. But we won't get to do that this year. No more International Day, when we go around to these stations all over the school and get to see stuff and even eat food from countries all over the world. I loved it when parents set up tables and displays all over the building and we had play passports they would stamp after we went to the country they would tell us about, like Guatemala or Senegal. Of course Music and P.E. and Art are already just lessons for the test now, and there are practice tests every week until the real test. If you are absent you have to make up the practice test during recess! Also the Student Government Association, the SGA, was going to have Spirit Week, where you get to wear your pajamas to school, and Whacky Hair Day, and then there's an assembly where kids get to show their special talent in this all homemade talent show.

Of course wearing your pajamas and Whacky Hair was every day in quarantine, and we had talent shows too, but it's different now that we're back. I was looking forward to having Spirit Day and the talent show and all that stuff.

Well not any more. It's all cancelled. It takes too much time away from learning. Plus all the SGA meetings are cancelled until after the test. The SNM has cancelled our government!

They sent home a letter today explaining about all the changes to the schedule. The interesting thing is that there isn't much in the letter about the SNM. It's all about success and academic support and you can barely understand what it really says. I had to explain it to my dad and he just shook his head when I was done.

Today the principal came in when we were doing reading groups and told Ms. Watchter she needed to talk to our class. I knew it wasn't going to be a good thing just from the look on Mrs. Drew's face.

Then Mrs. Drew told us we were going to the bathroom too much.

I am not making this up.

She said we had to maximize learning time and what that meant was we could go to the bathroom one time before lunch and one time after lunch. She said she would know if we went more often.

Somebody muttered "How?" which is just what I was thinking. She glared at us but nobody repeated it or tattled on who said it.

Ms. Wachter stared at the floor and looked mad.

Then after that Mrs. Drew got all fake friendly and she asked Jason what we were doing. He told her reading groups (like she couldn't tell that already, I mean we were all in groups around the room with books in front of us reading stuff and it wasn't Math and we only get to do Reading and Math these days so what else could it be?). So then she leans over one group and asks Mary Katherine to tell her what the story she's reading is all about. Now Mary Katherine is kind of shy around strangers and she really doesn't know Mrs. Drew except she heard her at the assemblies. All she really knows is, this is somebody bossy who says you can't go to the bathroom whenever you want to go. So she just sits there and looks at this real tall person the principal and says, "I dunno."

So the principal looks over at Ms. Wachter and says, "Shouldn't they know what they're reading?"

Ms. Wachter looks back at Mrs. Drew and says, "Mary Katherine, what's the main idea of the story?"

Mary Katherine says, "Oh, that the segregation law was wrong and that's why the four friends had to have a sit in, so they could make the law change."

Mrs. Drew looks mad for a minute, then shrugs and leaves and we're all glad.

Ms. Wachter goes and gets a big star sticker and puts it on Mary Katherine. Ahmed gives the signal that we use to mean you have to go to the bathroom and Ms. Wachter goes over, gets the pass, gives to him and smiles at him and says, "Be my guest, Ahmed."

And we go back to work reading. Sheesh.

I finally got to talk to my teacher about it. I had to talk about it or bust, that's how it was. So we were supposed to be talking about how all our research projects will be different now, basically turned into boring BCRs, and Ms. Wachter was asking me about stuff and I just started in talking. I said that the test was stupid, that it wasn't fair, and how come we had to all do it when everybody already knew who was going to do good on it and who wasn't and she just sat there and listened to me. I didn't even realize how loud I was talking until I stopped for a minute to think and I realized how quiet the whole room was. So then I didn't say anything else because I was embarrassed. So we just looked at each other and I thought of one more thing I wanted to say. I remember it exactly because it was coming from a deep place. I told her:

I understand about tests in school. If I was going to school in Cameroon I would have to take tests. If I were learning on the computer at home I might have to take a test like my sister used to do. There are all kinds of tests all the time. And you always say that we have to take the math tests so you can see what we know and what you might have to teach us again. But this test is not like that. You have to finish it in just so much time. If you don't answer every question in time you feel stupid. If you don't know the answer you're supposed to just try something and go to the next one and that makes you feel stupid. If you do know it and answer it too fast you have to sit there bored until the time is up. And what kind of rule is it that you can't read a book after you finish a reading test. That just doesn't make any sense. Draw on the scrap paper but oh you can't keep your drawing. Now let's take another hard test since you did that one. It's hard on purpose but there's this chance thing to it, so if you really don't know you might get lucky and guess right from three chances. So it's like throwing the dice, see what happens. If you just answer whatever and finish fast you can sit there and just wait for the pain to stop. So this test is really to see who already knows it and to make everyone else feel stupid and frustrated. It doesn't show what else you might know or how having an upset stomach that day or not much sleep got in your way.

My friends are smart and work hard but all this stuff is so hard for them. Especially these days, they are scared, and picking fights with each other like they never did before because there's just no break from any of it. Not even in Music class, not even to read a book just because it might be fun, not even ever. That's what it feels like.

Or maybe everyone always telling you to do your best on this test gets said so much it doesn't mean anything. I felt sorry for those kindergarten kids, when they see us in the morning on the bus they're telling us to go for it and try our best on the test and everything. Wait until they get to Fourth Grade and have to do this and have other little kids dancing and singing for them to do this stinking, boring, unfair, ridiculous test!

Ms. Wachter looked at me and just said in a very tired voice, "You're right, Darryn."

We walked into class today and there was a big new sign hanging over Ms. Wachter's desk. I thought it was going to be one of those big "Do your best on the State Test," but instead it said, STOP WHINING AND START A REVOLUTION. I don't know exactly what it means but I bet I can figure it out. It's not a computer sign from the printer. It's in Ms. Wachter's pretty handwriting but it is written really big on poster paper.

Ms. Wachter told us that she doesn't think we should take the test so she refuses to teach us how to take it any more. She says if she teaches us regular lessons that will be better than all this practice. And then:

"I want everybody in our class to go to college, get a good job and have a nice place to live. I want you to love to read your whole life. I think if you go to college you have a better shot at a successful life, but I don't think you should be required to go! You could go to a trade school, you could get on-the-job training, you might be in a special kind of craft that doesn't require college — I don't know, but you have the right to make other choices. And you shouldn't be made to feel like you have to go to college to be considered good. My parents went to college, and my brothers and one of my sisters, but my other sister didn't go and she was a success.

"When I was young and learning about computers and how to use them I had to keep getting shown how to do it over and over. Some of you are like that about some things. And I just don't believe in measuring intelligence the same way they did centuries ago just to figure out who should join the French army. Never mind about that. I'm just telling you, I don't trust or want to participate in a test that is unfair. Making you pick the best answer in a

244

multiple choice test is ridiculous, especially when it was made into law by two guys in the government who both went to private school and were both average students!"

Then she explained that if she didn't go along with the test, she would be fired and we would have to take it anyway. So no matter what we have to take the test. But we don't have to always do the fill-in-the-bubble sheets.

So what a day it was today.

Today I got into a big fight with both Rachel and Ahmed. It was so stupid.

Rachel was saying she was my best friend right to Maria, she was starting something on purpose. I could tell. This isn't the first time she's showed how jealous she is of the two of us. Maria didn't say anything back but Ahmed did (this was during math groups) when he should have just stayed out of it, but no. Ahmed tells Rachel that Maria is my best friend. So I told Ahmed to mind his own business and he said I'm just saying, and Rachel started yelling. I don't even remember what Rachel yelled, just that she was yelling stuff.

Naturally Ms. Wachter came over and wanted to know what was going on and nobody wanted to say, not even me, because telling her wouldn't help. She would try to fix it and it can't be fixed. So we all just pretended it was nothing to go back to figuring out the math and she walked away and told us to write about it and put it in the issue bin, so Rachel did that, wrote her note and came back and glared at everyone until math was over and she went back to her seat. I am so glad I'm not in her group. She would have tried to keep a fight up with me all day. Later on I put a note in the issue bin that said they were both my friends and what can I do? Because I know Maria won't put anything in the bin and none of it was her fault. Ms. Wachter will bring it up at the class meeting and there really needs to be something in there from my point of view.

We always end up talking about friends in class meeting. Even the boys get into it. I used to think it was just girls but it's boys too. I remember at recess one time when Shay-Shay was crying about nobody being his friend and one of the boys said it's because you act like such a sissy and Shay-Shay stood up and punched him a good one so I guess that settled that! Except it really didn't.

It hardly ever solves it to hit somebody but I understood why he did it.

I'm going to talk to Rachel about it on the bus today. I can't let this go on. All of us should be friends somehow, being friends is a forever important heart thing.

When I woke up this morning I was thinking about Rachel. I didn't get to talk to her on the bus, it was too loud and anyway I didn't want to talk to her. Then when I was waking up I was thinking about her and Maria and then I thought about how my dad didn't want to marry my mom. He never told me why exactly and neither did she but I know that she wanted to get married. Then I thought about what was in that letter he was writing. It was lots to think about.

One time I asked my mom in a letter what happened between them and she never wrote back anything. I started wondering if it hurts Rachel not to be my friend like it hurts mom that dad won't marry her. It's not the same thing at all, I know that, but when you don't get picked when you want to be maybe the hurt is the same a little bit.

When I thought about it that way I pretended I was Rachel instead of me and Darryn wouldn't pick me and when I thought about it that way it really hurt. I remembered that book Ms. Wachter read to us where the three little girls were friends and they weren't jealous of each other. I think that's because the first two were closer and the third one didn't mind, but maybe I'm wrong. Maybe they were all three equal fierce friends and it could be like that for Maria and Rachel and me if I work at it.

Because it will have to come from me, Rachel is already afraid I'm going to kick her to the curb and I'm just sick of her picking fights with Maria. Maybe Ms. Wachter will help us. Before I ask her I will ask Rachel, and I'll ask in a way so she knows that what I really want is to be her true friend. The last thing I want is to hurt her. She doesn't deserve that.

So tomorrow I will ask Ms. Wachter to help us with it and if she doesn't I will figure it out myself.

Ms. Wachter sat down with me and Maria and Rachel today and we really got it all out. I don't know how it happened exactly but somehow Ms. Wachter made us feel like it was safe to say what we were really feeling. So Maria got to tell about how she feels tense around Rachel because she doesn't know when Rachel will start something. Rachel got to talk about how she feels like we shut her out of the conversation sometimes and other times I tease her, which is true. I got to talk about how I feel like I have to pick one of them when I want both of them to be my friends and I pulled out the Betsy-Tacy book and told Rachel if we tried why couldn't we be friends like they were? Maria said, the book says they never argued, and Rachel said, well that ain't us then and then we all three started laughing. That's when I said Rachel I love how you make me laugh and would you believe she got embarrassed! And wouldn't look at me but she was smiling away! Maria said, then we will do it our way, this friendship, get aboard the Friendship!

I don't remember everything we said after that. The important stuff had all been said by then. These are my amigas and we will work it out.

Rachel is important for different reasons than Maria. I realized that today and if she were sure of it than we won't keep having this problem. For real.

So we have decided to call ourselves the Tres Amigas, which means the three girlfriends.

I like us having our own name.

These are the friends I always look for when we go outside for recess. These are the ones I want to sit next to on field trips, if we ever have one of those again.

We are going to get our pictures taken together in lots of poses with Maria's new phone. The best ones will get printed out and I will send one to my mom in Cameroon.

Today Ms. Wachter told us she had to talk to us about something very important. She looked so serious and kind of scared, a way I have never seen her look, especially the lines that were showing in her forehead. Then she just stood there for a little bit, looking at us. I didn't know what was going on. Then it popped into my head that she was going to tell us someone else had died from TB2, someone we knew, and then I thought maybe she had it, but then she wouldn't be here, they would have taken her to the hospital or one of the quarantine places still around, and I scared myself really fast before she even said anything.

Then after that she cleared her throat but she didn't say anything but just pointed to the sign that has been near the of the class door all this time. It's been there since the first day of school, I think.

The new sign says this:

No Bully Zone

She said she believed in the sign when she put it up and she still believes in it. She hates it when kids bully each other.

"It's just a symbol, really," she said, and then added, "but symbols are important if you believe in what they mean." She looked at everyone and I swear she looked a little longer at me.

Then she said the school superintendent is a bully. That he says that all the kids must practice lots of times for the big test. He says if a school does not do too good on the test that the teachers are in trouble and have to go to meetings to find out how to teach the test better. In these meetings they will look at charts that show how everybody did on the test and take the students who didn't do so good and teach them more and let the other kids do other work while they teach those kids. This is called a data meeting and it is really a sad bad thing to have to do. The superintendent also said that teachers have to challenge everybody with the next grade level's curriculum (whatever that is) and have to do the keys to college success and do really well so he looks good. Nobody ever gave me any keys to college. I have a key to the apartment. I don't go to college yet so what good would the keys do me?

She even said that if we do a good job on the tests, it means that house prices around here will stay expensive. I didn't understand that part at all but I didn't want to ask questions until she was done because she was really on a roll.

How if I do good on this test will that make a house worth more money? My dad says the houses around here already cost too much. That's why we live in an apartment. I already didn't want to take this test but if it means my dad can't ever buy a house then forget it. They want to give me keys to a college well how about keys to a house just down the street from the school. Then I won't have to take the bus and I can walk to school. Think of all the gas for the bus that will save.

So anyway Ms. Wachter has a plan. We are going to seem like we are taking the practice tests and all, but really we won't. We will actually be reading and doing our regular writing groups but we will have the practice tests on our desks in case somebody comes in when we are supposed to take it. We will do the first practice page together and help each other figure out the answers. That's how we do this test practice. Together.

She looked so fierce and scared at the same time when she said it. Then she said, really quietly but I could hear every word, "I am going to help teach you how to think for yourselves, so it really doesn't matter what is on this test. You'll be able to figure it out because of the strategies we'll learn. And we will prove how smart you are on this unfair, ridiculous, boring and biased test."

She went around and gave everybody a fist bump which usually looks kind of silly when grownups do it but somehow not this time. I don't know, it was like we all just got strapped in to a roller coaster ride and started to roll, even though we really weren't. It was the weirdest and coolest thing ever.

I would rather learn how to think than learn how to take a dumb test any day. So I approve of this secret plan my teacher has, to teach us to think instead.

Today was amazing. We worked like crazy on reading and math in our groups and then Ms. Wachter said, that's it, stop, we're taking a break. And we took a dance break, which was fabulous. We danced to some good stuff and some old stuff that Ms. Wachter likes. There was this song I Got a Feeling and it was pretty good for an old song. I asked her what the group was and she said the Black Eyed Peas, and I think I've even heard of them. What a funny name for a singing group, I told her. She said there was a group called the Red Hot Chili Peppers. So then we spent some time making up names for groups, only funny, like the Dried Up Mashed Potatoes, Burnt Microwave Popcorn, and then this group that can't get gigs anywhere called Liver and Onions.

Well, it's really hard when things go bad. Yesterday had been fun, and knowing we had a plan makes me feel much better. Not for long!

First off this morning they announced that everyone is losing 15 minutes of recess. Why? To practice for that darn test, of course. The SNM. The Stupid Numbing Mess. The State Nerd Measurement. Since we'll only have 15 minutes, no use going outside, by the time we get there, we'll only have ten minutes left. So all indoor recess instead. For a quick 15 minutes. Until after we take the stinky test.

Also we found out why we had to take so many practice tests. Not just to get us used to it, but to see who can't do it. They've been scoring these practice tests even though they told us it doesn't count towards our report card grades. Which it doesn't, but it sure does count for having any recess! The ones who are having the most trouble with the tests . . . they lose their whole recess, and practice for the test — with the French teachers! Who are going to teach them the lessons in English, which is okay somehow because these aren't their French Immersion students! And nobody is happy about it, not the teachers, not us, but there's nothing we can do about it. I heard the teachers talking about it, and one said, "After all the trouble we went to, to give them recess during quarantine, and now they can't go outside to move, it's absurd. It's not healthy! Michelle Obama told everybody that!"

I don't know what Mrs. Obama has to do with it, but it sure is true that we had recess when we were in the synagogue and now we don't. Also they said they couldn't change the schedule to do this unless it was for every grade, so everybody, even first and kindergarten, get shorter recess. The little ones don't even have to take the test. Talk about stupid.

So everybody is getting punished. This is going to make us want to do our best, you bet. It's just so wrong!

I am so lucky. Just call me the luckiest kid ever. There is no end to the luck in my life. NOT! It turns out just because I have been doing okay on these practice tests, I'm going to be working with another teacher in a small group in his room with other kids like me and we are going to practice writing BCRs together all the time and isn't that great, Darryn, you can do it, so let's give you more to do.

The thing is, I kind of like Mr. Tocs, the new guy that will be teaching me, but I don't want to go off and practice for this test even more than we already do. It's supposed to be this big compliment, that I'm going to be with these other smart kids working with the gifted and talented teacher, but it doesn't feel that way. At least it's not every day. A couple of the French Immersion kids are in the GT group so that's interesting too, I haven't gotten to do school stuff with any of them since the quarantine.

Mr. Tocs does not put up with any silly stuff. He used a very quiet voice to explain the rules to us for this class. He asked if there were questions and there weren't any because what he said was so clear. It all comes down to work hard and pay attention and we'll succeed. Then he passed out the practice test for today. Dionne and Alejandro were goofing around with a pencil while he was doing it and all he had to do was point his finger and they stopped.

I have to do it. That's pretty clear. Mrs. Drew was the one who told me and Alejandro and the other kids from the other class that we were going to be doing this. Ms. Wachter didn't say a word but she was not happy.

Mrs. Drew actually patted me on the shoulder like she was congratulating me. Sometimes I really don't like it when people touch me and this was one of those times. In my head I'm thinking GET OFF ME and my mouth is not saying anything.

So here's another thing I have to do so I can score really high on the test. Oh well.

At recess today we heard that a teacher quit. It was one of the French teachers. They hardly ever leave unless they retire. The kids said it was because of all this stuff about the SNM, and how that's all they are supposed to teach now. This teacher had been the one to plan all the field trips which are now cancelled. Plus she really loves to teach Social Studies, she taught all of us in the synagogue, and she's not allowed to teach it anymore that way she used to, only as multiple choice after reading. So instead of say, making model Eiffel towers and then presenting a report about it, they read two pages and write a summary and that's it. Which is the same thing that happened to our monthly research projects, instead of doing a big drawing (2 feet by 2 feet!) and a written research report that could include lots of information from many sources, we read about different mammals and wrote a BCR about the different ones and that was it. Kurt was really upset. He's a good artist and he really wanted to do a big picture. Last year's Fourth Grade got to pick a research topic and do the pictures and the reports they did went up in the gym. I remember because we went to see and they read us their reports and the pictures were so different so it was very interesting. Also I remember thinking that I might do a zebra when it was my turn.

They also got to do their own original musical for the school and they went on four field trips, but not us!

I can't believe how many things got taken away. If we were still having all the stuff we would be complaining about all the work they are, probably. The opera for sure. Now I want it all back.

Later on Ms. Wachter found notes in the Issue Bin that weren't signed but said things like:

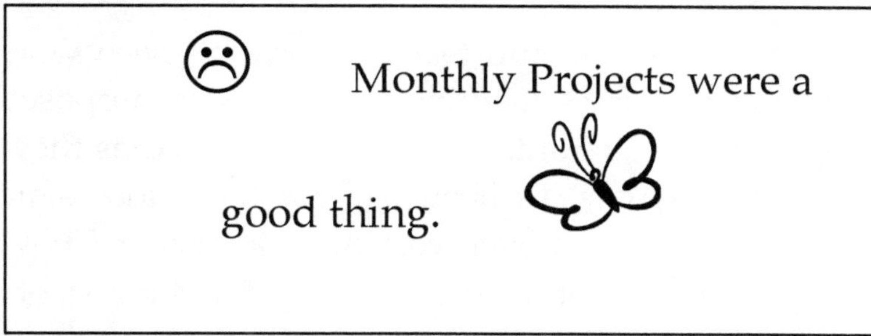

I know that was from Alana even if she didn't sign it. I know how she loved our butterfly project last year. She said she heard about lots of cool science projects from her friend. She knows because her friend Naomi did a queen bee for her big project last year.

I didn't tell Ms. Wachter who wrote it. I figure if she doesn't want to sign it, that's Alana's business. Anyone in our class can put something in the Issue Bin.

Somehow I forgot that the French classes did projects too. Now I remember seeing their stuff last year too, and it was pretty good, mostly. I didn't listen to them read their projects but they sure had lots of words on the pages.

When there was that awful assembly and we got told about half recess and no field trips, I didn't know it was going to be the same bad way for the Frenchies. I guess I just figured they wouldn't have to practice as much as we do, because they are supposed to be smarter than us, but apparently not. Seems like everybody has to do better and better every year until you reach 100% and everybody gets an A or B, that's part of the law No Child Left Behind. By a certain year everyone has to get proficient or advanced on the test which is the same thing as an A or a B, I guess.

And the parents and teachers have all been worried about the Frenchies learning what they're supposed to because of the quarantine but not as worried as they are about us. Anyway it's been bad for them too, which I didn't know. Now it even cost them a teacher. They are going to have a substitute, probably for the rest of the year. That's really too bad. It's bad enough we have to take this stupid test, but if Ms. Wachter wasn't here it would be even worse. The kids said that their teacher talked to them before she left and apologized but she said she couldn't take it anymore. They used some French word to explain it but I knew what they meant.

I also found out that one of the other teachers, Madame-something-I-forget, is leaving in two weeks because she is going to have a baby, but one of the kids, Griffith, who has a sister in that class says that the teacher is leaving earlier than she was going to because she is stressed out. I asked how he knew that and Griffith said he heard her talking on her cell phone when he went back to the room to get his lunch. I like this guy, he knows how to spy on adults without getting caught, just like me.

It's funny, I felt closer to the Frenchies after they told me about this. I don't think I ever felt like they had to deal with the same stuff we did. Well, they did in quarantine, but even then, they were having classes in French and I didn't know what they were learning. Since we didn't have separate classes so much I could hear them, but I couldn't understand what they were saying. They spoke English mostly at recess but they didn't talk to us much. Even in quarantine, where you could hardly get away from anyone. Now it's like we've always been talking to each other.

They hate the data notebooks we have to keep. There are so many things we have to track in them. If only it was just six or seven things. But no.

You have to put in the title of the books you read and how many pages they are. If a book isn't long enough it doesn't count. I never thought about it but they don't have as many books to pick from as we do to read because not all the books in the library are in French. So they have some good books but they don't have a Wimpy Kid or some of the Wayside School ones. They can still read them of course, but if it isn't in French it doesn't count for the reports. Everyone has to record their spelling tests and when they do spelling they have to put the accents on too or it's wrong.

For the math part they have the same timed test we do and some of them like it but most of them don't. The worksheets have all these problems on it and you do as many as you can in one minute. They have one girl in

French Immersion who cries every time they have a multiplication math minute. She starts crying the minute the teacher holds up the Math Minute worksheets. The teacher gives her two minutes but she still cries. She's not getting any faster at math but she's crying faster.

One thing they complained about that I never heard anybody in our class complain about before was that the teachers can use cell phones and we can't. Well, that was true before quarantine, that was the rule. They said they know it's not a new rule, they just don't like it anyway.

I told them about how mad Ms. Wachter has been and how we're not going to take all those practice tests anymore. One girl got all upset. She said we're going to get in trouble if we don't do all the test practice. I thought she was scared we wouldn't do well on the test, but no, she just thought we should be doing it because the principal said so! Then Maria, my Maria of all the quiet nice people, says, "The principal is the one who took away half our recess and the field trips and says we go to the bathroom too much. I don't feel like I should have to do this work because she says so. I don't trust her. All she cares about is this test and how it makes the school look good. She doesn't care about us and whether we are learning things. She is not a good leader!"

We all just looked at her for a second. I would never have thought Maria felt like that and would say it to everyone like that. Your friends sure can surprise you.

Then recess was over and we went back inside. I had lots to think about.

When I went to Mr. Tocs for the special tutoring class today, he looked real surprised. Apparently it was supposed to be cancelled because he has to go to a meeting for all the GT teachers. He was embarrassed because he was supposed to tell my teacher but he forgot, and he was still in his room and he was supposed to be gone already. Then Mademoiselle LaFontaine came bursting in practically shouting, "Voila, mon ami!" She didn't even notice me. She flourished this paper around, showing it to Mr. Tocs, and he said thanks to her, and she laughed and said, "You see, I was right, it is all our fault. We brought you the best food, wine and art in the world, but alas a Frenchman also began intelligence testing, you see. Then the Americans, they take it and they use it the wrong way entirely."

"Mikaela, I'll be late, give it to me."

She kept the paper and made him listen to the whole thing first:

> *In France, psychologist Alfred Binet worked at making tests to rate children's intelligence. In 1904 he was commissioned by the French government to find a method to classify some intelligence levels as normal and those who were intellectually inferior. Binet gave this I.Q. test to Paris schoolchildren and created a standard based on his data.*
>
> *Later, the Binet test was used in America to measure intelligence.*

"But then, the Americans made their own test," she told him, and he shook his head while she read on.

> *In 1917 America entered World War I. The military was faced with the problem of sorting many draftees into various Army jobs. To solve it, the Army put together a committee of seven leading psychologists to create an intelligence test. By 1919, over a million American men had taken the I.Q. tests.*

By 1950, intelligence tests were multiple-choice assessments that measured intelligence accurately. Things have changed since then, for sometimes data was distorted in certain populations tested over time. Standardized tests administered by schools do NOT actually measure intelligence, but are sometimes interpreted that way.

He said, "Okay, okay, now let me go so I can make my presentation about it!" and she gave him the paper. He grabbed his stuff and went out the door and that's when she noticed me. I explained what I was doing there right away, because she did not look like she was happy to see me. So I made sure she saw me gone.

Ms. Wachter has the coolest friends in the world. She has these buddies who are into something called improvisational theater. One of the things they do is get into being somebody famous, dressing and talking like them. Then they go and find an audience that wants to talk to that person. Ms. Wachter said it all started when her friend Andrea had a party at her house and came as Martina Navratilova, the tennis player. She dressed up like her and answered the questions the people at the party asked it and it was great. So now this group, which calls itself the Theater Conservancy, does this kind of thing all the time. And because Ms. Wachter is friends with them, they are going to come to our class dressed up as famous kids' book authors and answer our questions and tell us all about the author! So we are going to get to meet Beverly Cleary and somebody named Isabel Allende and Terry Pratchett and maybe a couple of others. Also one lady does Maud Hart Lovelace so I can ask questions about the Betsy-Tacy books.

Our part of the deal is we have to have read at least one of the books to ask a question. Also we can't tell about it because we aren't supposed to be having guest authors, even if they are just acting like them. So when they come to visit they are going to be classroom volunteers helping us learn to read. Which is true, in a way. It's too bad that the other classes won't get to hear these authors, but we can't take the chance. Mrs. Drew, that we call Mrs. P-U, said no more guest authors until after the SNM test. Well, these aren't the actual authors. That's all right, that's okay, we're going to do it anyway!

One of the performers in the Theater Conservancy is a guy called Dakota. The picture of him that she showed us is really cute.

Today Lewis, who hardly ever talks to me, kept asking me about Cameroon. It was like he was planning to move there or something. He wanted to know about the food and what people wear (clothes, what did he think we would wear?) and if they spoke a foreign language. I told him some things and then I looked up Cameroon in the Wikipedia about the language because I wasn't sure. I found out amazing things. I sent him the info by email:

Cameroon is home to 230 languages. These include 55 Afro-Asiatic languages, two Nilo-Saharan languages, and 173 Niger-Congo languages. This latter group is divided into one West Atlantic language (Fulfulde), 32 Adamawa-Ubangui languages, and 142 Benue-Congo languages (130 of which are Bantu languages).

English and French are official languages, a heritage of Cameroon's colonial past as both a colony of the United Kingdom and France from 1916 to 1960. The nation strives toward bilingualism, but in reality, very few Cameroonians speak both French and English, and many speak neither. The government has established several bilingual schools in an effort to teach both languages more evenly.

Most people in the English-speaking Northwest and Southwest provinces speak Cameroonian Pidgin English as a lingua franca. Fulfulde serves the same function in the north, and Ewondo in much of the Center, South, and East provinces.

What a complicated country it is just for talking! I had to look up so many words in the article, it was a pain. I told Lewis I was going to give him a quiz about it. He got upset and told me, "You can't do that." I told him I was only kidding.

The last thing anybody around here needs is another test!

I don't know what this part means at all: Cameroonian Pidgin English as a lingua franca. Who the heck is Pidgin? I can't tell Lewis about it until I know. I'll ask my dad.

There's a Cameroon saying: "He who asks questions must be prepared to hear the answers." My daddy likes to say it. Same thing goes for she who asks. You have to listen for the answers. But I did not like the answer about Pidgin English. It's like this strange English where you can kind of understand what somebody is saying and uses some slang words but it doesn't come out in the same way I would say it. I mean the way I would say it here in America. There's also Camfrangais which is like the same thing only in more French than English and it's all mixed together. My dad did a little bit of both for me but he didn't like when I laughed. So I stopped laughing. Still I'm not telling Lewis about pidgin talk. It's for the birds.

I think questions are important. Good questions make you really think about the answers. But Mrs. Drew does not even know how to ask direct questions! She doesn't ask, "Are you preparing to take the test? What are you doing?" She says things like, "What data do you have in your data notebook?" Then she looks through the notebook and asks kids questions about a spelling test graph. Or she asked Sebastian, "Did you have a quiz today?" He says yes and she says what about and he tells her and he just looks at her like so what. I know she's not ready for the real answers, which is that we are not going to practice every day for this SNM test, but we are preparing for it. We are preparing for it by learning how to think and write about what we read, and we are solving problems and telling how we solved them. Stop bugging us about the SNM. Or, like Jacob in the French class told me, "SNM préparation, feh! Est-ce que rien n'est sacré? Je suis intelligent. Laissez-moi tranquille!" (SNM preparation, feh! Is nothing sacred? I am smart, leave me alone!

During morning announcements Mrs. Drew told us that there's going to be a competition between classes to see who can get the best scores on the practice test. The class that does the best job will get a pizza party and extra computer lab time. We could hear them cheering in the portable next door. Nobody in our class was cheering.

I think she meant every grade level competes with other classes in their grade. So she's setting us against each other and for what? To try our best on this stupid test? For a pizza and computer time? Now that is some dumb kind of bribe.

Actually it isn't so dumb. I would like to have a pizza party and more computer time and I would like it if my class won. I wonder if Ms. Wachter is even giving her our scores, which we don't have.

The Frenchies will win it anyhow. They always do.

I don't want to compete about this. I don't like it that there can only be one winner, but most contests are like that. That's what happens on American Idol. This is just not my kind of contest.

I don't want this test at all, so that figures.

Every day brings more bad stuff and I can't do anything about it. I am so mad. I've decided that what we need is another Declaration of Independence. Only we need it for what's happening now.

Where's a piece of paper? Why can't I ever find a pencil in this desk? Okay, here we go. Time to write.

My Declaration

I think that we should not have to keep taking these tests. Here's why they are not fair. I can show my teachers that I know lots of things. But making me sit for 40 minutes and guess which one of the three answers is right. This is bad for my whole class. We can't have all our recess, we can't have music or Art or P.E. like we used to, we can't even go to the bathroom when we need to. Our principal is a real bully who doesn't care about anything but what is in our data notebooks. I know she doesn't care about us. She even cancelled all our field trips and the class musical.

The tests should be cancelled instead of the Fourth Grade field trips.

The law they made that says we have to take these stupid tests should be changed. We declare that the SNM is unfair and a big bore and we all hate it.

This is my Declaration of Independence from SNM.

Now what shall I do with it? I mean, I can't give it to the principal because it says she messed up. Which she did! I can't show it to Ms. Wachter because it says these tests should be cancelled. She already told us that's not going to happen.

Still I want somebody to read it. Who would I show it to? I can read it to Maria and Rachel. They would understand.

Rachel liked it but she says it isn't strong enough. Not strong enough! She also said I should call it the Declaration of Education, which I think is a really good title. Maria said I should try to write it so it sounds more like the real Declaration of Independence. She says I should start with "We the people."

So the first thing I did was a rough draft and it's still too rough.

At least they liked it enough to tell me I should work on it. If it was no good they would tell me. One of them would, anyway.

We went to the Media Center to look it up and it turns out that the Declaration doesn't start with "We the people." Our Constitution starts with "We the people" but not the Declaration. The librarian, Ms. Baxter, told us that the "We the people" part is actually called the preamble to the Constitution. So we found out what a preamble is, which is the special beginning of some writing, but anyway it isn't the Declaration. The Declaration starts with "When in the course." Then Mrs. Baxter told is if we wanted to know about the Declaration of Independence why not ask Bill? Which was a great idea except he's not in our class, he's in Mr. Etheridge's HFA class. So we sent a note to Mr. Etheridge and then asked Ms. Wachter and tomorrow we can meet with him when we go to the computer lab. We will have to give up some computer time but really Bill is better than a computer. Plus he can tell knock-knock jokes. Show me a computer that can do that.

This morning Mrs. Drew announced that some kid, I forget his name, scored the highest on the practice test for Fifth grade. She said, "He was always so smart and now we know for sure," and then she said, "I'm sure his class will win the SNM contest, but good luck to all the classes." Then she asked him if he wanted to say anything and he didn't and what a relief that was, and then she went on talking about the pizza party the class that wins will get.

It's enough to make you hate pizza.

Well, maybe not that bad.

Ms. DeCombe brought her French class over to ours today and we did our groups during reading together. I heard her say to Ms. Wachter that she misses being able to do lessons together like we did in quarantine. Another teacher said almost the same yesterday when we went to the cafeteria. I don't see why they can't just do it like they did back then. I liked working with the Frenchies then. I mean, whose classroom is it anyway?

I found out that Ms. Wachter is using our regular tests that we always do to tell Mrs. Drew how we are doing on our practice tests. She turns everything into a graph, how many spelling words right, how many sight words, how many math facts and how many problems we solved on a quiz. It's the same stuff on the practice tests only it's not something we do every single day twice a day and it's not guess the answer either. We track it in the data notebook but not with practice tests. How could you do that with the 25 books we have to read this year? It doesn't make any sense.

Ms. DeCombe also told us that kids can get smart if they work hard, it's not like Mrs. Drew said. Of course I knew that.

I finally got to talk with Bill. He really had a hard time understanding what I was doing at first. He just likes the actual original Declaration and he didn't get why I was trying to write something like it. But finally he kind of caught on and then he thought it was funny, which I guess it is, in a way. So we worked on it a little with everyone giving me ideas and Bill gave me a copy of the Declaration of Independence to keep which he called a facsimile and I will have to look up that word. His copy is kind of hard to read but it looks really cool. He said I can't put in "I," it has to be "We" all the way through. Then I went off to work on my own and Bill went back to his class.

Maria came back after a while where I was typing it up and said to put everything about Mrs. Drew in different sentences instead of one long sentence which I like to write like this one. She said if I did that it looks longer and more like the real thing. Then she reminded me of some other stuff Mrs. Drew did that I forgot to put in. I tried to put it in that old timey language when I added the other stuff.

I didn't actually put Mrs. Drew's name in it. It makes me feel a little less nervous about it. You never know where she'll pop up, coming in our class and looking around to find stuff she doesn't like.

I know she wouldn't like to see me working on this, even if she can't tell it's about her. She LOVES the SNM. She must think it's the best thing ever. She talks about it enough. I wish that she would be fired and Mrs. Hayes-Roberson would come back. I have respect for Mrs. Hayes-Roberson. In the beginning I wanted to have respect for Mrs. Drew but no way Jose like Maria always says.

Rachel came over and helped me re-write the part where it says "We hold these truths to be self-evident." I didn't want to write that exact thing in mine. She said that part means "We hold this truth to be obvious duh," but I didn't want to put in the duh part. So we talked about it and instead we put in that "We think that it's seriously obvious that all this testing is wrong."

Then I told her to go away and she got all hurt and I had to tell her it's not personal, I just can't write steady the way I want if other people are standing around or sitting around watching me and talking to me while I do it. For once she got it that it wasn't personal it's just the way I write and she was okay and went away. I was so grateful she didn't bring a drama I got three more sentences done.

The Declaration of Education
By Darryn Yochangko Thomas

When it becomes necessary for students to refuse to take tests, we should tell everybody why we don't want to do it.

We think it's seriously obvious that all this testing is wrong. We believe we have a right to education. That's why there are schools. But not tests all day every day.

Students have the right to protest when all they do anymore is take tests to prepare for another test. Schools that do this should be stopped.

Our principal is a real bully who doesn't care about anything but what is in our data notebooks. She even cancelled all our field trips and the class musical. She should be fired and the tests should be cancelled instead of the field trips. The law they made that says we have to take these stupid tests should be changed.

We declare that it's obvious that the school is not a good place to be any more. So if the government is making the schools bad then just like in the revolution there should be independence from the government. Or something, because this isn't working.

We declare that the SNM is unfair and a big bore and we hate it. We make this Declaration knowing we're going to get in trouble but it's the principle of the thing, we therefore pledge our Time, our Lunch Money and our Friendship.

I typed it up and asked Maria and Rachel if they would sign it. Rachel said we didn't need the part about lunch money. I showed her the part in the original about "our lives, our fortune and our Sacred Honor." She said so? I explained that Bill told me that fortune meant

269

money. Rachel said so, again. I said what do you mean, so? She said, so it means money, but I don't have any and I don't have any lunch money, my dad sends a check and what do we need to promise money for anyway? Then I was really surprised that Maria agreed with her and then Maria says to me, you don't have any lunch money either, which is true, I get free lunch but that's nobody's business.

So I changed it to Resources because we know we have those. I put in time because it sounds stronger and is truer because these tests take so much time away from actually learning something new. Then I re-arranged some sentences because they didn't make sense. I added some other stuff I thought about and took some stuff out. Besides I really don't want a whole new government. I want the old one to get rid of a bad law.

So I spent all my time in the computer lab working on this but it was cool, I got into it. The second draft is much longer since I put in more of the old language when I could get it to make sense.

Then I put it in this cool looking font and almost lost the entire thing because I hit the wrong button. So then I saved it and I sent it to Bill as an e-mail as a backup.

I wanted to print it out so I could put it into my writing portfolio. I went to ask Ms. Wachter if I could print it out so then she came over to read it.

She looked at me so strange when she finished reading it.

I just looked back at her.

I don't know what her problem was, but she let me print it out. I made two copies, one for me to put in my portfolio and one to take home.

Osumare taught us this new game at indoor recess. It's really an old game she says, but most of us have never played it before. It's called Mancala and you really have to have a good pattern strategy to win it. The idea is to get rid of all your seeds and that's how you win. You put the seeds in cups and, well, I can't explain it very well.

Which is probably why Osumare beat me three games in a row. It didn't help that Rachel kept talking to her about her hair, where did she get her braids done, and all that. I thought her braids looked nice but so what?

But I'm probably just aggravated because I didn't win. I'll get better at it. Whenever I work at it, I usually get better. Ms. Wachter told me that about word problems and she was right. Sometimes I have to show somebody how to do it and share my special strategies that I would rather keep secret, just so I can get somebody to play it with me. Nobody in class can beat me at Boggle or dominoes.

Well, maybe Eamon can beat me. But not every time.

Today in writing class we started a new project called the Backpack Project. This is going to be one of those long projects that actually we're not supposed to have time to do any more. Since we are secretly not spending all our time preparing for the stinky test, we're doing the Backpack Project. What we get to do is design our own original backpacks. Then we create an ad with a drawing and words that tells people why they should buy it and then we write three paragraphs telling people all the reasons ours is the best backpack ever. This is all pretend so we can make up stuff like our backpack has rockets or an MP3 player or whatever we want, as long as we have three paragraphs at the end. We also get to write a letter to a customer with three sentences with three different reasons why they should buy it. The letter can have the same things that are in the ad and in the long essay.

This whole thing is a part of writing class called Writing to Persuade. The whole idea is to persuade people about something. For this project it's this imaginary backpack and the idea is you learn how to persuade people about other stuff by giving them reasons why.

If we get all that done, Ms. Wachter says that some people can also do a Power Point. The Power Point is what she calls the challenge part, which is usually the part I like the best. But you can't do the challenge part until you finish the rest, and you have to finish the rest by this day next month, so I would need to complete it before the due date. Which I bet I could do even in time though this one looks like hard work except that Ms. Wachter wants me to do something else even first!

She finished explaining the directions and the rubric and gave out the packets for the Backpack Project. Then people got started talking about what they wanted to write about in small groups. Then Ms. Wachter came over to talk to me. I thought maybe I was in trouble but that wasn't it.

She brought my writing portfolio. She took out that Declaration I did. I kind of forgot it was in there. We both looked at it for a hot second.

Second draft of The Declaration of Education
By Darryn Y. Thomas

When it becomes necessary for students to refuse and resist unfair tests, we should tell everybody why we are impelled to rebel against such tests.

We think it's seriously obvious that all students can learn, however not in the same way every day. We believe we are endowed with good brains. We believe we have a right to a public education. To secure this right, schools have been built and funded with money from taxpayers. Public taxes pay for all the resources required by the school. Schools are then responsible for teaching students in such a way as to most likely effect their Safety and Happiness.

Students have the inalienable right to protest and petition the government for relief when schools cease to teach students how to think and instead teach them how to take tests.

Schools that create suffering instead of success should be abolished.

When a long train of Test Abuses evinces a design to hurt people under Data Despotism, it is the right and duty of the student to throw off such torture. Students have suffered patiently and the history of the present principal is a history of repeated injuries and a Tyranny over all. Power is used for the single goal of making the school look good on the mandated tests.

To prove this, here are some Facts:

She has refused to allow field trips.

She has suspended all the activities of the Student Government Association and events scheduled by the Parent Teacher Organization for the sole purpose of having all students spend all their time preparing for the SNM.

She has been mean to many of us and the teachers too.

She has deprived us of months of recess, cut off any education in Art, Music or Physical Education and limited how often we can go to the bathroom.

She has favorites and treats them better than the rest of us.

She acts like she hasn't done anything wrong and it's all our fault.

She made us compete with each other to make us do better on the test. But the way she did it doesn't work.

We asked our teachers to make her stop but they weren't allowed to stop her. She is wrong and should be stopped.

We therefore declare that these tests aren't fair and we should not have to spend months taking them. We declare that students can and should take tests and complete projects but not have all the fun sucked out of school because this test is so important to grownups.

We declare that not everyone can be above average and that an average score is not shameful anyhow. We think it's better to accept this rather than try to make everyone the same. We are created equal but we're not identical.

We further declare that any one test that claims it shows everything a student can do and what the teacher taught, is wrong. We're not going to give in and keep taking these tests all the time.

We make this Declaration knowing we're going to get in trouble but it's the principle of the thing. We therefore pledge our Time, our Resources and our Friendship to this.

Louise Parker Kelley

Darryn Y. Thomas
Maria Ramones
Rachel Baker

Then she asked me how I got the idea for it and I explained about being mad and remembering Bill saying the Declaration of Independence all the time while we were in quarantine. I mean the Declaration was practically a rap song by the time he got done. Then I showed her the first thing I wrote, the rough draft in my journal and she read it and smiled. Then I explained how Bill gave me the facsimile and how Rachel and Maria helped me and said it should be more like the original thing. I showed her all the vocabulary words I had to look up and put in my writing journal that were in the Declaration (the one Jefferson did, not mine). I forgot to tell her about sending a copy to Bill as an e-mail but it doesn't matter, we have the printed version right in front of us. I showed her the first draft on the computer, and then could tell her about the changes I made.

"Did your dad help you with this?" she asked me.

"No!"

He doesn't even know I did it. He wouldn't like me saying the school should be abolished, which means ended. Also I said we shouldn't have to take these tests. I wrote that the principal should be stopped, actually I think she should be fired but I wrote stopped in the second draft. Either way he wouldn't like it.

The amazing thing is that Ms. Wachter liked it.

She told me it was very impressive and I should be proud of it. You could have knocked me over with a pinkie eraser when she said that.

Unfortunately she likes it so much she wants me to work on it some more instead of the Backpack Project. She said it is already a super example of writing to persuade. So of course I went right into persuading her I could do both because that Backpack Project looks awesome. We compromised and I can work on the Declaration some at the beginning of class and the rest of the time on the Backpack Project.

This thing is already longer than the paragraphs I have to do for the Backpack. By the time I get done it will be even longer.

She wanted to make some editing comments on it on the computer version and she wanted to know if that was okay. Like I'm going to tell her no she can't edit what I write. Well I guess I could but I like it when she tells me how to make it better. Usually she asks a question and I figure out what it needs from that. Anyway I told her to go ahead. She put the draft back in the portfolio and asked me if I would put my first rough draft in. I'm kind of embarrassed about the rough draft but I put it in anyhow.

Then she looked strange again for a minute and asked me if I was going to give the petition to Mrs. Drew. I looked at her like she was crazy. I told her no. I didn't write it for that mean principal at all. I wrote it for me, and my friends. I totally forgot that Ms. Wachter read it when we were in the computer lab. I'm still a little shocked that she liked it.

What I did was make more work for myself. Oh well. At least I can do it during writing class. I'll still get to work in my writing group. The Backpack Project, not the Declaration, I don't want to make it a group project. It was bad enough when Maria and Rachel made their criticisms and suggestions. Besides, it's weird, I don't feel like it's just me writing this. It's like all the kids here that are sick of this stuff are inspiring me to do it and it's stronger than it could ever be if it was just me complaining. It makes me feel like I'm really doing something about the situation.

I wonder if Jefferson felt this way.

One of the French students ran away today. They were doing a regular math unit test and he said he had to go to the bathroom and he took off. The teacher knew he was gone and told them in the office and the assistant principal, Ms. Black, went out in her car to look for him. They had to call the police because they couldn't find him and somehow he got two miles away on a highway. It was really scary and when they got him back he said he was going home because he was sick of school.

The other kids said he ran away last year once but not as far and he was not as upset. So maybe it's because of the test and maybe not. He left during a regular math test too. Maybe he would hate school no matter what. I don't think the regular math tests are that bad but some kids hate them. I guess it's just like anything else. If you can't do it and it makes you feel stupid then you will hate it.

Now this kid, I wish I could remember his name, can't go to the bathroom without another kid along. I don't see what good that is, he could take off if someone's with him just as easy. Maybe they think they can catch up with him faster if there's someone to tattle.

What's really bad is that it's not safe for a little kid to run out there like that. There are bad people that could hurt him. He's hurting so bad inside I guess he doesn't care. He sure scared his teacher. She was talking to another teacher about it in French but I could kind of understand what she was saying because I heard his name.

He never tried it when we were in quarantine. That's when I wanted to do it!

Poor kid. He's not going to get to do anything on his own from now on.

I wonder what he was thinking?

Today Ms. Wachter said it was time to go with Mr. Tocs and something snapped. I told her I didn't want to go. Because. I wanted to stay right in my class and work in my group.

It turned out I had to go anyway, but I stared at the ceiling the whole time. Mr. Tocs looked very disappointed and gave me warnings, but too bad.

Rachel is sick. It wasn't a big deal when I first heard, but then I thought, what if it's TB2? Then I was really upset and I wanted to call her house to see how she was and what she was sick with but of course we not allowed to do stuff like that. Make phone calls during school. So I asked Ms. Wachter to find out about her and she said yes and called after I told her I was afraid it was TB2. And it isn't. Thanks be to God.

People are idiots. You think things are going along fine and then once again somebody has to be an idiot. We had the dumbest ever argument today. My friends are idiots. I'm probably one myself for even talking to them.

I tell Rachel that I was afraid she might have had TB2. She laughs and says no, just a fever. Maria says fever is one of the things you usually get when TB2 starts. Rachel says she doesn't have TB2 so don't worry, she's not going to die. Maria says if you died we would come to the funeral.

Then Rachel says "I bet you would be glad since then you could be friends with Darryn without me."

I told her I thought we settled all that, we are the three amigas and that's that.

So Rachel tells me, "You thought it was all settled but I'm talking about after I die you won't still be my friend, you'll be her friend."

Maria says back, why are you worried about after you die, we will go to your funeral and you'll be in heaven and it won't matter to you who is your friend because you will be friends with God.

Rachel argues back friends always matter whether you are dead or not.

Then I said, "You will be my friend forever even after we are dead, my sister is dead and she's still my sister."

Maria, even Maria who should know better, she says, "Yes but she's your sister so that's different."

I asked, "How is it different, love is love!"

Rachel says, "So now you love me, huh, now that I have died you love me."

I said, "Yes I love you and hey, look you're not dead."

Maria, I guess she starts realizing how dumb this is, she says what are we talking about love after you are dead anyway.

Rachel gets mad, yells "You don't care if I died from TB2 or not."

Maria says, "I just said we would go to the funeral."

Rachel starts crying and told her, "That doesn't mean anything I went to my great auntie's funeral and I hardly even knew her except once when she came to visit her stomach made the most amazing noises ever."

I said, "Once and for all Rachel can you stop talking about what will happen after you're dead, it's not going to happen for a long time."

And she said to me, she actually said, "How can you say that, your sister died."

That's when I walked away from both of them. I could see Angelique's face in my head. I went off by myself and I didn't cry but I wanted to and I got a face ache all around my eyes.

These are my friends that I am going to spend eternity with and they are idiots.

Today I finished the last version of the Declaration, at least I hope so. I fixed a couple of the things Ms. Wachter wrote about, but some of them I didn't change. I like some of the stuff the way I said it the first time I wrote it. I noticed that Ms. Wachter didn't write much feedback on the part about Mrs. Drew. She isn't totally okay with what I wrote but I think she knows that for me it's the truth. She did ask me when we talked about it if I really thought Mrs. Drew should be fired for cutting our recess in half, and I told her no, it's not just that. I pointed to all the other reasons and she just sighed. Then she told me that if I left that part in, she probably couldn't put it up in the Publishing Center.

I hadn't even thought about that.

I could see her point, though. Mrs. Drew is the boss of the school and maybe you can't put up a thing that says she should be fired. Not if you want to keep your job.

Now that I know I might not be able to publish it I want to do it! Plus I'm kind of disappointed that Ms. Wachter doesn't think it's a good idea to publish it.

Oh, I don't really know what she thinks of it except she gives me time to work on it so she must think it's good. I kind of don't care if she approves it or not.

That might be one of the reasons I don't want to work on it any more. What's the point, if people don't get to read it? The only ones who really know it so far are Maria and Rachel and Bill.

There's no reason why I can't show it to people though. I could let Dave read it, and Osumare too. Osumare is a pretty good writer herself even if she doesn't write the way I do. If she likes it then it really is okay.

I could print it out the next time we go to computer lab. I'll find that font that looks like handwriting and make it look more like the Declaration. I better do spell check. If people are going to read it I don't want them stopping because it has a mistake.

First I'll give it to Osumare and if she likes it I'll show to Dave and some of my other friends. Rachel might have thought it wasn't strong enough but maybe it's too strong now. I might tell Halima about it. Even though she's so old she's not in school any more so maybe she wouldn't care. She's still my half sister, so maybe she would find it interesting. We'll see.

After I thought about it I went to Ms. Wachter and asked her straight out if she didn't want to put it up in the Publishing Center because it wasn't good. She got a real funny look on her face and kept starting to say something and then not saying anything. Finally she said that it was good, it just wasn't a good idea to publish it right now. Right now? She took a deep breath and said we could publish it after the SNM was over. She looked a little scared when she said it.

So, it's good.

I knew it was good, really. I just needed to find out what she was thinking. Her opinion matters even when in my heart I know I'm writing it right. So. It's really good!

Halima read it and said it was good but kind of long. That's true. However it needs to be long.

It was strange, but for a couple of minutes today I just sat down and read it real softly out loud to myself. Just sat and read it over. It's different when you say it than when you write it. I really enjoyed reading it out loud.

I used to read the stories I wrote out loud to Jamarr and I could tell when I needed to change something. Not just when Jamarr would say, "That doesn't make sense" or other stuff like he did sometimes. Actually I could tell myself and sometimes I would change it right then when I was telling him the story. Another thing that helped when I read things to him was I could tell if it didn't work because he would get bored.

Ms. Wachter calls telling people what works and doesn't work about writing feedback. Jamarr was good at feedback. I didn't always like it but he was good at it.

I'm going to read this to him tonight after dinner. If I can get him to pay attention for a few minutes then I'll really know if I got it right. It's good but maybe it can be even better. He won't say it's good if it isn't. He's very aggravating but reliable that way, my little brother.

Jamarr liked it. He says they have too many tests in First Grade too. The part about the principal made him laugh and then he got mad.

My brother, my sister, my friends and my teacher think it's good. I knew it before they did, though.

The most awesome thing ever happened. Several awesome things one after the other. When I showed it to Dave at recess, he read it and said, okay, then he said, have you got a pencil so I can sign it? It never occurred to me he would want to sign but he wanted to, and we got a pencil and a clipboard from Ms. Garcia and he signed his name. First name and last name, because he said there are other Daves out there and he want everybody to know it's him.

Alana read it and she wanted to sign it too. Then Ahmed came over to see what was going on, and when I gave it to him to read he said he couldn't read the fancy letters and could I read it to him. So I did, and . . . wow.

I gave myself goose bumps. I usually never read my stuff to people unless it's a school assignment and I never read anything like this before. Today I just read it like I meant it and I only made a few mistakes, it was as if I almost had it memorized. You would think I would know it by heart by now but I didn't know I did, or maybe it was my heart talking.

When I looked up from the paper the second time, there were a few more kids listening, and Jeannie gave me a little nod like, don't stop.

Shay-Shay was there and he, or she, looked fierce.

Abby was listening too, and Minah.

When I was done, they applauded. I am not kidding, they did. Then Rachel and Maria came over to see what was going on, and meanwhile Ahmed was signing it and then, OMG, they all lined up to sign it! Dionne didn't even listen to the whole thing, she got there late, and she got in line to sign it! I wasn't even sure she liked me, and there she was, asking for the pen.

I just stood there. I couldn't say anything, couldn't move.

By the time we had to go inside, twelve people had signed it and more people wanted to. And Bill told me I just had to give him his own copy so he can read it again and the High Functioning Autism guys in his class can sign it if they want to. Because some of them have recess at other times. I told him I already sent him one by email and he looked confused for a minute, and then he said "Good" like he meant it.

Whoa.

This is getting to be a big deal.

So everybody, or at least some people, wanting to sign it was cool, but now what do I do with it? I went to ask Bill about it. He said they sent the original Declaration to the King of England. I don't think this is quite the same. He told me I should send it to Mrs. Drew. I don't think that's a very good idea. There's that part where I say we know we're going to get in trouble, but I don't want to get everyone in trouble. I don't want to get in trouble with her right now, to tell the truth. I don't trust her.

It was time to take some action to keep it from being big surprise trouble. So I showed it to my dad. He read it and he looked at me. It wasn't the look that Ms. Wachter gave me. It was a real thoughtful kind of look, like who are you Darryn, what are you made of, that's how he looked at me. No words, looking, but sizing me up with his eyes.

I couldn't wait for him to say something, anything, but I just sat there. I realized that what he thought mattered more than anybody else. Of course if it was wrong to do it he's also the one who can punish me.

He said, "You wrote this?"

I nodded. I couldn't talk.

He said again, "You wrote this," and I nodded again. "No one helped you write it?" Another nod. I must have looked like one of those bobblehead dogs.

Ms. Wachter wanted to know if he helped me and he wants to know if she helped me, and they really ought to talk to each other more.

Then I said, "Oh, Rachel helped me some, and Maria, and Bill. They told me how to make it better. Stronger. Clearer. Especially Bill."

"Is Bill a teacher?"

"No, he's a kid, only in another class. The HFA class."

"But he is a child."

"Yes." (I'm not supposed to say "Yeah" to my dad. He doesn't like it. It's yes or don't say anything.)

Dad knows Rachel and Maria, I didn't have to explain about them.

"Your teacher did not help you?" he asked.

"No, she just told me some stuff I could improve, and told me how to figure out my spelling and here, I used the wrong word but she knew what I meant so now it's right. She knew I was trying to make it like the Declaration of Independence."

"Yes, I know. In my citizenship classes, we read the Independence Declaration. We read it in high school in Cameroon too. It is a very important thing."

"Yes, it is."

Then, I couldn't stand it, but he read it again.

Then he looked at me and smiled. I could see almost all his teeth, the smile was so big. He read it again, or maybe only part, and he chuckled a little.

"Why did you show this to me?" he asked.

"Because I don't know if it's good."

"You do know."

"I do?"

"Yes."

He was right. I did know. I wanted him to say it was good too but he just smiled and that was better in a way.

I still don't know what to do with it.

He didn't say anything about what I said about Mrs. Drew in it or how schools that don't teach kids enough should be abolished. Which is a fancy word for closed down. Maybe he doesn't think I need to do anything else with it. No, I'm not going to go back into wondering what people think. It's my writing. I get to decide what to do with it. Maybe I'll just put it in my writing portfolio and that's that. It would be the simplest thing, that's for sure.

Bill printed out a copy of the Declaration I gave him and all his HFA buddies signed it. I don't know them as well but everyone in his class signed it. He also got some of the French Immersion students to sign it! I noticed Veronica signed it Veronique, and I couldn't read Maureen's signature but Bill told me it was her. He even got somebody named Nanette, she's in Third Grade, and then there were Kelly, Veronica, Charlene, Lisa and Linda, and one I couldn't tell what they wrote but it was a signature. Most of the kids didn't put their last names but that's okay.

I am embarrassed I never even thought to show it to the French kids. Bill says they are mad about the injustice of it all too.

Bill's signature is really big. He did that on purpose. He said he wanted his to be like John Hancock, who had the biggest signature of all the signers of the Declaration of Independence. The thing is, his handwriting is not as good as John Hancock's but I decided not to mention it. After all, mine isn't either.

I went back to see how Jefferson signed his, since he wrote it. He didn't even put his whole first name. He just put "TH," which stands for Thomas of course.

I just realized his first name is my last name. Hmmm.

Bill didn't ask me what I'm going to do with these signed Declarations and I'm glad he didn't because I still have no idea. He said his teacher, Mr. Etheridge, read it and said, "I wish I could sign it!"

Next week is the SNM test. The power went out at school and I heard a teacher say, "Oh no, we have to do the test practice today, we can't have no power!"

I couldn't help it but I thought, we've never had power when it comes to the SNM.

John asked Ms. Wachter today why we have to take the test. He talked to me yesterday about it, saying we should get a break because we were in quarantine. I really didn't want to hear that. This test sucks in some kind of way for every single kid who has to take it. I am sure of that. Then afterwards, if the results aren't what folks want, then they blame the teachers and the kids. They don't think, what is this test supposed to prove? People who are not kids want the test to be hard and want it to prove that everyone in school in America is smarter than kids in other countries, as if Americans have different brains. Except Americans hate to lose, so they blame something else when it doesn't work out that way. This is what I heard Maria's auntie say about the war we have been in in Afghanistan for more years than I have been alive, that Americans can't stand to see when they've lost so they just keep going. So this test is supposed to prove something about schools and when the result isn't good, it just cannot mean the test is not fair. So yes, we have to take it, even if we were in quarantine, John.

I suppose John should have put a note in the issue bin instead of asking it out in class. I remember she gave us lots of reasons the first time we talked about it. This time she looked at John and said, "Because it's the law," and then she went right back to teaching us about theme. So I guess that's the theme of the standardized test: "It's the law."

We all have to pass the test. That's what is expected. Required. That's the law. It's not likely that we'll all pass it, but it's the law.

My teacher is looking at me. She can see I haven't even opened the test booklet. What a stupid word, booklet. Like a book that was born too small to count. But this booklet is big, a big deal, it's supposed to measure me, my teacher, my school and just how much I learned this year. This booklet cancelled all the art and music and physical education classes. It changed the lunch schedule, got rid of recess, scared teachers and kids without making a single sound. Pretty big booklet. Don't want to open it.

I don't want to do this test. Even though I did it last year and it wasn't a big deal then. I think it was shorter, for one thing. But if I don't do it this time, if I just refuse, it won't really mean anything. They will just ignore it. Ms. Wachter already told me that.

I've got my plan, my secret, but it might not work and I could get in big trouble. Even if I'm really careful. But if I don't do it, I won't be able to stand myself.

"You may begin, " she says, and everybody starts looking at the test booklet, except me.

I don't want to begin. I'd like to throw something instead.

There's nothing like a long reading test to ruin a good story. Or your whole day. This is the reading and writing test we are going to take for next TWO HOURS and then another TWO HOURS tomorrow. After that there's one day break, then the test will ruin all the fun of math for the next two days after that and then it's OVER.

Right now I wish I could just refuse to do it but then they would just flunk me. They'd tell me I didn't do my best. Do your best on the big test, it's all over the school, big posters made by kids who won't take the test, and some of the words on the posters aren't even spelled right! So what's that about, besides making the little kids make posters about a test they don't have to take and can just fear for a few years?

A kindergartener asked me this morning, "Did you eat a good bra-fast?" He was worried about me because of this test because whether we have a good school or not depends on how we do! Why should a five-year-old be scared about that?

Or a ten-year-old like me, for that matter.

When we were all stuck together in quarantine I liked Fourth Grade.

Well. Parts of it. Worrying about catching TB2 was not fun. Sharing a bathroom with that many people was horrifying. But actually doing school that way was amazing most of the time. I think I learned more than I ever had before, faster too.

But I never thought the next part of Fourth Grade would be like this.

I'm looking at my teacher while she writes the time the test is starting on the board. She looks like a stranger today. She won't help me at all. Not allowed. How is that possible?

This is the woman who was so strong and good to us when we had to go into quarantine. This is the woman that I followed on that bad mad day, the one I lived with for months, and I thought I knew her.

My friend Maria is busy working on the test, so maybe I should do the same.

No! I won't give in! This isn't right and if I just give in, it's as if I agreed that we get to be treated this way. It isn't right.

Rather think about something else. Even something bad.

That scary day months ago when it started, when we had to just get up and go. Not allowed to take anything with us, just go. So weird. I will always remember it. Never forget it, ever. Parts of it were terrible, parts were great. Never thought I'd wish I were back there. Wish this classroom and the test would just fade away.

It's done. Now it's the end of the first day of the test and we are celebrating. Ms. Wachter turned on the music and we're having popsicles later and I'm so glad the first day is over. The test isn't too bad for me but I can tell it's hard for some other people. It sure is boring. It's like doing six of those mazes in the fun activity books one after the other. By the time I do number five I'm sick of mazes.

The first part took half an hour. The longest half hour in the history of the universe. Then we got to stretch and drink a little cup of water and then we did the next test, which was longer and even more boring, except this one part with a poem, that was kind of interesting. I wouldn't have minded reading that and talking about it in class.

I don't remember much of it. Which is fine.

Ms. Wachter collected our scratch paper. We can't keep it, it's against the rules. Kurt was upset. He drew a really cool dragon. He showed it to me when we were on our next break. I don't understand how a picture of a dragon is a problem. Maybe if it was eating somebody in our class.

The second day of the reading and writing test is worse. Everybody knows how it's going to be. I just kept getting madder and madder inside. When we finished the first one, I just leaned back and stared at the ceiling. Ms. Wachter has put posters and our word wall on the ceiling. I was staring at this one poster, about cause and effect. I started thinking about my Declaration, and how I wanted to cause something with it, I just didn't know what. Then I looked over at Ms. Wachter's desk and she still has that sign up, "Stop whining and start a revolution."

I looked over and Rachel was staring at the board looking bored and tired. I saw Maria looking even more tired and she was twisting her hair like she does when she's upset. John was chewing on his pencil and looked aggravated.

We got up to do the stretch and touch our toes that we can do in between the tests, and I thought again about how hard this test and getting ready for it has been on everyone.

That's when I decided that enough was enough. I stood up from "touch your toes" and went and sat down. When she gave me the test I turned the pages until I found the first box for a BCR. The question was something about what was the first event in the story. Instead of writing about that, I wrote . . . the first part of my Declaration.

I had to write it really small and even then I could only fit the first long sentence in the box. There was a little room left but not enough to fit the rest of it. I couldn't remember most of the second paragraph but I remembered the part about schools teaching us how to take tests instead of how to think. I put part of that in the box and the rest underneath the box. If you don't fit it inside the box it doesn't count, but mine won't count anyway, so who cares? I tried to write what I could of the rest of the first part, about Data Despotism, I got that in. Then I signed it!

Then I went back and did the rest of the test as fast as I could because that took a long time. I got most of the questions, at least I answered them, but there wasn't time to answer the last two. I answered the second BCR in it the regular way but I made it really short. I did it mostly to show I do know how to do a BCR! Of course I wrote several yesterday, but still.

Anyway when she said "Pencils down, time's up," I stopped. I closed the test book. I looked straight ahead and tried not to show anything on my face. Then I put my head down like I was tired. Which I was, but not normal tired. It was what-have-I-done tired and there was a little tummy ache with it.

When she gave out snack I didn't want to eat it and it was my favorite, rainbow goldfish. I did drink the juice box. I was really really thirsty. I thought about asking if I could go to the bathroom but decided to wait. She might ask me if I was all right. Teachers always want you to answer the questions honestly. I can't tell her.

I started in on the next test, the last one, just reading and answering the questions. I just wanted to get it done. But then there was this BCR. The question was about character traits. And this time I figured I could fit more in the box, since I'd had a little practice, and it was at the bottom of the page, so I could put in more words there.

So I wrote about the character traits of the principal, as much as I could, and I wrote the last sentence of the Declaration only a little shorter and I signed that one too!

Madame Blanche was looking at me and I realized I was smiling. So I stopped doing that and got busy with the rest of the questions, which would make anybody stop smiling. This time I think I missed at least three of the questions but I'm not sure because I stopped when she said to stop, didn't even turn the page to see what was left.

Ms. Wachter collected the tests in the box and all our scratch papers and pencils. She told us what to do while we put the desks back the regular way. The assistant principal, Ms. Black, came and got the tests. She didn't look in the test books. Neither did Ms. Wachter. All they checked was how many there were and whether our names are on them.

Alejandro dropped some of his cheese goldfish and Ms. Nickles, the ESOL teacher, stepped on them by accident. I looked at the crunched fish and thought, that's going to be me when they find out.

Maybe they won't. Maybe they just send off the tests — Ms. Wachter said they don't grade them, they get scanned by a computer and then some other people read the BCRs and decide what's a 3.

So I'll just get a zero.

I don't care. It was worth it.

I went to the bathroom today and it was a mess. There was stuff all over and bad words on the stalls. Some of the bad words were about the test. Some of the bad words weren't spelled right.

I mean really. If you're going to write a cuss word at least spell it right, come on. Of course it was kind of a long word.

This morning I was walking up the school steps to go to class today and just for a minute I remembered a day when we were in quarantine. I was in the lobby of the sanctuary, looking out from the chained doors at the big steps in front. First I was thinking about how Maria would like to decorate those glass doors. She makes a kind of art called stained glass and she could make that plain glass into a pretty design. Then I stared at the steps. The steps out. These were such long, interesting steps, like there are in front of the Lincoln Memorial but not as many as that, all interesting grey stone. I was looking at those pretty steps and hating them because I couldn't go out and play on them, run up and down them, sit on them and talk to my friends in the sunshine. I felt trapped and the synagogue and its steps were horrible.

Mr. Rabin came in and asked me what I was thinking, and so I told him.

He said to me, "I understand, but these steps and this place can be wonderful. We have this special time, called Simhat Torah, where we go outside and we dance down the steps. We hold hands and we celebrate our book and being the people Israel and we sing. Over there, you can't quite see it, across the street there is another synagogue, and they stop the traffic and come over here to us or we go over to them and we all dance and have fun on that night. If you could do that on these steps, you wouldn't hate them."

I didn't say I agreed with him but I did think about it. Perhaps if they were my steps to dance on I wouldn't hate them.

Now here I was, on the steps to my school, much smaller of course, but I used to like these steps. I would run up them. I wanted to get inside, get breakfast, go out to my portable classroom, see my friends and learn something new every day.

Instead I am going up the steps very slowly and wishing I was somewhere else.

I hate these steps. I wish I had the other ones back.

Math tests are not as hard as some of my friends think. I didn't mind the math SNM too much, until the third test today. By then I was tired and even having the snack right before it didn't help that much. There were three problems I had no idea how to answer it, so I just guessed. When I had to do the BCR for that I just drew something. It sort of had to do with the problem. If I leave it blank I won't get any points but if they see I put something maybe I'll get a point for trying.

Michael was working away at it, he was doing much better than we were doing the reading tests these past two days. I shouldn't have been even looking but I wasn't trying to read his paper. I was just noticing. The way we moved the desks around, I couldn't read it anyway, he's too far away.

The math tests are more like the ones we have at the end of the units. The practice tests were harder than this. We only did one practice test but I remember it was hard. Going back over the whole thing in class was even harder.

I know we're going to relax and take it easy this after-noon, but I'm pretty pooped. I wish I could take a nap or something. I don't even want to go out for recess and that's not right, since we finally got our whole recess back.

Ms. Wachter says we will have the last test on Mon-day of next week and that's it. She said we're going to watch a movie and have popcorn when it's over. We're not supposed to watch movies. The parents complained that we were always watching movies at indoor recess. That was last year, not this year, but they decided that we shouldn't see movies much any more. If we do, it's supposed to be connected to the lesson, like we got to see Charlotte's Web after we finished reading the book. It was after we wrote the summaries, which was kind of hard to do for a chapter book. It's true that if they could just watch the movie instead of reading the book that's what lots of kids would do. But America makes some of the best movies, it should be patriotic to watch movies!

Besides, it's fun.

Bayra was crying today when we started doing the last of the math tests. Then she wanted to go to the bathroom but she couldn't since the test started. Then Ms. Wachter looked at Madame Blanche, who is always in here when we take the SNM tests, and Madame Blanche threw up her hands and Ms. Wachter closed Bayra's book and told her to go ahead, go to the bathroom.

She whispered to Madame Blanche that Bayra could take the makeup test if she was gone for a long time.

I didn't even know there were makeup tests. It figures. No matter what you can't get out of it. Maybe if you got TB2. Or if you're dead. If you're dead you don't have to take the test. It's too hard to hold the pencil!

We came in this morning and I couldn't believe it, there were practice tests on our desks! The SNM was supposed to be over yesterday, and here are these things again! At least it's a small one, not many pages, it's even one that we already did. We already scored it. I know what I got. I probably remember most of the answers. We're going to do it again, for what? I just can't stand it. This is not morning warmup. This is morning meaness.

She told us we wouldn't have to do all the practice tests before the SNM, so I guess she wants us to do them now. It's no fair!

I raised my hand to tell Ms. Wachter this wasn't fair and she ignored me!

She said, "Everybody pick up your test by the top right hand corner. Now turn it sideways so it is horizontal."

I can't believe she's giving us directions on how to pick up the stupid test. This is as bad as when we had to check the back of the real test to make sure our names and student numbers were on it. And horizontal? You can't even read it that way. She's even saying the directions that same dull way like she did for the test.

And then she said, "Now rip it down the middle!"

And we did!

"Now tear it again!"

And we did!

And she brought around the trash can and we threw it away!

Now that's what I call finishing a test.

What a wonderful Friday!

It's so good to have school back the regular way. In music class we had a music lesson. In Science Lab we did an interesting experiment creating water pollution in beakers. We have a project for homework. We solved math problems. We went to lunch and recess and got to eat and have some fun. After lunch we read stories and did spelling games. In three weeks we're going on a field trip.

The Special Education teacher came for the Special Ed kids and they wanted to go because it was going to be learning to read, not endless test practice. Not the tall ESOL teacher. The other one, the special education teacher, Mrs. Marjorie Meredith, who is always helping kids learn new stuff.

Some kids were complaining about the homework project. Other kids were arguing about who had what job again. Kateri said it was her turn to pass the papers and Dena said it was hers. It turned out Kateri was right because we looked on the job board. The point is, we had to do that. Nobody has argued with each other about jobs for weeks. I think we were too depressed or stressed or something.

In reading class we had reading groups and a group got in trouble for talking instead of finishing their work. We got a ton of papers to take home because it's Friday and they always give us all these papers to give our parents to read about all kinds of stuff. John threw and eraser at Ernie and Ernie threw it in the trash can and they both got a time out.

It's been glorious. School is back!

I can't even remember where we're going on the field trip. It doesn't matter.

Oh, it's time to line up and she had to flick the lights so we'd get quiet! Yippee!

Instead of going to our special I got told to go to the principal's office today. I was scared it was about what I wrote on the SNM, that part I remembered of the Declaration. But it wasn't about that.

That reporter that interviewed me for the radio during quarantine was there, and she wanted to do another interview with me for her blog. Mrs. Drew was smiling about it and acting like she thought I was the best student ever. Mrs. Drew doesn't even know me. Boy do I wish Mrs. Hayes-Roberson would get better and come back.

Mrs. Drew wanted her to do the interview right there in her office, probably she wanted to be interviewed too. But Liz Hunt said it would be better to go somewhere else, where there was background noise of other kids doing something. This makes radio more interesting. Then Mrs. Drew got a little huffy and said we didn't have a noisy school. You can tell she spends most of her time in her office now.

Liz Hunt showed Mrs. Drew a letter from the Superintendent that must have said it was okay for Liz to talk to me.

Anyway, we left went to sit outside the music room since my class was in there making music. Well, sounds, anyhow.

Mrs. Drew stayed in her office. Which was fine.

We talked about what it's like back at school and being out of quarantine. I don't know exactly how we got to it, but I started talking about how I missed parts of being in quarantine, and she wanted to know why, and I told her that the lessons were more fun then. How come, she wants to know.

Naturally I explained about having to spend every blessed minute lately getting ready for the SNM. So I had to tell what the SNM was, and I couldn't remember what it stands for, except Standard Measure, but I remember what I called it one time, the stupid nasty monster and I told her that instead. She laughed. Then she asked me what it was like to take the test after all that practicing. So I said it was okay but boring and I hope I did okay on it. Which is true. I hated getting ready for it but after all that, I still want to win.

Of course I didn't tell her that we didn't practice as much as some of the other classes. I didn't want to get Ms. Wachter in trouble.

I didn't want to get her in trouble, but somehow I wasn't worried about myself. Because I ended up telling her about what I did on my BCRs, about the short version of the Declaration of Education.

Liz Hunt is so easy to talk to, you end up saying more than you meant. Naturally she wanted to read it, see what I was talking about, and I should have expected that. I got nervous. I mean, it really is pretty strong writing.

The test is over and it isn't such a big deal any more. Nobody has asked me about my Declaration since the test. Ms. Wachter never did put it up in the publishing center and I forgot to remind her.

Well, maybe I forgot on purpose.

Liz said we wouldn't read it out loud if I didn't want to, but she still wanted to read it. So we went to class and my class was still in Music so we were the only ones in the classroom. We were lucky the door was unlocked. I got out my writing portfolio and showed it to her.

She read it and she looked at me and she said, "You really are angry at the injustice of it, aren't you?"

I was glad she didn't ask me if I really wrote it or anything like that.

She understood, right away, first time reading it.

I remember dad telling me that I knew it was good. Suddenly I wasn't nervous about it. I was proud of it and I was so glad I wrote it.

So when she said, "Do you want to read it so people can hear it on the radio?' I said yeah. That's what I did next. She recorded it as part of our interview.

The Declaration of Education

By Darryn Y. Thomas

When it becomes necessary for students to refuse and resist unfair tests, we should tell everybody why we are impelled to rebel against such tests.

We think it's seriously obvious that all students can learn, however not in the same way every day. We believe we are endowed with good brains. We believe we have a right to a public education. To secure this right, schools have been built and funded with money from taxpayers. Public taxes pay for all the resources required by the school. Schools are then responsible for teaching students in such a way as to most likely effect their Safety and Happiness.

Students have the inalienable right to protest and petition the government for relief when schools cease to teach students how to think and instead teach them how to take tests.

Schools that create suffering instead of success should be abolished.

When a long train of Test Abuses evinces a design to reduce people under Data Despotism, it is the right and duty of the student to throw off such torture. Students have suffered patiently and the history of the present leader is a history of repeated injuries and a Tyranny over all. Power is used for the single goal of making the schools look good on the mandated tests.

To prove this, here are some Facts:

Our principal has refused to allow field trips.

She has suddenly suspended all the activities of the Student Government Association and events scheduled by the Parent Teacher Organization for the sole purpose of having all students spend all their time preparing for the SNM.

She has been mean to many of us and to teachers too.

She has deprived us of months of recess, cut off any education in Art, Music or Physical Education and limited how often we can go to the bathroom.

She has favorites and treats them better than the rest of us.

She acts like she hasn't done anything wrong and we are to blame for the test outcomes.

She made us compete with each other to make us do better on the test. But this doesn't work and is not fair.

We asked our teachers to make her stop but they weren't allowed to stop her. She is wrong and should be stopped. Her boss, Superintendent South, must stop this mandatory testing.

We therefore declare that these tests aren't fair and we should not have to spend months taking them. We declare that students can and should take tests and complete projects but not have all the fun sucked out of school because this test is so important to grownups.

We declare that not everyone can be above average and that an average score is not shameful anyhow. We think it's better to accept this math fact rather than try to make everyone the same. We are created equal but we're not identical.

We further declare that any one test that claims it shows everything a student can do and what the teacher taught, is wrong. We're not going to give in and keep taking these tests. We believe the Superintendent is wrong and we request that these tests be changed immediately.

Darryn YochangkoThomas

I am proud of it but I wanted Liz Hunt to promise not to tell Mrs. Drew all about it. She said she was surprised Mrs. Drew didn't insist on having a teacher along with us for the interview, but she wasn't going to tell her every detail. She said it might get cut out of the interview at the studio anyway. Then she winked at me.

She asked me if I wanted her to erase it off the tape. I was looking at the Declaration, and this was the one everybody signed, and I thought no, I don't want my words erased. I want them heard.

But I still hope Mrs. Drew doesn't listen to NPR.

I told my dad about the interview. He gave me a hug. He didn't say much but I knew. He's got my back.

I hope I wake up from this nightmare soon.

The interview went out on the radio.

It got mentioned online in the newspaper and on some blogs.

Somebody sent parts of it around to teachers as an e-mail after that.

Then it got put on something I never knew about called a list serve, which is this online e-mail group that is for the PTA.

I don't know exactly what happened after that, it just kept going around to more places. Somebody in Baltimore made a video and they were dressed up in the clothes they wore back in the old days with the three cornered hat and all and they read it and posted it on YouTube.

Somebody sent it in to people in Congress. Somebody else, a grownup whose name I forget, said they wrote it and got in trouble because they didn't write it, I did.

It got put on a T-shirt. It got a mention on Twitter. Somebody wanted to make a documentary about it. Huh?

Some reporter tracked down Mrs. Bonuss, who taught me in kindergarten. She said I was one of the best students she ever taught and could do long sentences even in kindergarten when I was just learning English. Then she said that the tests have gotten ridiculous, that it was about time something was done about it. They asked her if she wasn't worried about getting in trouble for talking to the media and she laughed and said, "I'm retired, I can say whatever I want. What are they going to do to me?"

On another station, on the radio, there was an interview with some teacher from our school who said Mrs. Wachter was an excellent teacher and she believed that I wrote the Declaration myself. The person on the radio said they were keeping her identity confidential. I couldn't be sure, but I think it was Mrs. Meredith, the Special Education teacher. Maybe she figured it was safe to say things on the radio since they can't see you?

It was very odd, hearing people talk about me on TV and on the radio, even if they were saying very good things. It made me feel kind of nervous. I had to have a coke to calm my tummy down. I mean, Mrs. Bonuss actually knows me and she knows what she's talking about. She was a pretty good teacher but in a way I'm surprised she even remembered me. I know I had fun learning with her. Her room was full of interesting things to do, from the sandbox to the clay center and all the lovely books. She was also very calm, which is important when there lots of little kids doing things all over the place and sometimes pretty loud. Well, I was loud, that was for sure, I was glad she didn't tell them that in the interview.

Elizabeth, the little kid from when we were in quarantine, found me in the bus line at dismissal. There was this tall cute teenage girl with big fluffy hair and a long face next to her, and Elizabeth introduced us, "Darryn, this is my cousin Clare and she has something, she wants you to, well, you tell her!"

Turns out Clare has a copy of my Declaration that she downloaded and printed from who knows where, and she wants my *autograph*. Wants me to sign it. So I did, and the next day there were three more older kids I didn't know at dismissal and they all wanted me to sign theirs and a teacher came over and was all worried because they didn't go to our school and why were they talking to Roosevelt students? When she found out she got even more upset about it and got on her walkie-talkie to tell the office and the next thing was Mrs. Drew came zipping out to tell them off or something, only by then I'd signed the papers and they were gone.

So now I get escorted to the bus line and no one is allowed to talk to me even if it is another kid that just wants my autograph and I'm not supposed to talk to any of them but excuse me but I will talk to them if I want.

But mostly I just felt like, what the heck is going on?

Somewhere in the middle of all this I got in big trouble and so did Ms. Wachter. Or maybe it was trouble from the beginning.

First they told my dad that my test scores would not count. I think that was the first thing. They tried to kick me out of school but they couldn't do it yet because Liz Hunt found out and she told them she would put that they did that on the radio and how could they justify doing it? Because they were going to have to find reasons that would stand up in court.

Mrs. Drew wants to get rid of me. Or shut me up.

They said I cheated on the test. Ms. Wachter asked how could they know that when the tests aren't even finished being scored yet.

Oh, I'm getting a big headache just remembering the stuff that busted loose from this. Right now I'm sitting in the counselor's office waiting to talk to her again. Even the counselor, Mrs. Bondanza, says there's nothing the matter with me except I've been accused of something and it may not be true. She winked and said, "It's good to be able to have a counseling session that's not about how much everything has changed for the worse since TB2. I know people need to talk about that, but you are something else!"

I think she likes my Declaration, actually, but she can't say that because, well. She can't. So I have to talk to her again. The Tyrant Drew is still in charge.

It's mainly Mrs. Drew. Besides me, Mrs. Drew is trying to fire Ms. Wachter since Ms. Wachter let me write it in class. Or didn't stop me from writing it. Or Ms. Wachter wrote it and told me to put it in my test. The story keeps changing but they, or Mrs. Drew, have not gotten to fire Ms. Wachter yet. There is no proof I cheated since I didn't.

Rachel's mom, Mrs. Baker, is the one who told us about some of it because she is a leader in the PTA and they have a list serve where people text all the time now about all this.

Mrs. Drew told me not to talk to the media because she's says it's a violation of my privacy. Really.

She must be crazy. She's not worried about my privacy or my anything. She's mad as she can be and she wants to shut me up. She wants to kick me out, it's called "expelled." But she hasn't done it yet.

What she ought to be is embarrassed. All I did was say all the things she did and, well, I did say she ought to be fired.

They, meaning Mrs. Drew again, won't let any reporters on school grounds. All the teachers are on what she calls a media lockdown and what the teachers call being muzzled. Mrs. Drew also posted a request that parents not talk to reporters. Mrs. Baker says they can't do a media lockdown, it's against the right of free speech. Other PTA folks say that a reporter should never have been allowed to talk to a student even before, when we were in quarantine. None of these folks said anything about me not talking back then, they're only saying it now.

Some of the famous grownups have their own shows and they can say anything they want about me and there is nothing I can do. They all seem like they are angry all the time. One guy even made fun of my *family* and he said "The idea that this cab driver's family who should be grateful to be allowed to stay in this country and get a free education criticizing our wonderful school system is preposterous." People got mad at that and he apologized. But I don't believe him. He still thinks what he said is right, he just said he was sorry because the people who sponsor his show probably told he had to say it or get fired.

Some other people have been doing interviews and have said stuff like "This girl just doesn't want to take the test and she's lazy really," and I probably would have flunked it if I'd just taken it like everyone else.

"She wrote that, if she did write it herself, which is hard to believe, to hide the fact she can't handle the standardized test," one woman said on the local news, and I felt my hands curl up into fists so tight it hurt.

Somebody was interviewing some fat-faced old man in a suit online and the man said that, "The public schools in this country are broken beyond repair and this controversy is proof. All of them should be closed and replaced with charter schools and private schools with some public subsidies so that parents can be certain that their tax dollars are being used effectively. Their children will gladly take these tests because the results will hold schools accountable."

There are things being said on Twitter and Facebook and all over the place and most of them are horrible. Some people wrote posts that said dad and me should be deported back to Cameroon. I guess it is only a free country where you can say what you want to say if you are born here. Otherwise forget it.

One man was really mad, and he had about the strangest things to say. He said he has a job with one of the testing companies and he said what I was doing was going to "take away jobs. Stopping all the testing will destroy education in America." Then he cursed me and they bleeped it out but I know what he said. It was kind of scary.

I was not being any of the things they said. My name is Darryn. I am not a bad person. I am smart enough and I nearly always make an effort in class. Making your best effort is supposed to count. I know I can be stubborn. But I am not stupid or lazy.

These mean people don't even know me! I don't know who they are talking about, but it sure isn't me.

If I was smart I'd never have gotten into this mess in the first place.

However, Maria and Rachel think I did a great thing. Maria found me this great song and the verse says, "Truly *scandalo*!" She says she is so proud of my *scandalo*. Abby wrote me this note that is nothing but praise for what I wrote. That was a surprise. Alana came up and told me she was glad I did it. So did David and Ahmed. Sebastian saw me in the hall and gave me a fist bump. Kateri gave me a whole sheet of stickers! On the bus two fifth graders came over and told me they thought what I wrote was really cool and how did I ever think up the Declaration? The speech therapist, I can't even remember her name, stopped me on the way back from the bathroom and said I was her hero. Me! A hero to a grownup!

I told her I can't remember how it began and I really can't. What I remember is being fed up.

Now Mrs. Drew is fed up with *me* and I don't know if I'm even going to be able to stay in my school.

Or whether Ms. Wachter will get to keep her job.

We can fight back. They can't just kick me out.

My dad wrote a letter to the editor of the local newspaper. He said his daughter did not cheat and he thought the declaration I wrote was very good. It wasn't a very long letter. It didn't need to be. So cool, to read a letter from your dad about you in the newspaper, and there is his name, Mr. William Yochangko, right there in the paper.

The only thing I think about the Declaration now is that it's too long. I should have made it shorter and to the point, like my dad did with his letter.

Once upon a time I wrote something and showed to a couple of my friends and three of us signed it. It was just something that I wanted to share with them, that was all. To think that once I didn't want Ms. Wachter to know I wrote the Declaration on the test, and now hundreds of people know.

Including Mrs. Drew, the poophead.

Hee hee.

What a wonderful thing! Liz Hunt came through for us. Ms. Wachter was able, because of her teachers' union lawyer, to bring a recorder to the meeting with Mrs. Drew and that other dude Superintendent South. There was another teacher there too, just to be sure they were fair to Ms. Wachter. She's called *the union rep*. Her name is Ms. Maharani and she teaches fifth grade and she is the union rep too.

Then Liz Hunt took part of the recording and made it part of her radio show. Those two are so embarrassed! You can tell they just want to fire Ms. Wachter and they can't. Here is the best part of what I heard on the radio that they said:

Mrs. Drew: We find it difficult to believe that a child could write such an essay on her own. In fact, we are certain she had help.

Superintendent South: Help from an adult.

Mr. Daniel Hunter (the lawyer): Are you now accusing Ms. Wachter of writing the Declaration?

(There's a quiet part here where Mrs. Drew doesn't say anything, neither does anybody else.)

Ms. Maharani: Because if you are, you need to say it directly.

Ms. Wachter: Darryn wrote it. I have her portfolio and her journal here and can show you her first draft and subsequent drafts and my comments.

Mrs. Drew: Please don't refer to it as the Declaration. An essay by a ten-year-old is hardly the same as the real Declaration.

Mr. Hunter: Everyone calls it the Declaration of Education, Mrs. Drew, thanks to the publicity. And that's what Darryn gave it as a title. This essay by a student in your school. Are you changing your mind, to say she did write it?

Mrs. Drew: No she did not write it. When I spoke to her, she even mentioned that she had help from an older student.

Ms. Wachter: She did? Who helped her?

Mrs. Drew: Several people helped besides this boy, but he did help, he said as much when I asked him. His name is Bill.

Ms. Wachter: Bill? Who — oh, Bill in HFA, that's who you mean.

Mrs. Drew: So you know he helped her.

Ms. Wachter: Bill taught her about the original Declaration of Independence. He's memorized it, he's been to see the original document downtown, he knows all about how it was written, he knows about Thomas Jefferson — it's Bill's thing. He'll recite the whole thing himself if you give him a chance.

Mrs. Drew: Yes, he's very bright, and he did recite it for me. So he probably wrote more of this, this satire, than she did.

Superintendent South: What's HFA? Wait, I know this one, High, High Formative, what is it?

Ms. Wachter: High Functioning Autism.

Superintendent South: So this boy, is, is —

Mrs. Drew: Autistic, correct.

Superintendent South: So you think the autistic boy wrote it?

Mrs. Drew: No, I think her teacher wrote it but this boy and others helped.

Mr. Hunter: So you are accusing Ms. Wachter of being the author.

Mrs. Drew: No, no, I'm not accusing her, I'm merely saying it's my opinion that an adult must have helped her, and perhaps the most likely person is her teacher. Probably not her father. You see, this child, this girl, has a problem. She's attention-seeking, and manipulative. Ms. Wachter is probably not even aware of how she has been used. Her behavior has not been professional with regard to Darryn and probably happened as a result of the experience of quarantine. That was stressful for all, naturally, but more so for this particular teacher.

Ms. Wachter: How do you know? You weren't there. But somehow you know all this, and can diagnose it. Did you get your medical degree recently? Perhaps while we were in quarantine?

Mrs. Drew: I am merely sharing my insights based on my observations.

Mr. Hunter: Ms. Wachter, excuse me. I'd like to see if I understand what's just been said by Mrs. Drew. Because the union won't allow you to fire this teacher because you have formed an opinion with no proof, Mrs. Drew, especially since Ms. Wachter has the artifacts that prove that Darryn wrote it herself. Clearly this is a gifted student, it's not impossible that she could have thought this out for herself.

Mrs. Drew: She's an immigrant from Cameroon with English as a second language!

Mr. Hunter: She's clearly fluent in English and has been learning it since she came to this school in kindergarten. Be careful, Mrs. Drew, your implications are troubling. You've made other charges as well. You told Ms. Wachter that she violated test security —

Superintendent South: You told her that?

Mrs. Drew: I told Ms. Wachter it was possible that she had done so, and that there would need to be an investigation.

Mr. Hunter: And did you then tell her she should consider leaving her position?

Mrs. Drew: I believe I mentioned to her that if, and I did say if, Mr. Hunter, that there was an investigation and she was, uh, impacted by it, she might want to consider resigning before that happened so that her career would not suffer negative consequences. I suggested that perhaps teaching was not a good fit.

Mr. Hunter: I think what you said is that she should quit before you made certain that her contract was terminated because she helped a student cheat. That she had no business being in a classroom. Isn't that what you said?

Mrs. Drew: This isn't a courtroom, Mr. Hunter.

Superintendent South: Mr. Hunter, would you turn off that recording device please?

Mr. Hunter: Why would I do that?

Superintendent South: Very well. If you can't do that, would you excuse the two of us, Mrs. Drew and I, for a few minutes? I need to speak to the principal privately.

Ms. Maharani: Will you then examine this portfolio of Darryn's writing that Ms. Wachter has brought with her today?

Superintendent South: Certainly, certainly, and any other evidence you wish to show us. I'm willing to examine it. But if you could just excuse us for a few minutes . . .

I don't know what that Superintendent talked to Mrs. Drew about but I think she wasn't supposed to say what she said. It sure made me mad.

When they went back in Mrs. Drew hardly said anything and Superintendent South was nicer than he had been before. They didn't say much after all that.

Afterwards Liz, Ms Wachter and Mr. Hunter went and sat in the library to wait and talked about what happened. Mrs. Drew stayed in her office. The Superintendent wanted to talk to her some more. Then he would come back and talk to them a little more about "next steps."

Then Liz Hunt interviewed Mr. Hunter the lawyer and they joked around about having similar last names. He said to Liz that they didn't have a case and they would have to prove that Ms. Wachter dictated the essay to me during the test. Which they can't because there were two witnesses in the room during the test who never heard her say anything to me that she didn't say to everyone, like, you may begin or time's up. One of them was the French teacher, Madame Blanche, who was helping Ms. Wachter give us the test. She was what they call a proctor. Then there was the ESOL teacher who was helping a kid take the test. I totally forgot there were other people in there that day.

Also Ms. Maharani said that the librarian, Ms. Baxter, said she would do something that's called an Affy David that we came into the library to research the Declaration and she told us to ask Bill. Bill's teacher will testify that he brought my Declaration in to class for his buddies to sign and Bill told Mr. Etheridge, his teacher, that I wrote it. There's a teacher who all she does is the computers, Mrs. Hornlaw, and she said that she did the research and can show the dates I worked on the computer and first started writing it. I never knew the computer could remember that stuff. But Ms. Hornlaw will be able to prove it because she knows about computers and is the I.T. specialist.

Anyway I wrote it and we can prove it and that's that. Too bad for you Drew!

Liz Hunt let me listen to the whole interview from the office. I appreciated that.

She also said the assistant principal went and collected the tests and took them to the testing room to Mrs. Jones and both of them confirmed that they didn't hear Ms. Wachter tell me to do anything, which she never did, so no wonder.

Liz Hunt also said that Ms. Maharani told Ms. Wachter that "There's a lot of love for you, Kathy, in this building," and Ms. Wachter cried.

I will never understand grownups. I can't believe I'm going to be one, someday.

My dad told me that he keeps getting letters from new lawyers who want us to hire them to sue the school. He called the school secretary, Miss Kay, to find out if she is giving out our address. She said no, they are probably getting it by doing research to find it, but he still doesn't understand how they could figure out where we live because they know my name. He just wants them to stop.

We even get phone calls from them sometimes. Dad says that there is nothing to sue about and anyway I don't want to sue Ms. Wachter. Dad explained that we wouldn't be suing her, it would be the school. Well, I'm not mad at the school. The building and the kids never did anything to me.

I wouldn't mind suing Mrs. Drew. I told Dad that. He smiled but didn't say anything.

He talked to Ms. Wachter all about it today after school. She said if they did expel me, and it looks like they won't, then maybe he should consider a lawsuit. I was in the room listening to them even though it looked like I was reading and I wondered for a minute what a lawsuit was, do you wear it? Then when they kept talking I realized it just means going to court and suing, which I don't understand exactly anyhow.

Ms. Wachter said Dad might want a lawyer eventually. He asked if he could hire Mr. Hunter and she said she didn't know. Then they started talking softer and I couldn't hear what they were saying except for "conflict of interest" whatever that is.

If we had to have a lawyer Mr. Hunter would be okay.

Dad says it will be hard for them to fire Ms. Wachter. She may be against all the testing but she did have us take it and she didn't break the law. The law doesn't say you have to *practice* for the test all the time.

It does say everybody has to pass the test in a couple of years or teachers can get fired. Or if students don't do so good on the test the school has to change the staff all over, but Dad wasn't too sure about that part. Seems to me that the main thing is that nobody is allowed to fail.

Not students, not teachers. But I can't get 100% all the time, and I'm good at tests. What's so bad about making mistakes? Ms. Wachter says that's where we can learn.

Well I hope I don't get expelled. Staying home with Auntie all day would be so boring.   All my friends and even that nuisance Jamarr would be at school and there wouldn't be anyone to play with.

School will be over in about a month. I can't wait. My friends keep asking me to read the Declaration out loud and I'm getting sick of it. I tell them they get to do it instead and now Rachel is saying that we should ask Mrs. H to put it to music and sing it at a school assembly. As if, please.

I'm sitting in this room which they call a green room but it isn't green. I'm sitting here waiting to go on TV with Ms. Wachter. I'm sitting here but I'm so nervous that I'm bouncing, I guess you can't call it sitting.

We are going to be interviewed on the Ellen De-Generes show.

How is this even possible? How did I get here? Okay, a phone call, and they asked us to, I know how it all happened, and yeah, but still, how is it really happening. We agreed. We went out to the airport. We got here. They sent a limo to pick us up!

I never even get to watch the Ellen DeGeneres show myself. I'm in school when it's on, usually. Except I saw some on the internet after they invited us to come on as guests. She seems very nice. I watched her dance with the president. That was fun to see. I wonder if we will dance when we go out there?

All because of something I wrote.

This is a good thing but it's also scary.

They tape the show and show it later. But there's a real audience out there, even though we can't hear them in here. It's kind of strange, they sit there and listen to us having a conversation with somebody else.

They invited my dad but he didn't want to do it. Jamarr said he would go in dad's place but dad said no he couldn't. Thank you dad.

Ms. Wachter had to make sure ahead of time they couldn't fire her for going on TV first. Mr. Hunter said it would be okay, since my dad signed a release for me to do it so she could talk about how I wrote it and all. Otherwise what happens in the classroom is *confidential and private* and she shouldn't talk about it to anyone outside of school.

Whatever else it is, my Declaration is not private anymore!

They asked me what kind of snacks and drinks I wanted before we got here and here they are. Every single thing I wanted. Mrs. Wachter is having Dr. Pepper and I'm having coconut and pineapple juice and candied ginger and Cheez Its. Except my throat is so dry I'm not having many of the crackers. My stomach is sort of jumpy.

I can't wait to meet Ellen.

Still, how did I get here? It's ridiculous. I'm just me.

Ellen: Darryn, why do you think you wrote this Declaration?

Darryn: First I just wrote it for me, because I had such strong feelings about having to take this test. All I wanted was to use my writing to make me feel better. And it was very satisfying to write it down.

Ellen: Then what happened? You showed it to your teacher?

Darryn: No, I never meant to show it to her.

Ms. Wachter: (Laughs) Really?

Darryn: No, no disrespect. But it wasn't an assignment, I did it for me, and then I decided to show it to Maria and Rachel. They liked it, but they said I should make it stronger.

Ellen: Stronger? Saying no more tests, schools should be closed, and your principal fired wasn't strong enough for them?

Darryn; I didn't say she should be fired in the first one. Or that schools should be closed who don't teach kids enough. I don't even think I put the word *abolished* in the first draft. I only learned that word later.

Ellen: What did you say in the first one?

Darryn: I don't remember all of it, but it wasn't that. I said the tests weren't fair and the principal was a bully.

Ms. Wachter: I have a copy of it.

Ellen: With you?

Ms. Wachter: I have copies of all the drafts with me in this folder. I thought something about how and exactly when she wrote it might come up.

Ellen: Ya think? (Everyone laughs.) Okay, let's see it. Darryn, would you read it?

Darryn: Do I have to?

Ms. Wachter: You are the author.

Ellen: Yes, in spite of what some people have been saying.

Darryn: Okay, I will. I did write it, you know.

Ellen: Yes, we do know.

Darryn: Well it's really short. I forgot how short it was to start with. (Clears throat).

The Declaration of Test Independence
by Darryn Y. Thomas.

I think that we should not have to keep taking these tests. Here's why: they are not fair.

I can show my teachers that I know lots of things. But making me sit for 40 minutes and guess which one of the three answers is right.

This is bad for my whole class. We can't have all our recess, we can't have music or Art or P.E. like we used to, we can't even go to the bathroom when we need to. Our principal is a bully who doesn't care about anything but what is in our data notebooks. She doesn't care about us. She even cancelled all our field trips and the class musical.

The tests should be cancelled instead of the field trips.

The law they made that says we have to take these stupid tests should be changed.

We declare that the SNM is unfair and a big bore and we hate it.

This is the Declaration of Independence from the SNM.

(Applause. Darryn hands the paper back to Ms. Wachter and gives her a hug. Smiles.)

Ellen: Thank you, Darryn. When we get back, we'll talk about the impact this essay has had across the country. We'll be right back.

Being on TV was very interesting. I don't think I've ever had anybody listen as close to me as Ellen De-Generes did. It was like there was nobody else there sometimes. Later we found out what happened when she told people watching to send e-mails to Congress. It was thousands of people and they blew out the server when they did it! Unreal, that people could shut down the computers of Congress after seeing me on TV. Well, actually, it was more than just the people watching. What happened is that people watching called or sent tweets to other people, #DarrynDeclaration, and then — I don't know, just a whole lot of other people heard about it and sent texts and e-mails. Ms. Wachter said that people have been wanting to do something for a while and so when they heard, they all did it at once.

It's cool. It's about time.

Mrs. Hayes-Roberson is back! She has lost weight and looks tired, I think her glasses are different with thick lenses but she is still herself. So glad to see her. There isn't much left of the school year now but at least she is back and that Tyrant is gone.

She came around to every class and said hello to everyone. I wondered what DeCombe's class next to us was cheering about, then she walked in. I have missed everything about her, how she is calm and dignified, her soft accent, how she looks at me like she likes me. I don't even know what country she's from, but I feel like we are from the same place.

She came over to me and leaned down and said something like, "I've been hearing about you lately," and then she laughed so big and it was all right again.

Then she went over and shook Ms. Wachter's hand and said, "Congratulations. You sure taught somebody how to write," and Ms. Wachter disagreed, no, no, I was a writer before I got to her, and Mrs. Hayes-Roberson said, "Yes, but you helped her get stronger."

Ms. Wachter told her, "We missed you," and then they were both kind of crying for a bit and I decided to look at the word wall for a bit because I almost cried myself.

Maria passed me a note later. It said that Mrs. Hayes-Roberson was the best principal ever. I agree.

We had a party last night because, just because, my dad is so proud of me he wanted to have a party for me. Everybody came. We filled up the party room at the apartment. I got to pick the music and everything. Jamarr even hugged me. Even that was okay.

When the song came on, "We Are Family," I danced and danced. I pretended, like I always do with that song, that Angelique was dancing beside me. I miss her so much, but I can still dance with Halima and Rachel and Maria and all the girls who are strong like me.

The fudge cake was incredible. I don't know where Dad got that cake, but it was in the shape of Cameroon! and kind of near where I was born, they put my name, like it was the name of a town! Then they brought out another cake, which was all made out of ice cream, my favorite flavor which is chocolate chip, but that was the inside and the outside was cherry frosting (which does not sound like it would go with chocolate but it actually does) and the ice cream cake was in the shape of the United States! They took pictures of the cakes and they cut the Cameroon cake very carefully so I could have the piece with my name. Which was too big a piece really so

I shared it with Jamarr, he's been getting upset that I'm getting so much attention.

I love my dad. I love my family. I am so lucky to have such a family.

We throw good parties!

It is really amazing to have my own website just because I wrote the truth. We got thousands of hits after we were on TV and every time another school has a walkout or a protest about the tests, we get more. But I am not telling folks to do anything, they are doing it for themselves.

Like Bill says, that's because that's how we are in America. If we don't like what is going on, we get together to change it.

I didn't expect it to turn out this way when I sat down to write. Some days I still can't believe it. It never gets in the way of being glad, though.

Today we put up a new selfie of me and Rachel and Maria all in those old three-corner hats they used to wear back in the colonial days. Rachel had a song to go with it: "My hat it has three corners. Three corners has my hat. And if it had not three corners, it would not be my hat." Now I can't get that silly song out of my head, thanks Rachel.

So this cool pictures shows us in the hats. I am holding a pen made from a feather (the pen doesn't really work) and a scroll that is supposed to be my Declaration (but it is just a scroll). I love the picture. We are all smiling but not being too goofy. It's funny and serious all at the same time.

Wheee! I'm in a limousine. With my friends and others. Me and Rachel and Maria and Maria's mom and this woman, Ms. Crockett, we are all talking a mile a minute. What a wonderful day this has been. We're going to meet Whoopi Goldberg! We flew on a plane to California! They picked us up in this limo and Ms. Crockett is telling us all about what we're going to do when we get to the studio and there is going to be a show all about us! Rachel is talking about the buildings and Maria is holding my hand so hard it almost hurts and they even have a thing in the car which has sodas we can drink and I'm just so happy I don't think I could ever get any happier.

Bill was invited to go with us but he said he didn't want to do it. I will make sure to tell about his part and how he helped. He asked me not to talk about that he has autism. It's not anybody's business. What he has, is friends. That's all.

I thought I could not be any happier but I was wrong.

Whoopi Goldberg talked to all of us and we had a good time talking to her. She asked us to read the Declaration to the cameras and we all three read it together like we practiced. She wanted to know what kind of games I liked best and I told her anagrams. That's how we found out what an anagram is, when you switch the letters around in the word to make a new word. We tried making some up and everybody said my middle name, which is my dad's family name, Yochangko, was the best one since you had so many letters in it you could made more words and phrases from it. Thomas wasn't so good that way. We did Hotmas and Smatho though.

Then we waited while there was a break while they moved cameras and stuff around. Still talking a little.

And. And And.

Whoopi looked at me all twinkling and said she had a surprise for the little lady who started the revolution. I thought it was going to be, I don't know, maybe a computer to write with? I didn't have much time to think about it.

Because Mom walked out on the set and I couldn't think about anything.

Mom was sitting down next to me.

And and and.

She was holding me in a hug and I couldn't breathe but I could and there she was.

She touched my face with her hands and I cried and she cried and we sat there still holding each other for all the rest of the show.

She talked to Whoopi and Whoopi talked to me but I don't know what they said and didn't talk much. I looked and looked at mom.

I didn't need to talk, and besides I couldn't. The words went down and hid in my heart and didn't go up near my mouth.

Which was fine, since I love you had already gotten out from both of us and that was all we needed to say.

She's here. Whoopi got her here. Whoopi is going to make sure she stays here, I don't know how, she talked about how some important people she knows in Congress will help but I couldn't understand it except the important part, which is, mom is here. With me.

She is going back to Washington with us and going to live with somebody Whoopi knows there. I can go see her all the time. She can come see me.

She is going back on the plane with us.

Thank you Whoopi! Thank you for bringing Imani Thomas to America. I did say it to you on the show but I will say it again for the rest of my life.

It's unbelievable. They want to write a book about me. These two people called my dad and want to write a book about me. I forget their names.

He told them no, I can write my own book!

I told him, if they will pay us money, we might want to let them. Then we had to laugh.

I can't write it yet myself. Well, maybe.

This is ridiculous. Even though I am enjoying it.

Now somebody wants to make a movie about me and Ms. Wachter. Mostly me, but she will be in it. And Maria and Rachel. And my mom. And Bill if he wants to. This woman who makes movies was very nice and I hope dad says yes. We could do it over the summer. I wonder how they would do it. They couldn't show me writing the Declaration because I already did it.

It's an interesting life lately. Somebody wants to make a movie about what happened, that's amazing!

How can they do that when it's already happened? I guess they have a way.

One day Bill asked me if I was sorry that I wrote the Declaration. He says he would hate people always talking pictures and asking for interviews and all that stuff. There are people who feel like that who don't have autism, so it isn't that. I don't like some of it but I'm not like Bill, I like most of it. Actually I pretty much like people in general. I don't always say good things about all of them, but I like people mostly.

They're not going to pay attention to me for too long, anyway. Someone else will do something and that will be the next big deal.

I'm not sorry I wrote my Declaration. I'm sorry that kids still have to take a test that doesn't measure what it says it does, and that it messes up some of the best parts of school. The SNM would be bad enough if it didn't take so much time and be so painful. I'm sorry that the law that makes schools do this is still around.

If I hadn't written it, Mom would still be living in Cameroon.

So I'm very glad that I wrote it.

Mrs. Baker asked me if I would do it again. Yes. If I had it to do over, I would. I had to take a stand.

Right now I have to go call Mom. We're going to the National Archives to see the Declaration of Independence! Then we're going to a museum.

I don't know which one but it doesn't matter. I'm going somewhere with my mom. That's what matters.

Liz Hunt called me today. I love it when I pick up the phone and it's someone I actually want to talk to. We had to get caller ID because so many times it isn't someone we want to talk to any more. Our phone rings much more than it used to . . . .

Congressional hearings are about to start about the NCLB law. The government has been giving out something called waivers, and at the same time giving out more money to schools that agree to do more tests. So the grownups are still crazy. Do they have to take tests all the time for the jobs they do? Do the people in the Congress have to take hours of tests to keep their jobs? I bet if they did they would hire somebody to do it for them and make that the law for them!

Liz thinks I should go hear the hearing, ha-ha. Somebody called Marian Wright Edelman is testifying there today. So this lady runs something that sounds cool, the Children's Defense Fund. Liz said she'll explain what that is to me.

Liz wants me to come to the U. S. Capitol building and she wants to interview both of us after the hearing is over. I guess she must be important or Liz wouldn't want me to meet her. I have to ask my dad if I can do it. Maybe this time he'll let them interview him too.

I think I'd better go now. I wouldn't want to be left behind!

Acknowledgements

Thanks to Jessica, Carolivia and Epic Publications, Jackie U and Kean Kaufmann, every student I ever taught, and my entire family. Thanks to my friends at TI, SAS, TTC, GLCCB, Bunker Hill DCPS, SCES, WAES, SSMAPCS, Montgomery College and Trinity University of Washington DC.

Thanks: Denise, Andrea, Gobie, the Ritters, Martha, Mickey, Charlene, Leon, Jackie, Andrea, Sharnita, Sue, Georgia Herron, Dr. Rodriguez, Rabbi Ethan Seidel, Dr. Dorr, Rev. Dr. Asher, Rabbi Avis Miller, Jared, Sr. Hope, Cheryl, Mary Dietz, Yasmin, Rev. Kathy Baker, Dr. Hunt, Beryl, Ginny Apuzzo, Michele Sumka, Pearl & Larry, Margie & Carl, Esther & Gene, Bernie & Debra, Ann, Richard, Mardie, Louis, Ellie, Terry Dalsemer, Joyce Kramer, Virginia Kelley Mills, Dr. Howard, Gerry Meredith, Marjorie Grays, Myra Roney & Bayard Rustin.

Thanks to Shelly, Darren, Halima, Juwan, Darryl, Nora, Sarah, Chandini, Jamir, Malcolm, Jackie, Maria, Eric Hernandez and his mother, Frankie, Luis, Anaiah, Lisa, Jackson, Jenice and her brother, Naomi and her sister Rowyn and their parents, the original Shay-Shay, FGWs, The Flames and the Stars Kids Original Opera Company.

Thanks to Ann, Diane, Terry, Marita, Jennifer, Travis, Debbie, Kirsten, Susan, Cynthia, Lara, Barbara, Jessica, Cassandra, Sue, Veronique, Miriam, Dena, Angele, Lainey, Jill and Frankie.

Thanks to my dad, who encouraged me to write, and my mother who loved to tell me stories. Thanks to my brothers Dave and Jimmy, who taught me about teamwork and taking a stand, and their fabulous wives, Jackie and Kathy. Thanks to all nieces and nephews and their spouses and children, a special shout out to first reader Elana Marens and Christine Michos Rider for feedback and editing help. Thanks to Erin, Marion, Matt, Liz, Carrie, Andy and Rachel for inspiring me.

Thanks to my admirable array of cousins, their superb spouses and children; deep gratitude to the late Marie Antoinette Sherrett, eloquent advocate for those with autism.

Author

Louise Parker Kelley is a writer, editor, leader, playwright and teacher. Her crowded life, full of wonderful friends, colleagues and family, inspires her writing. She lives with her wife, writer Jessica Weissman, in Silver Spring, Maryland.